HAUNTING THE HUNTER

HAUNTING THE HUNTER

Book One of the
BOUND DUET

HANNA HARP

SIMON MAVERICK

New York Amsterdam/Antwerp London
Toronto Sydney/Melbourne New Delhi

SIMON MAVERICK
An Imprint of Simon & Schuster, LLC
1230 Avenue of the Americas
New York, NY 10020

Portions of this novel were previously published on Substack in 2025.

First Simon Maverick trade paperback edition November 2025

Interior design by Kyle Kabel
All illustrations by the author

Manufactured in the United States of America

5 7 9 10 8 6 4

The Library of Congress Cataloging-in-Publication Data has been applied for.

ISBN 978-1-6682-3000-8 (pbk)
ISBN 978-1-6682-3014-5 (ebook)

I made him to ruin you, and you begged for more . . .
So spread those pages, little ghost—he's ready for you.

THE PLAYLIST

Play with Fire—Sam Tinnesz
Let the World Burn—Chris Grey
Drive You Insane
—Daniel Di Angelo
Dangerous Hands
—Austin Giorgio
Worship—Ari Abdul
Desert Rose x Renegade x Streets
(Gobaith Mashup)
Taste of the Divine—Shaker, with Azee and COBRA
Who Are You—SVRCINA
Fatal Attraction—Reed Wonder and Aurora Olivas
All You Need—Midnight Blu
Chokehold—Sleep Token
The Death of Peace of Mind
—Bad Omens
Flatline—Jared Benjamin
Hotel—Montell Fish
If I Had You—Chris Grey
Her Name—Beneld, Cheyanne, and Omido
The Summoning—Sleep Token
Waves—Normani
Blood on Her Lips—Raven Knight
Best Behaviour—Beach Season
Take Me Back to Eden
—Sleep Token
Haunted—Chris Grey

THE MENU

"Trigger Warnings"

This is a fourth wall–breaking story, where you, my darling, are the love interest. Turn back now if you don't consent to a book character becoming obsessed with you. This is your warning. Now, onto our menu . . .

- Explicit sexual content
- Violence
- Blood and gore
- Torture
- Demons
- Inappropriate use of a gardening hose
- Mentions of past childhood trauma
- Light stalking
- Forced proximity
- Vines of the provocative variety
- Demonic possession—including, but not limited to, a toaster
- Manipulation
- Murder
- BDSM themes
- Mental health struggles (for the characters)
- Light dubious consent from a poltergeist
- Delusions
- Possessive demon
- Fourth wall break

PROLOGUE

ALABASTER

Well, well, well, what do we have here?

Mmm, my pretty girl . . . Hair as black as the charred edge of that grimoire she keeps too close. I want to thread my fingers through it and see if it leaves ash on my hands like the pages do. How poetic.

The golden rays of the sun seep through the sheer curtains of the library window, and she looks as if she is glowing. Reminds me of an angel.

Innocent.

Pure.

Powerful.

Makes me want to corrupt her all the more.

There is something about a creature so perfect that makes me want to taint it. Even if it's just for the fun of it. I've watched this one. And haunted her dreams long enough. I'm getting bored, and I want more.

I watch as Callisto picks up a strange pendulum from behind the grimoire—funny, that wasn't there before. Curious. She holds it in her hand, looking it over, and speaks under her breath.

"Where did you come from?" She holds it up in front of herself, smiling. "I suppose you'll do for what I need." Moving over to her little makeshift altar, she kneels and speaks, holding the item close to her chest.

"Spirits, hear me." Her voice is soft but steady. "I call to you across the veil: Find Cade. Bind yourself to him. Watch him. Protect him."

I chuckle to myself. She's so cute when she's desperate. The thought of her desperation pleases me. I picture how pretty she would be pleading like that to *me*.

She continues—rambling on about how her brother doesn't know what he's getting into, and how much she wants to help.

As if the universe cares about her little wish. Yet, as she speaks, a ripple in the air prickles against my senses. It's faint, but it's there.

How interesting . . .

A new player in my little game.

I can feel you, human, yes.

You.

The girl is mine to haunt. Mine to possess. Mine to do with as I please . . .

My thoughts snap back to her as a tear slips down her cheek. Her hands tremble as she pleads—

"Gods I hope that worked."

An iridescent haze fills the space and she appears to breathe it in, head leaning back ever so slightly. I watch as her long hair falls off her shoulders—unable to pull my eyes away.

I hesitate. That feeling again—something heavy and unfamiliar twists inside me. Curiosity, maybe? No. Something else. Against my better judgment, I step closer, reaching out a hand.

Just a little closer—

Her breath catches, eyes snapping up . . . directly at *me*.

Impossible.

I freeze. She can't see me, not if I don't allow it. And yet, here she is—staring, mouth open in a silent gasp. Pretty rose pink lips parted.

For a moment, neither of us moves. She tries to speak, but the only sound she manages is a small, broken squeak.

The pendulum.

It must be the pendulum. Artifacts like that are unpredictable, and I can feel its pull tugging at the edges of my form. Strange. I let my hand fall and step back, watching her carefully.

She swallows hard. A single bead of sweat drips down her olive skin, and she visibly shakes it off before scrambling to her feet and rushing out of the room. Pity. I would have liked to lick it off her.

I follow—keeping to the shadows. She doesn't need to know I'm here . . . Not yet.

She glides quickly down the hall, the navy rug muffling her steps as the wood creaks faintly beneath her. Approaching her brother, Cade: the little hunter. He towers over her with his broad shoulders and chiseled features. Overrated, if you ask me. Not to mention he's a total asshole. I'm clearly superior.

He looks down on her as if she's a child. She presses the pendulum into his hand, her voice tight with urgency. "Take this—it'll keep you safe."

I can't help but notice how dainty her hands are, and how pretty they would look wrapped around my—

"Please, Cade."

Please, Cade. My eyes roll into the back of my head. The only person she should be saying please to is *me.*

Something in her voice makes him pause. He sighs, taking the pendulum and shoving it into his pocket; not another word shared between them.

Yes.

Follow him, and stay the fuck out of my way. He doesn't deserve her and neither do you. But you could deserve each other . . .

So, the skeptic has a magical object now, *that's hilarious.*

CHAPTER I

CADE

The heavy bass is a dull thump through the walls as I slip through the back entrance and look around the gaudy mansion. The whole place is ringed with hedges and elaborate sculptures. Even had a fucking staff entrance hidden on the side of the property, perfect for me to get in undetected.

A myriad of golden hues splayed from floor to ceiling. Too fucking much. My heavy boots echo against the marble floor in the quiet hallway.

Footsteps reverberate off the walls, and I quickly press myself into the wall near the entryway, silently setting my trap.

Just as the shadow of a man enters, I loop the cord around his neck, yanking tight till I feel the pull cutting off his air. He spasms, clearly shocked from my assault. I'm sure he didn't expect *this* kind of choking at a party like this. The poor bastard. He's clawing at his throat, which will end in—Five. Four. Three. Two. Out.

I grab him by the ankles, dragging his unconscious body further into the room near a closet. Stripping away his clothes takes effort, but I get them off, tossing them aside. I grunt, wrestling his dead weight into the closet.

I grab the clothes and hurry out of the room, farther down the hall, slipping into one of the back rooms and planting the clothes under the chaise lounge—I'm gonna need those for later. Walking over to the full-length mirror, I run my fingers through my hair, messing it up on purpose, and walk out, into the party.

The room reeks of sweat and arousal, a heady mix that turns my stomach. These people disgust me, but I haven't come to judge.

In the writhing masses, bodies are tangled in slick, desperate motion among the silk pillows scattered across the floor, but they're nothing more than background noise among the variations of blues. My focus remains sharp against the dimly lit euphoria.

I scan the room and head toward a bar in the back corner, sitting on one of the empty stools. I raise my finger up, capturing the bartender's attention.

"What can I get you?"

"Whiskey, straight," I reply.

The bartender moves with quick hands, sliding the drink to me. But I'm distracted by a stunning woman in lingerie. She's carrying a tray out to a man fisting a woman's hair as he aggressively fucks her mouth. My eyes shift away and meet the gaze of a short blond-haired man, his features delicate yet confident, as he seats himself next to me.

"You are way too hot to be alone right now," he says in a sultry tone, eyeing me up and down.

"I'm not alone. You're here." I smirk and take a sip of my drink.

"You like what you see?" he says, biting his lip.

I look him over. His small frame is covered in . . . glitter. Nope.

Redhead, long hair, short hair, big dick, a pussy I can sink into. I'll fuck it all, but no fucking glitter.

In a dim corner, a blond in a silver mask gasps, and shudders. Her body taut beneath the hands of a faceless stranger.

I watch as the man squeezes hard into her love handles, her massive titties bobbing back and forth over a woman motorboating her. Now that's a thing of beauty.

"Sorry, I've got my eye on someone. Unbothered, I saunter over to the trio. Tilt her chin upward teasingly, and her breath hitches.

"Mind if I have a turn?" I ask, smirking as I meet her gaze.

Her eyes drift downward, lingering on my chest before wandering lower. A smile plays on her lips as she rises to her feet, slipping her hand into mine. I lead her out of the room, feeling the weight of her curiosity in how she studies me.

She hesitates for only a moment.

"Have we met before? You seem familiar," she murmurs quietly.

"I don't know. You got a name?" I look down at her.

"We don't do names here."

Perfect.

I guide her into the empty back room and press her against the wall, my lips finding the curve of her neck, teasing and tasting as my hands explore her body. A deep moan escapes her throat and echoes through the room, raw and unguarded. I lean in close—

"We may have never been formally introduced," I whisper, low and deliberate. "But for now . . . I'm yours."

She trails her hands up and down my biceps. "Fuck, your tattoos are so hot," she says, then pulls my face to hers and kisses me. Her tongue rolls over mine as my hands trail down her subtle curves. Gripping her thighs, I lift one of her legs over my forearm, locking it in place. She wastes no time unzipping my pants and dropping them to the floor. Her fingers wrap around my cock, guiding me to her entrance, and the moment I feel her warmth, I thrust in deep, burying myself inside her.

"Fuck, you feel so good," I growl, my voice rough.

I lift her higher, making her take every inch of me as I carry her to the chaise near the window. Laying her on her back, I pin her down, pounding into her without restraint.

"Oh my God, don't stop!" she cries out, her back arching as she trembles beneath me. Gripping her hips tighter, I pick up the pace, driving into her ruthlessly. She fucking molds to me as I angle myself lower and find that perfect spot—

"Don't stop, oh my God—please, I'm—" I feel her pulse around my length as I slow down to savor the feeling. Fuck . . . I'm gonna come and it hasn't even been five minutes.

Weak.

Reaching under the pillow, my fingers close around the knife I planted when I got here. I groan, still riding out her pleasure, her moans becoming reckless and unguarded beneath me. I take the knife and cut the front of her bra, freeing her breasts. She shudders at the blade's cool touch and looks up at me.

She meets my gaze, breath hitching, eyes blown wide, dark with something sinister. Then, in a whisper, she says, "I like to play." Well, fuck me, that just made my dick twitch. If I'm going to get this done, I might as well get some enjoyment out of it.

Her bright hazel eyes roll into the back of her head as I thrust into her with reckless abandon, the chaise now loudly thumping against the wall. I throw my head back, wiping the sweat that's trickling down my brow, my abs flexing as my hips move more erratically. Her moans drown out the cries of pleasure just outside the door.

A deep, guttural cry rips from my throat as I let go, filling her, my body pulsing against hers. My breath is ragged, muscles taut as I hover over her, drinking in the sight of her blissed expression.

I exhale, eyes downcast, my charcoal hair tickling her chin, lips curling into something that isn't quite a smile, my voice just a breath, blunt. "Okay." And before she can react, the blade sinks into the soft flesh of her neck.

Her eyes go wide with terror and confusion, her swollen lips open, but no sound comes out. I stay there, watching, waiting—until the light in her gaze finally flickers and fades.

Gone. Fucking finally.

I stand, my breath still heavy as I pull away from her lifeless body, the warmth fading fast. I turn my head and look out the window, at the lanterns that line the empty pathway outside it. The night is a quiet contrast to the room outside the door, so . . . Why do I feel like I'm being watched? Moving with practiced ease, I crouch under the chaise and grab the clothes I stashed earlier—from the poor bastard working the party. He's probably still out cold.

He'll wake up . . . eventually.

Now that I've changed, I can blend in as a staff member of the party.

I leave the room, feeling smug, knowing the next step of my plan has been executed. As I cross the threshold, though, an overwhelming feeling of anxiety washes over me. A high contrast array of colors—my eyes squint in an attempt to focus. Was I drugged? No . . . But I don't feel like I'm here—an overwhelming sensation of eyes on me, but nobody is looking.

What the fuck?

"I need to get the fuck out of here," I whisper, my voice strained.

Walking down the hallway I steady myself on the wall, my skin glowing unnaturally in a neon hallucination from the ultraviolet lights. I focus my sights on the end of the hall. My vision tunnels on the door.

I pull open the door to the exit the staff uses, sucking in the fresh air. I straighten my black blazer. This is not the place to lose my cool. I walk past two guys smoking cigarettes, talking about how badly they wish they could participate in the activities inside. I keep my stride confident; it won't be long before someone finds her body. Not that they'll know it was me. She was so covered in cum; there would be no way to tell whose DNA was the one to take her out. Convenient for me.

I hop into the truck I hotwired earlier, my pulse thumping in my ears as I slam the door shut. The engine roars to life, and I shift into gear, feeling the tires grip the pavement beneath me. As I adjust the rearview mirror, I'm suddenly freezing, like the temperature in the truck dropped ten degrees.

What the fuck is going on?

I scan my surroundings: no other cars on the road. It's late. And I'm probably the only motherfucker who leaves an orgy early. No one saw me, no one is following me. And there's no way this piece of shit is being tracked.

Despite my rationalizations, my gut tightens at the thought. That's not possible. I took precautions. I'd gone out of my way to snatch this truck from a small-town hick while he was too busy attempting to pick up two very unwilling women at the bar.

There is no way anyone would have bothered to look twice at it. It's just another beater, blending in with the employees' cars parked nearby.

So, how the hell could it be bugged? It's not. And I know damn well I wasn't drugged. I've gone crazy. There's no other goddamn explanation.

I rub my face, trying to shake off the creeping paranoia.

I tap the brakes, swerving the wheel slightly as the unease builds, and I pull off to the side in a movie theater parking lot. I should change cars just in case. The area has a few in the lot. I grab my duffel bag from the passenger seat and set my sights on a beat-up old wagon two spaces down. I try for the door. It's unlocked. How convenient. The thing looks like a forgotten relic from the eighties. Rusted, unkempt, and totally under the radar.

Perfect.

I toss my bag in and slam the door shut. My fingers tremble as I hotwire it as quickly as I'm able. Tiny wires are not my thing. I fumble a bit with them before the engine sputters to life. I hate this shit. If anyone is following me, they won't think twice about this piece of junk. I shift gears, and the seat rattles beneath me as the wheels hum under the vehicle. Thankfully it holds together long enough to get me close to the airport. I ditch it near an abandoned gas station and walk the remaining way to my hotel. Tomorrow, I'll be back in Washington—safe, secure, and out of sight.

I jump at a sudden vibration in my pocket, fumbling to pull the phone out. It's Jack, right on time. Fuck, I need to get a handle on myself. Attempting to steady my fingers, I swipe the screen to answer.

Jack's voice comes through, loudly chewing something as he speaks. "Yo, is it done?"

I drag my hand down my face. "Yeah, it's done," I answer, trying to push the unease crawling up my spine back where it belongs . . . What the hell is wrong with me? I grit my teeth, forcing my mind to focus.

"You good, Cade?" Jack asks, his voice dropping slightly, sensing something's off. When I don't respond immediately, he continues, sounding serious, "You'll be happy to know I found our next target, and it took me less time than I expected."

"These assholes aren't exactly hiding, Jack." I smirk to myself despite the rising feeling. The Covenant created me in their own image, a weapon. Their dutiful soldier.

"We're going to get them, Cade."

I tilt my head back, taking in a long breath.

A smirk tugs at my lips despite myself. "Yeah, but the higher-ups in the Covenant won't be so easy."

"Keep an eye on the target." My purpose returns in full force. Fucking *finally*. The thrill of the hunt, of tracking them down, of getting to the ones pulling the strings—it steadies me. "I'll get the full details when I'm back."

"Got it, boss."

I hang up the phone, letting the silence settle in, but the weight of everything lingers.

And it's not just the mission anymore—it's something else I can't quite place

I head into the hotel, each step heavier than the last. My hand trembles, feeling distant—like it's not my own but still familiar. This is fucking annoying. It's like I'm watching myself from the outside. I struggle with the key card, fingers numb as I slide it into the slot. It clicks, the light turns green, and I step inside.

The room feels too quiet. Too empty.

Stripping off my clothes, I move mechanically toward the bathroom. The shower knob turns quickly under my fingers, the rush of water filling the silence.

Staring into the mirror, my eyes trace the scar on my face that reaches from my cheekbone down to my jaw. The reflection blurs. Like I'm not here but instead watching from the other side of the glass. I focus on my hair . . . It's been too long since I've had it cut properly. Then I see it, a shiny silver strand caught in the black mass.

"Are grays normal at my age? Must be stress . . ." I mumble. My voice sounds hollow, like it's not even mine.

I lean closer to the mirror, inspecting the silver intruder. The closer I get, the more disconnected I feel. My face seems . . . off. The edges of my features seem soft and out of focus, like my reflection doesn't belong to me anymore, my dark eyes unfamiliar.

As the steam fogs up the glass, further distorting my reflection, I squint, leaning in. It almost looks like another face is overlapping mine . . . like a shadow over my own, or an overlay of someone else's expression.

I wipe away the fog, but the other face vanishes, leaving only my own, strained and blurry. I rub my eyes, trying to shake the feeling off. It was just the steam. A trick of the light.

I step into the shower, hoping the water will ground me, bring me back to something real. The heat pours over me, hitting my scalp, my back, rinsing away the day's grime and tension.

Under the steady rhythm of the water, my body relaxes, lost in the comfort it provides. Time slips away, but in the reprieve, my mind drifts, too quickly, back to the mission.

Flashes of my parents' bodies tangled in their bed.

The cold sting of the ritual room.

Artifacts glinting under dim light.

The memories bear down, heavy and unwanted.

No. No distractions.

Not now.

I was groomed to take over the Order of the Covenant. So, I know how to end them. My next target is within reach, and now that I've gotten rid of his daughter, gaining access to him should be easy. I force my mind back on track. *Concentrate. There's still work to do.*

I step out of the shower, wrapping my towel around my waist as I crawl into the bed. The cool fabric against my skin, a stark contrast to the heat of the night. Sleep drags me under, and my dreams are fragmented, distorted—nothing that makes sense, everything twisting.

Except for one thing.

I see someone. They're holding a book, eyes focused on the pages, but as if they sense me watching, they look up.

They don't have a face.

Just an empty space staring back at me, like there's a black hole in the place where a face should be. But before I can truly process . . . oh fuck no . . .

The blackness pulls at me, swallowing me whole, deeper and deeper until it feels like I'm falling—endlessly falling into the void. Eyes surround me.

So many eyes.

Waiting.

Watching.

I can feel them on my skin. They're everywhere, and it's fucking suffocating. Then, I hit bottom, but it's not what I expected. It's soft. A familiar warmth, like the feeling of being caressed, even though I can't see anything.

My body tenses, but the touch is gentle—delicate. Hands glide over my skin, tracing my chest, neck, and arms. Electricity pulses through each touch, and goose bumps rise as my body responds, even though I can't explain why.

I feel myself growing hard, the touch both foreign and strangely familiar. Hands explore my body, moving lower, their fingers grazing my hips and then my thighs. It feels too real, too intense, like something I've always wanted but never let myself acknowledge.

"Fuck . . ." I mouth in a breathless whisper. "Who are you?"

There's no answer, but they continue to touch, intimate and precise. The sensation overwhelms me. On instinct my hips begin to rock into it, as if I am no longer in control of my body. Then, without warning, my cock is freed from the confines of my pants and I feel it being taken into their mouth. A blurred aura. Lips moving up and down in rhythmic precision, too perfect to be real.

"Oh my God . . ." The words escape me, muffled by the pleasure. "So good, too fucking good."

I reach my hands out to find something, anything, but my searching hands meet only air. Nothing tangible.

"What is this?"

I throw my head back, lost in the sensation, but the moment quickly severs, as if it was never actually there. In the next moment I'm met with a caress, and it almost feels like lips meeting my forehead. Ethereal. It snaps me awake.

My brows furrow, and I jerk upright, sheets tangled around my legs. The room is still as my heart pounds in my chest.

I look over at the clock on the bedside table: 3:33 a.m. I gaze down, my body still betraying me—hard and wanting. My stomach twists in disgust when I noticed the sheet is stained.

"Wet dreams now?" I grumble to myself, exasperated. "I'm fucking losing it."

CHAPTER 2

CALLISTO

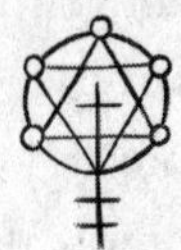

I jolt awake from a dead sleep, drenched in sweat. The memory of the towering black mass, the image of its golden eyes and massive horns, is burned into my mind. My heart pounds as I scan the room, moonlight filtering in through the curtains. It's quiet . . . too quiet.

I reach for my phone: 3:33 a.m.

The witching hour.

Again.

The same dream every night for over a week now . . .

"My little witch. Are you here to come again?" I whimper at the contact, sharp fangs grazing against my collarbone.

"Please." I can feel his low rumble as I look up at him, my demon.

"You always beg so pretty. Now open your legs for me." I do, Gods I do. The covers shift as I do what he asks, strong, thick fingers dragging over my core. Teasing as his claws slowly trail up to my breasts, one thumb brushing my nipple until it hardens under his touch.

"Always so responsive for me," he breathes, so low, I almost don't catch it. Like he is in awe of how I melt for him, crave him. The smell of amber and earth consumes me. Warm, grounding, ancient. Like freedom. Like stepping into a world I've never known . . .

My thighs press together at the memory. "Guess I'm up now," I mutter, sighing as I push the covers aside and swing my legs over the edge of the bed. A strange heaviness lingers in the air, an unsettling feeling like something is watching me. I can feel him, my monster of sorts.

From the moment I found that pendulum, I can't shake the presence it has left behind. The way it just appeared one day sends a chill up my spine. At first, it felt gentle and almost comforting. But then . . . The darkness I felt was overwhelming, as if it would consume me if I let it. I prayed that whatever I called didn't open the door to something else . . . Something more dangerous.

I'm still new to this. I've always been aware of my magic, but haven't a damn clue how to control it. That was the last thing my parents wanted me to learn, lest I use it against them, but not knowing leaves me dangerous. It breaks through when my emotions are high and grows stronger by the day, showing me visions in my dreams I can't escape. I have no idea what this power is capable of or how to use it.

Giving the pendulum to Cade was the right call. It vibrates with magic—that even he shouldn't be able to deny. He needs to know what's out there, to feel what our eyes can't see. I am convinced that whatever came through the veil will do just that, both for him and for me. I just wish these nightmares would ease up.

I rub my eyes and lift myself off the bed. My body is heavy and sore from the poor night's sleep. I head to the bathroom and turn on the faucet to draw a bath. Sweat-damp leggings cling to my skin, and I shiver as I peel them off . . . *Gross*. I grab my favorite bath salts and sprinkle them into the steaming water, hoping the heat will wash away the lingering unease.

The lights flicker—once, twice—accompanied by a faint buzzing that makes the hair on the back of my neck stand on end.

I freeze. It's not me. I can tell when it is.

"What the fuck?" My voice is barely a whisper. *It's just a faulty wire. Nothing to worry about.*

Wrapping a towel around myself, I scan the bathroom, pulse pounding in my ears. Something caresses my shoulder, almost like a breath that pebbles goose bumps over my skin.

No . . . Not me.

"Who's here?" I call out, trying to sound braver than I feel. Earthy tones fill my senses—*the scent from my dreams.*

Heat blooms over my skin, and it isn't from the steam. My chest tightens, the air feeling thick and heavy. I close my eyes for just a second and an image flashes in my mind: a towering black mass looming in a corner. It appears to move, almost as if it's pointing to me, when I hear an eerie whisper—

"*Mine.*"

My eyes snap open, gaze darting to the corner. Nothing's there.

I bolt from the bathroom, my bare feet padding against the cool hardwood as I rush toward the kitchen. The sensation of something right behind me fuels me to move faster. My heart hammers as I turn the corner—and slam into a solid body.

I scream, the sound ripped from my throat, my heart slamming against my ribs.

"Shit, Calli! It's just me," Jack says, gripping my arms to steady me.

"Damn it, Jack!" I snap, trying to catch my breath. "You scared the hell out of me."

He raises his hands in apology. "Sorry, I couldn't sleep . . ."

I flick the kitchen light on, and as his voice trails off, his gaze drops to the towel clinging to my body.

"Next time, turn on a light if you're up," I scold, brushing past him to grab a glass from the cabinet. "Unless you want to give someone a heart attack."

"Yeah, right. Got it," he mumbles, eyes darting anywhere but at me.

I fill the glass at the sink, gulping down the cool water in an attempt to calm the heat still crawling over my skin. Out of the corner of my eye, I catch him sneaking glances, but he does that with any woman with a pulse, a hopeless flirt. Something I easily fell for when we were young.

We don't talk about it, knowing Cade would murder Jack if he ever found out I lost my virginity to him when we were teenagers. We were isolated, bored, and left alone. And I wanted to know what it felt like to be the center of someone's attention. Jack was more than willing to provide that attention. Though I know he wouldn't do anything now.

We have evolved. He's the closest thing I have to a friend, and both of us decided it was better this way—friends.

"Cade will be back later this afternoon," he says, breaking the silence.

"For how long?" My voice is sharper than I mean it to be, but Jack just shrugs.

"Not long. I found Allen White. He's not going to miss his chance to get to him."

My stomach twists. I get why Cade is doing this, but that doesn't make it any easier. The Covenant is no joke—they have a literal *God* on their side. I haven't seen it myself, but my parents did. And for all their neglect, they never lied to me.

I drift back to the night Cade found out I was meant to be sacrificed. Deep down, I had always known, and I had accepted it. But not Cade—he refused.

His rage was explosive.

Our parents said I should feel *honored*, like I had been chosen for some grand purpose, but Cade didn't buy their bullshit. Ever since, he's been obsessed with tearing the Covenant apart, but he doesn't understand the supernatural side of it. He has no clue what he's really up against.

"I'm worried about him, Jack," I admit quietly.

"Don't be," Jack says, leaning against the counter with a confident smirk. "If anyone can take down the Covenant, it's Cade. Your brother's a badass."

He isn't wrong. They trained him in hand-to-hand combat, made him a person capable of tracking, hunting, and capturing people. They had unknowingly built the perfect weapon against them. Cade never trusted our parents—and he never stopped protecting me. In his own fucked-up way, he's the only one who's ever really had my back. Though for many years I didn't realize it.

"Yeah, I guess you're right," I say, setting my empty glass in the sink. I turn and start back toward the bathroom, but Jack catches my arm before I reach the hallway. His deep blue eyes burn into mine, an attempt to calm me.

"Trust him, Calli. We know what we're doing," he says, his voice steady. I lift an eyebrow at him but nod.

His mouth curls into a teasing smile. "By the way, what the hell are you doing walking around in a towel at three in the morning?"

I roll my eyes. "None of your business," I snap, but after a beat, I sigh, his hold still firm on my arm. "Fine. I had a bad dream and woke up sweating. I felt gross and needed a bath."

"Need any help with that?" he jokes, his eyes glinting with mischief.

I glare at him, about to fire back, when I see the cabinet behind him swing open. A glass flies out, hurtling across the room. The sharp sound of it breaking shatters the moment.

"Shit! Calli, get back!" Jack moves between me and the mess, and I step away from the scattered shards. My breath catches as I attempt to put logic to what I just saw.

He kneels to clean it up. "Go on," he says without looking up. "I've got this."

That wasn't me. I *know* that wasn't me. My feet stay rooted for a moment too long—any doubts in my mind have been quelled; this is full confirmation to me. I'm being haunted. My eyes dart around the room, trying to see whatever is clearly trying to get my attention, but I find nothing. Gripping my towel to my chest, I back away. I'm used to weird shit, but this is ridiculous.

Just my luck.

I head back to the bathroom, only to find water spilling over the edge of the tub, soaking the floor.

"Fuuuuuuuck."

After spending twenty minutes cleaning up the massive mess I made, I give up on the bath and opt for a shower instead. I attempt to wash away the lingering unease under the hot water, to get myself to feel a little more human.

Freshly dressed and somewhat calmer, I settle onto the living room couch with my favorite book, *Death*, the last book in the Four Horsemen series. I flip it open, hoping to lose myself in the words—but after reading the same sentence four times, I drop it in my lap, frustrated. This sucks. Of course I would attract a fucking poltergeist. I've done nothing my entire life. No job. No purpose. No luck. Just existing in the background.

Easy to overlook.

My only redeeming quality is my dreams. They have always held weight—flashes of things before they happen, like a twisted form of déjà vu. I've always been able to sense when something is coming, like a strong gut instinct. Maybe not the best judgment . . . But it's always given me a sense of pride.

And right now? My gut is screaming that something is *here*.

Setting my book aside, I head back to my bedroom and pull open the top drawer of my nightstand. My fingers brush against the cracked leather of the old grimoire. One of the many artifacts my brother took after we left the house where everything fell apart.

I sit down on the bed, my heart pounding. I take a steadying breath before opening the book at random, the pages crackling beneath my fingertips as they settle on a section about demons. Thinking back to my dream, my stomach twists.

Oh, hell no.

Nope. Nope. Nope.

Snapping the book shut, I press my palm flat against the cover.

I may not be the brightest crayon in the box, but I sure as hell know a red flag when I see one. Maybe I can ignore it. If I don't feed into it, then it will get bored. Because unequivocally: *Fuck. That.*

"I do not claim any bad energy. You hear me?" My voice is firm, but there's a tremor beneath the surface I can't quite hide.

Silence.

Not even the hum of the fridge or the distant tick of the hallway clock. A bitter laugh escapes my lips as I push myself upright. Soft golden light spills through the window. Morning already. I could really use some breakfast.

I tuck the grimoire back into its hiding place and head toward the kitchen.

A sudden creak breaks the silence, the sound crawling up my spine like cold fingers. The air thickens and my heart pounds as I turn to find the drawer cracked, grimoire lying open again . . . this time on the section about a demon named Alabaster. I linger on the image for a moment, stuck on his eyes—his golden eyes.

CHAPTER 3

ALABASTER

Oh, this is almost too perfect. Her fear makes this all the more enjoyable.

Don't worry, pretty girl.

You'll have me soon enough.

I can't help but fixate on her heart racing, knowing it's me it's working so hard for. I hover behind her and look down at the cursed book in her hands, watching as she gawks at the terribly drawn portrait of me. This is how they know my name . . . As frustrating as it is that I am there in the first place, they could have at least done me justice.

My nose looks nothing like that.

My initial enjoyment is quickly broken when I feel an unwelcome presence approach from behind.

"Your obsession with this one is concerning."

I smirk to myself, flashing my teeth. Alok knows I've been watching her. He finds it curious that I've been creeping in her shadow for so long . . . longer than any other human I've watched.

He can stay curious.

"What are you doing here?" I ask in a clipped voice, sitting at the far end of the room.

He sits down next to me, his long pale-blue hair cascading down to the floor. An ugly grin stretches across his too-perfect face.

"How about you come back with me, and we can team up again? You used to be so much fun."

"I am disinclined to acquiesce to your request. I have no interest in going anywhere right now."

"You better be careful, Kai. Don't want to end up like Ashur."

Ahh yes. The scary story all of us are told to keep us in line. The big bad Ashur who fell in love with a human and went mad after she died—like they tend to do.

Dumb bastard.

Then there was that whole thing with him taking immortals and trying to fuse them with his wife's spirit to bring her back. But what the fuck did the guy think was going to happen?

Humans are flesh-bound. We exist beyond that limitation. Our essence is not confined to a vessel. We move between the physical and metaphysical as easily as breathing. Humans have to die to be free, but we were never caged to begin with. And without a body, they are nothing more tangible than smoke. Anyone who knows anything knows the price you pay for love is loss. Ashur couldn't handle it and lost himself. I'm nothing if not self-aware, and I don't need the reminder.

Ashur was an idiot, and I'm not falling for a damn human.

"Let me have my fun and leave me be," I say, brushing him off.

"Ah, and here I came all the way to this miserable cesspool of a planet to see you. And, of course, to see what has you so occupied." He glances over at Callisto.

I reach for his throat and shove him onto the ground, his horns clacking against the wooden floor.

I hear Calli gasp, and she turns in our direction. I catch the look of horror on her face before she runs from the room. I hover over him, rage boiling in my eyes.

"Oh look, you scared away the human."

"This one is mine—you do not get to look at her," I say, venom seeping from my words as my claws dig into his neck.

I know what would happen if he decided to follow her. We tend to hyperfixate quite easily. Immortality will do that to you. But Alok is known for his brutal ways when handling humans. He has little restraint, and I'm not in the mood to share.

He laughs through his sharp teeth and shoves me off. Standing, he offers his hand. I smack it away. He's only slightly shorter than me, but he's older, and stronger. I know he could tear me apart if he wanted to—but I don't care. He looks me over with a glint of authority in his glowing white eyes.

"Find me when you're done with your new plaything." The air vibrates around him, and he waves his arms. His form fades away in a spiraling mist, leaving behind a faint shimmer in the air.

So dramatic.

I'm surprised he didn't put up much of a fight—but I'm glad. The fun is just beginning, and no one needs to know why I'm here. Not yet at least.

That goes for you, too—you'll take what I give you. Now go back to your hunter, little pest.

CHAPTER 4

CADE

The seat of the truck squeaks beneath me. An F-250 highboy. Such a beauty. It will be missed by its owner, but I couldn't resist. My phone vibrates in my pocket and I roll my eyes, shifting to grab it.

Calli.

Again.

I silence it. She can wait another thirty minutes until I'm home.

Outside, the mountains roll by like they're trying to calm me down. It's beautiful here, but none of it gets through. Not really.

The unease hasn't left since last night. Since the party.

That wasn't my first kill, and it won't be my last. But something about it won't leave me alone. There were no bugs, no tails, and no loose ends. I checked. But that dream . . .

That fucking dream.

Goose bumps crawl up my arms and neck, and I grip the wheel, letting myself sit in discomfort for a moment. The cheap leather of the Ford's seat cracks. That same feeling of being seen, of being touched, of something slipping past every defense I've ever built.

I fucking hate it.

I speed up, my jaw clenched—the road winding through the trees like it always has. I know every curve, but today it feels different.

I pull into the driveway and kill the engine. Home sweet home. A two-story scenic modern fortress, tucked away in the mountains of Washington. The perfect place to keep Calli hidden. Personally, I would have moved to a place like this regardless. I prefer my solitude. I hop out of the truck and see that Jack is waiting for me on the front step.

"She's waiting for you," he says, voice flat, but there's something under it, a tightness in his tanned skin. His shoulders are set, eyes sharp, concerned. I don't fucking like it.

"Where is she?" It comes out sharper than I mean, but he doesn't flinch at my tone. We've been friends long enough to know that just because I'm an unfeeling asshole to the rest of the world, it doesn't mean I don't give a shit about him.

"Balcony. But listen . . ."

I stop and turn. She's in for an earful. Calling constantly when I'm on a mission could have put her at risk, or me. What if I fucking lost my phone? The wrong person could have caught wind of her.

"She's been off, man. Jumpy—and not her typical Calli-weird. It's like she's paranoid."

The back of my neck tightens, and I knead the tension that seems to always be there, growing each day. I narrow my eyes at him, not because he deserves it, but because I'm an asshole. What can I say?

"She has every reason to be scared. She's not safe until everyone in the Covenant is dead."

Jack gives me a more serious look. "Nah, man, this isn't about them." *What?* He nods his head, defeated, tired. "Just go talk to her. I'll be in the office when you're done."

I nod and walk past him.

The house feels hollow, my boots echoing on the stairs as I climb. I don't knock. I never do. She's out on the balcony, book in hand, feet up. The moment I open the door, though, she startles, dropping the book.

"Dammit . . . I lost my page." She sighs, picking up the book and setting it down as she walks straight into a hug. Her arms around me feel smaller than I remember.

"What happened? How are you?" Brown eyes and heart-shaped face, already scanning me with worry. *Just put a smile on, reassure her, Cade. That's all she needs.*

"I should be asking you. Jack says you're being weirder than usual."

"Fuck you. I'm serious, Cade."

And my smile drops. It was wishful thinking that this reunion would be pleasant. "You don't need to know shit. Stop asking questions. I'll tell you what you need to know."

She stiffens in my arms and then moves to sit again, hugging her book to her chest.

"Sorry," she says quietly. "I just . . . I had a dream . . . a bad one."

I sit across from her, my eyes on her face.

"Like I was being watched," she continues. "Not like paranoia, or anxiety, but like something was in the room with me."

I freeze.

"And it didn't feel wrong, not at first. It felt familiar, but it was horrifying."

The air in my lungs tightens but I keep my face still, not giving anything away.

"I swear I saw something, Cade. Something is here with us."

There it is . . . More talk of ghosts and magic. I lean back.

"Nothing's here, Calli. You've gotta stop feeding into that shit—it's clearly getting to your head."

Her face hardens, eyes narrowing at me.

"Don't you fucking patronize me, Cade. I'm not stupid. We grew up with this shit. You think just because you're bigger and stronger and quieter about it that it didn't fuck us both up?"

Running my hand over my face, I deflect. "It almost killed you."

"Because of *them*, not because of me. Not because of what I am. You don't get to rewrite that." I clench my jaw so hard I swear my molars will crack.

Goddamn. Why does she have to make this so difficult?

"That symbol they carved on the back of your neck wasn't a game, Calli. They didn't see you as a daughter. They were deranged, and their belief in this bullshit is what started it."

"I know that! And I've lived with that longer than you have—because I didn't get to hide behind training, and rage."

I stare at her. Her voice is rising, breaking with emotions.

"I stayed here, in this fucking house. With the aftermath. With the silence. With the ghosts of our parents and with the grimoire." She throws one of her hands up, nearing hysteria. "It's fucking *alive*, Cade. I didn't ask for this. Any. Of. This. But I see things. I feel things. And just because you can't beat it into a wall, doesn't mean it's not real. I believe in what I do because of what I've *seen*."

She pauses, breath catching, then whispers shakily, "I see them when I sleep. I see you, covered in blood. Screaming for something you'll never let yourself have."

"Magic is not real, Calli—it's all in your head."

I want to reach out, to comfort her. To do what a brother would. *Should*. But I'm broken. She clings to magic and fairy tales, but I live in the real world. The one where a psychotic group of fucked-up people are hell-bent on murdering an innocent girl. All because they believe her death will bring them a power that doesn't exist.

"I see with more than my eyes, and I don't care if you believe me or not. Just because you can't see it, doesn't mean it's not real."

"That's the *definition* of things that aren't real." I brush off her words, standing to leave.

"Don't walk away from me."

She's shaking now, still clutching her book. "Let me in on this—I need to help. Because if I don't . . . If you keep shutting me out, I'm going to fall apart. I'm hanging on by threads, Cade. This house, this silence, pretending I don't know what's coming. It's killing me. I don't have your armor. I don't have your rage. All I have is this . . . this belief that maybe, if I can help you, if I can do *something* . . . I won't disappear completely. I'll matter. Just let me matter."

We stand in silence, staring at each other. Two broken, fucked-up souls.

Her hands are trembling, pressed into the book, knuckles white.

I study her. She's unraveling—not from fear, but from hope. Or a lack of it. She needs to believe this means something . . . that *she* means something.

I watch her. The weight of her words hangs between us, raw and sharp. She's not delusional—she's desperate. This isn't a belief. It's survival.

I blow out a breath. "You're only twenty-one, kid—you're still so young. I know it's a lot. But I'm only doing this so you have a chance."

"Don't speak to me like I'm a child, Cade. Twenty-nine isn't that big of a difference."

The world an awful place, and she doesn't understand. I'm only hard on her because I care. Granted I'm not the best at showing it. But she knows I won't pretend with her. I wasn't raised that way. I was raised to be a machine, a leader. Not a nurturer.

I stare at her for a moment. I've never understood magic, never really wanted to. But I understand this.

"You're only seeing what you want to see," I say, and her shoulders flinch like I struck her.

"How could you say that to me?"

Fuck, I'm fucking this all up. I just want to keep her safe. Why can't she just stay out of my way and see that's all I want?

"Look, I'm sorry, okay?"

"You're supposed to be my brother, Cade. It's just us. We are all we have in this world."

I exhale, the weight of my own words twisting something in my gut. Why do I care so much that she believes? Why do I feel the need to protect that belief, even if I don't buy into any of it myself?

Damn, these fucking dreams are getting to me.

The truth is, I don't understand what she sees—but for the first time, I want to . . . And that scares the shit out of me.

I exhale, steadying the sharpness in my voice.

"That's what I used to think and maybe I still do. But now . . . I get why." Taking a breath, I try again. "After everything, I don't blame you. I see you need this. You have to believe there's something bigger, something that makes all of this have meaning."

I pause, my voice lowering. For all that I am, I do genuinely care for Calli. Hell, I'm doing this all for her. So I continue, trying to see things the way she does. "I won't pretend I believe it, but I won't tear it down, either. Not if it's what's keeping you alive."

She looks up and her eyes are glistening—but she's not quite crying.

"I guess that's the closest thing to support I'll get from you." She forces a smile, but it doesn't reach her eyes. There's a flash of something else—disappointment, or maybe resignation. Like she hoped for more, even though she knows better.

"Probably," I say seriously.

I've seen her cracks; I know how deep they go. And for the first time in years, I don't feel angry about it. I feel responsible.

"I just don't want to feel alone," she says, lowering her head.

"You have Jack."

"That's not what I mean, Cade . . . I want in," she says stubbornly.

"You're not coming with me."

"Then share what you know. Don't lock me out. I promise I won't get in your way."

I hesitate but she stares me down. A small sense of something akin to pride wells in my chest, even though I'd prefer her to stay out of my way. She's not budging on this.

"You'll take what I give you. Stay out of Jack's way. And stop calling me every hour like I'm going to vanish."

She smirks, victorious. "I can accept that—for now. So . . . how did it go?"

After feeding her only the bare bones, I leave her and head to Jack's office.

He's not there. I sink into his chair, the cushion exhaling under my weight. His monitors glow—multiple news feeds, satellite footage, and his usual mess of surveillance chaos. I glance over it, but I'm not really paying attention. My thoughts are still stuck in that moment with Calli.

The way she looked at me, like if I didn't validate her belief in something, she'd vanish. And maybe that's what's fucking with me the most, because that look? It's the same one I've seen in the mirror more times than I care to admit. She's not the only one clinging to something just to survive; I've just gotten better at pretending mine doesn't exist.

And the worst part? I can't stop thinking that maybe she's right . . .

Jack walks in with a bag of spicy chips, crunching one before he even speaks.

"All right, so . . . don't be mad," he starts, voice casual, like he didn't just leave me alone with ghosts in my head.

I raise a brow, unimpressed.

"I had eyes on Allen up until this morning, then he ghosted. No pings—he just went dark."

What the fuck. "You let him slip."

"Hey, I didn't let shit slip! The guy probably flew to L.A., got into a private estate with Order ties, and left nothing behind," he defends, like the fucker didn't just let this monster slip through the cracks.

I lean forward, scanning the monitors now as footage rolls, blurry at the edges. Locations that don't mean anything to me yet. Jack keeps talking, detailing guard rotations, escape patterns, the logistics I usually live for—but my mind is slipping.

My eyes catch on one of the monitors. The color is all wrong. Too blue. Too bright. The letters begin to bleed at the edges. I blink, but it doesn't stop.

I turn my head slowly, letting my gaze fall to the galaxy prints framed on the wall. Deep space. My breath slows, chest growing tight—not from panic, but from something stranger. It feels like I'm unraveling from the inside out.

There's a voice in the back of my skull, pulling on my mind. Like a thread under my skin, dragging me inward. I lean into the feeling without realizing it, letting it take me.

Those hands . . . They're not real, but I feel a brush over my chest, creeping to my throat. Curious and familiar. My skin prickles with the feeling.

It's that presence again, the one I can't name. The one that touched me in that dream . . . The one I haven't stopped feeling since.

"Cade?"

Jack's voice cuts through the static.

I blink hard, snapping my head toward him as the room slams back into place.

He's pointing at the screen.

I follow his finger. *Focus.*

TRAGEDY STRIKES: BILLIONAIRE ALLEN WHITE AND DAUGHTER OLIVIA FOUND DEAD IN CRASH.

You've got to be fucking kidding me.

CHAPTER 5

CALLISTO

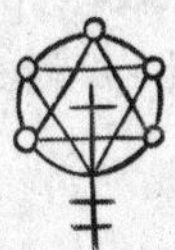

I know he isn't telling me everything, but from the little he did say, I don't think I want to know. How he talked about the location sent shivers up my spine.

I pull out the tin of coffee and place three scoops of grounds in the filter. I flick the switch on the side of the machine, the red light flickers on, and the machine roars to life.

Resting my elbows on the countertop, I run my fingers through my hair, staring out the window. I look out at my garden, wishing it wasn't fall—taking my one source of solace from me.

"This is so fucked up," I mutter.

Cade has been planning this for years, carefully strategizing the perfect attack plan, but now that it's actually happening . . . I don't like it. Right now, I'm more concerned about how this is going to affect him. You can't do the things he's talking about doing and walk away the same.

My brother has been through a lot . . . too much. He was always training when I was little, and he always seemed so sad. Or angry. I could never really read him. To be honest, it was a huge surprise when he reacted the way he did after finding out what the Covenant had planned for me. Our parents had done a good job isolating me from the world. The only friend I ever had was Genevieve, if I could even call her that. We played a lot when we were kids—she was kind to me. That's been a rarity to me throughout my life ... kindness.

Finally, the robust scent of coffee fills the air, providing my senses with a much-needed, though temporary, relief. I grab my favorite mug from the cupboard—I need a spoon for the sugar, but *of course* I forgot to empty the dishwasher. When I turn back around my mug is ... gone?

Hold on.

I rest my hand on the counter where the mug *should* have been, as if it would magically appear. Confusion twists my face as I look back and forth between the island and the counter. I give up, and open the cupboard to grab another. And there it is. My mouth drops open ...

I grab it gingerly, carefully setting it down. Like it might explode. Or disappear again.

I pour myself a cup of coffee, adding one and a half spoonfuls of sugar and stirring carefully as I hold the handle tight to ensure it doesn't get up and walk away.

Nothing.

I cautiously try a sip. Nothing.

My headache begins to quell with the hit of caffeine.

I genuinely don't know how much longer I can take feeling like I'm constantly on edge. Just waiting for shit to happen. And now I've got a poltergeist. But why do I oddly find that comforting?

With a breathless laugh, I say, "If you're going to do something, just get it over with." And now I'm speaking to the air. It's too quiet. I gasp, feeling a sense of contact along my collarbone.

A whisper. *"Do I scare you?"*

Yes.

"No," I reply.

Cade and Jack are still upstairs going over their *master plan*—as if there is such a thing—while my demon surrounds me. I'm about to take my coffee back upstairs, ignore what is so clearly happening around me, when I hear:

"*I should . . .*"

In a blink every cabinet door flies open. I suck in a breath, heart pounding, as I stand there for a moment—wide-eyed and in shock—before rushing over and closing them one by one.

I grab my coffee and run to the library down the hall, slamming the door shut behind me. I place my back against it and hold my hot mug of coffee to my chest like a safety net.

I take a few deep breaths as I try to calm my pulse—feelings of dread sinking into my bones. I slide down the door, hands trembling, still gripping my cup, eyes shut tight.

I feel the floor begin to vibrate under me, the room closing in on me.

I hold my breath as blackness dances across my vision, limbs chilling as the vibration picks up, like an earthquake isolated to this one room.

There is a roaring. I'm convinced this is all in my mind . . . I need to control myself. Fuck.

As my heartbeat increases, I can feel the energy build, and then—it bursts out of me.

All I can do is keep my eyes shut, pray that I can hold it back. But the room is in chaos, thudding books flying off the shelves, falling to the floor.

Stop. I plead.

"Stop!" The scream rips out of me.

I feel a banging against my back, and my eyes jolt open as I gulp in deep breaths.

"Calli? What the hell is going on?" I hear Jack's muffled voice from the other side of the door.

I look around the dark room, books littering the floor around me. I set my mug down and slowly stand. My face is wet from tears. I didn't even know I was crying. I open the door slowly.

Jack looks both white as a sheet and ready to take on the world. When my eyes meet his, I'm met with concern.

"Are you okay? Calli, your nose is bleeding." He runs back to the kitchen and returns with a washrag. He flicks the light on and begins wiping my nose. I grab it from him and back away.

Holding the rag to my nose, my shoulders droop. "I'm sorry. I—I don't know what happened."

He looks around the room, examining the mess, and walks over to me. He wraps me in a tight hug, and it only takes a moment before I sink into him. I'm still crying. My chest heaves as I let it all out.

"I'm . . . scared, Jack," I say between breaths.

"Shh . . . It's going to be okay," he says, holding me tight as he gently cups my head with one hand, the other tenderly tracing circles on my back.

No. No, it won't be okay. He would never believe me if I told him what happened. Neither of them would.

I'm in hell.

Trapped in this house, this cursed body, this life. I'm losing whatever little of myself I had left. The only word that comes to mind is *despair*. My tears begin to ease as the familiar numbness washes over me. I stand in his arms, staring at the wall behind him. My nose burns from the blood still trickling into my sinuses.

How depressing. Who the fuck do I think I am? I'm lucky to be alive at this point, even if it means miserably going about my days without purpose. A broken thing, a ticking time bomb. Nausea bubbles in my gut. I despise self-pity—and this pathetic state I find myself in.

I keep falling, keep backpedaling—every step forward I take, my mind and body push me back three steps. I'm not alive. I'm *surviving*.

Constantly waiting for the next bad thing. My arms are cold and heavy. The pain in my chest reverberates through my body.

Everything Cade is doing, whatever the fuck is haunting me, it's petrifying, but even that takes a back seat to the overwhelming anxiety. I barely eat, I can't sleep without the nightmares waking me up. I need to show them I can handle this. Even if it's just to prove it to *myself*. I'm done wasting away.

I pull away from Jack. Accepting that there is nothing he can do. I'm on my own with this.

It is what it is.

"Are you gonna be okay?" His voice is almost stern, wanting a genuine response. "Should I be worried?"

"I'll be okay. I'm sorry," I say in a quiet voice. "I'm gonna go to bed. I'll clean this up in the morning."

I walk away, leaving no room for a response.

When I make it to my room, I allow the weight of my body to sink into the mattress. I'm not okay, I've never been okay. But I will be.

CHAPTER 6

CADE

Flashes of bodies and blood. The sharp sound of screaming tears me from sleep—but it's not a dream, it's a memory.

The first sacrifice I witnessed.

Shoving it away, I wake. Sort of. Eyes wide open, but my body won't move. I'm stuck staring at the ceiling, limbs heavy, chest tight.

Panic stirs low in my gut as I adjust to my surroundings. The room is dark but not empty. I notice something in the air, like smoke. It moves with intent, graceful and fluid as it hovers.

I try to move, but my muscles won't respond.

Why the fuck can't I move?

Just then, the haze shifts, the shape warping until it almost looks like . . . hands. I try to shut my eyes, but I can't even do that. Then, I feel pressure, cool and weightless. As I focus on the touch, it's featherlight, but I feel it.

A hand rests on my chest. It eases my breath. The panic doesn't vanish, but it dulls. The form shifts again, circling around to my side. One hand stays pressed over my heart, grounding me, while the other traces down my body—slow and careful. My mind races to catch up with my body. I want to ask what this is. I want to scream, but I can't.

And then: a kiss. Soft. Just at the crook of my neck. A chill races down my spine, but not from fear. From something else.

Something *worse.*

I feel safe, and my eyes are able to close, finally. Just for a second. What is this? Comfort? I want to lean in, but I still can't move, can't speak. I can't do anything but exist in the blissful, terrifying silence. It's just a dream. It has to be. Not real. I struggle to vocalize my thoughts.

"You're not real, ghost."

Just a trick of my fucked-up brain. The thought hits hard and bitter. Immediately, the pressure lifts. A withdrawal. Like I hurt it.

No.

No, don't go. But no sound escapes. No plea reaches it. My body jerks and I bolt upright, sweat-soaked and breathless once again.

"No!"

I don't know why I said it. Instinct, maybe. My hand flies to my neck, fingers grazing the exact spot I felt those lips. The skin is cool. Sensitive. Too real. I scratch at it, hard, trying to replace sensation with pain. I look over to my bedside table. The clock reads 3:33.

Again.

This is fucking annoying.

Lying back down, I stare at the back of my eyelids for too long, tossing and turning every so often, but sleep never finds me. Eventually, I check the clock again—5:15. Dammit. I throw the covers back, swinging my legs out of bed and grabbing my jeans from the chair near the window. As I pull them on, I feel it again. That stare.

Eyes. On me. Always.

I grab my shirt. They must like what they see. I'm an attractive guy, what can I say? A dry laugh slips out—but it fades just as fast. Because I'd be crazy to derive pleasure from the look of something unseen. *Right?*

I yank the shirt over my head and sit on the edge of the bed, hand covering my mouth. This isn't normal. This isn't right. There's no possible fucking way any of this is real. I'm paranoid. Stressed.

Spiraling. It makes sense. It has to make sense. I push the thought down, burying it under the usual weight of logic. Only the logical is trustworthy.

Coffee. I need coffee.

The comforting smell of fresh coffee grounds fills my nose. Bitter and earthy. Calli always makes it strong. I make my way to the kitchen and pour myself a mug, leaning against the counter like it's the only thing keeping me upright.

I can feel myself slipping. The line between what's real and what's not blurs more every day. The anxiety, tight chest, blurred vision, my hands that won't fucking steady.

I grip my mug tighter. Maybe it's hallucinations, or panic attacks. It doesn't matter—I have to push forward. But this presence, this thing in the dark that won't leave me alone. Even now, I feel it. Despite my logic, I don't want to break it apart like I do with everything else. It makes me feel safe.

I don't know what that says about me. I constantly remind myself to focus. To be better, stronger, less distracted. But this *ghost* is there every time I close my eyes. Something that *should* be an unwelcome distraction, but if I'm honest? I don't want to lose it. I shudder at the thought, recalling the events of last night.

"Jesus, Cade—you look like shit." My eyes shoot to Calli, who is already sitting at the table. Snapping out of my thoughts, I grunt and take a long sip of my coffee, ignoring her.

She stares and doesn't drop it.

"What?" I finally snap, sharper than I intended.

Her eyebrows lift. "Nothing. You just look . . . off. Didn't sleep?"

"Don't start," I growl.

And there's that look she does. The one where her mouth wants to fight but her eyes know she's already lost. She shrinks a little in her chair and I instantly feel like shit. Not because I yelled, but because she's used to it.

She exhales, attempting to deflect my misdirected anger. "So . . . What's going on with the mission or whatever?"

I sit across from her, mug between my hands. "Allen White's gone dark."

Her brows pull together. "What do you mean gone dark? Isn't he the guy whose daughter—"

"Yeah. Olivia White. I was waiting for the news of her death to drop. Instead? They ran a story saying both she and Allen died in the crash. Same day." Honestly not surprising. What were they going to say? *Heiress stabbed in the neck during orgy*? That'd be fucking hilarious.

Calli blinks, surprised. "What the hell?"

"Exactly. It's bullshit. He faked his death. Slipped out under a new alias. Jack tracked him to L.A. and then—nothing. Radio silence."

She frowns. "You think he's with the Covenant?"

I nod. "Or he's hiding with one of their upper-ring bastards. Either way, we'll find him."

There's a pause. Then she leans forward slightly. "What about his wife?"

I raise a brow. "Rosa?"

"Yeah. Could she be a way in?"

I shake my head, dismissing the idea. "Nah. Rosa White's all flash. Parties. Spending money. Showing off. She was never close with Allen in the cult's inner circles." I breathe the next words through my teeth. Pissed off, not at her, but that he's slipping through the cracks. "Not that I ever saw."

Calli tilts her head, unconvinced. "Still might be worth looking into."

I roll my eyes. "Sure. I'll keep that in mind."

The moment stretches, tense but quiet. Almost bearable.

Then Jack strolls in, humming some ungodly pop song, and goes straight for the coffeepot. Shirtless, barefoot, bedhead in full glory.

"You two look chipper this morning."

Both of us groan.

Calli mutters, “It’s not even seven. Why are you like this?”

Jack shrugs, pouring his coffee. “Some of us are emotionally well-adjusted.”

I snort into my mug.

Calli shoots him a death glare. “Touché.”

He leans on the counter, sipping with a smug grin. “So, what did I miss?”

Calli doesn’t even look at me. She just says flatly, “We’re gonna look into Rosa White.”

Jack blinks. “Really? Her?”

I sigh, finishing the last of my coffee. “Apparently.”

But the words taste wrong in my mouth. Like I already regret underestimating her.

Jack and I take our coffees and make our way to his office, Calli trailing behind us. The second we cross the threshold, I shoot her a stern look that she knows means I’m in no mood for her shit.

“I won’t touch anything,” she says quickly, hands up. “I’ll stay quiet.”

I give a clipped nod, pointing. “You stay over there, no breathing down our necks while we work.”

“I get it. I’ll stay on the back wall.”

Giving her my back, Jack drops into his chair and starts tapping away at the keyboard. The wall of monitors lights up like a command center.

“All right, let’s see if our fashion-obsessed widow is up to anything interesting,” Jack mutters to himself.

The next few minutes are a blur of code, surveillance footage, and low-level cyberstalking.

“Her socials are still active, but the posts are off. Inconsistent time stamps. Locations that don’t match. Either they’re scheduled or old shots. She’s not where she says she is.” Jack’s fingers fly over the keyboard. “There! A wire transfer from one of her shell companies hit a burner account out of New Mexico yesterday. Weird timing.”

I step forward, staring at the screen. "What's the account tagged to?"

"Anonymous, but the routing path links back to a private defense firm with known off-record affiliations. The kind of group that launders secrets and builds tech for people who don't officially exist. That screams Order."

"But it's not Allen?"

Jack shakes his head. "Nope. Tracked the signal through three proxies. He's not with them. He's alone."

A smile slowly spreads across my face. "Perfect."

Jack frowns. "Still doesn't tell us where—"

Calli speaks for the first time since entering the room. "He's probably holed up somewhere eating cold Chef Boyardee out of a can like a scared little rat."

Jack freezes. "Say that again."

Calli blinks and repeats slowly. "Chef . . . Boyardee?"

Jack spins back to the keyboard. "No—the hiding. He's not in a facility. He's off the grid. He's being cheap, scared. That narrows the radius. Think motels. Cash-only rentals. No cameras."

He clicks a few more times, scanning databases.

"Boom! Got him. Last-known credit card swipe was at a gas station half a mile from a rundown motel in Nevada. He's not laying low with the Covenant. He's hiding in plain sight, and he's panicked. Amateur."

Jack turns the screen, revealing a grainy still from a motel parking lot.

"Nice work, Cal."

I stand up slowly, gaze fixed on the screen.

Calli eyes me wearily. "What are you going to do?"

I smirk. "Get some answers. Through his teeth or his fingernails. Whichever gives first."

CHAPTER 7

CALLISTO

The look on my face could probably tell a thousand words. *What. The. Fuck.* I went from feeling proud of my remark actually leading to Allen's location to feeling sick to my stomach.

My brother is crazy. I know the way we were raised was entirely different—he a weapon, me a sacrifice. But is he certifiable? Something is definitely off with my brother. I have no doubt that it has something to do with the pendulum—I don't even know how it got here. It just kind of showed up . . . One moment there was just the grimoire and the next it was laying there like it was always there.

But something in my gut told me that I needed to give it to him, that calling on the spirits—or whatever is connected to that thing—might help him, might save him.

I hate the idea of this mission—I hate his entire goal. But I promised myself I would try to understand the position he's in, that I would do anything I could to try to be helpful. We're all we have, after all.

But I'm unstable.

My nerves are frayed and exposed. Too sensitive to the touch. I know the second I allow myself to feel everything, I could lose control. And I don't know what that looks like. Trying to fix what's broken is hard, and having hope . . . well, that's even harder, but I'm trying.

Despite all my efforts, the dread is still there looming over me, waiting to creep in when I least expect it. The concoction of fear and anxiety is creating this potent and toxic perception in the depths of my mind.

An unholy configuration that separates me from who I think I am.

I don't even know who I am.

I've never had a chance to find out. But I do know:

I am more than my trauma.

I am more than my pain.

I. Am. More.

I exhale a breath in an attempt to center myself and prepare to attack this head-on, with logic instead of emotion. Jack and Cade may not want to hear it, but they *will* know my thoughts on the matter.

I grit my teeth. "Cade."

"What?" he snaps.

"I, uh . . . I think if you're going to do this, you should focus on choosing your location. The desert would be a good place . . ." I stumble over myself, wanting to retch at my next words. "Bodies decay quickly in the desert, and if he's in Nevada, it wouldn't be too difficult to smuggle him to one of the abandoned mine shafts out there."

Cade quirks a brow and looks over at Jack. He looks almost impressed.

Almost.

Jack goes back to clacking on his keyboard. "I can pull a list of some of our best options." His fingers move even quicker. "Better than your idea of winging it," he says sarcastically, with a glance at Cade.

"I just want to say, for the record, I don't like this. Torturing a man? This feels like you're taking it too far. And I know you don't want to hear it, but I need you to," I say, looking at Cade.

He steps over to me and places his hands on my shoulders, pushing them back as he looks down at me.

"I appreciate your concern. I know this seems wrong to you. But I need you to know how essential it is that I get whatever information this man has." He speaks with sincerity. "I've seen a boy barely younger than you fall to that man's blade. He doesn't deserve your empathy, Calli."

"It's not him I care about, it's you. It's what spending every moment planning and executing these missions will do to you."

"And as much as I appreciate that, I feel that you underestimate my ability. I'll be fine. You just focus on yourself," he says, walking back over to Jack and making a hand gesture for me to leave.

Fine.

I'm not even sure there was any point in telling him how I feel. He's going to do what he wants anyway, my feelings be damned. I walk away, toward the door, when I hear Cade speak once more.

"That looks like a perfect location." He turns his head toward me. "Good call."

I give him a tight-lipped smile as I shut the door behind me. I could use some air.

Heading to the front porch, I sit on the swing Cade built for me, my focus shifting to the tree line beyond. It's beautiful here, I have to admit. This may be my prison, but a lovely prison it is.

The chill in the air bites at my nose and I wrap my cardigan around myself and pull the sleeves down over my hands. I lean my head back, sighing heavily. The wind begins to pick up, and goose bumps rise over my skin. The wind howls, bringing with it an eerie sound. As if it's calling my name.

I look toward the trees. I scan the area and my eyes focus on a shadowy figure near a tree. A figure . . .

It must be almost seven feet tall, a black mass of curling smoke. I blink. It's the shadows playing tricks on me again. It shifts—moving side to side and pulsing, as if to show me it's there. It *wants* me to know it's there.

I'm completely frozen as it approaches. Afraid that if I do turn around to run inside, it will be on my heels, that same scent from earlier flooding my nostrils: amber and earth. My heart is pounding out of my chest, but all I can do is stare, immobile. As if I'm in a trance, waiting for it to do something.

It doesn't seem to have any features. At least none that I can make out. I can't tell if it's looking at me or facing away in its approach. The sky is starting to darken, the shadows stretching, and the figure becomes too difficult to focus on. For a moment I feel a jolt of panic rush through me, or is it anticipation, for what my shadow will do. I can't look away as we come face-to-face, *his* hand reaching out and caressing my cheek—like a lover would.

"You are mine, and soon . . . I will own every part of you."

It's in that moment that I instinctively yell for Cade in an ear-piercing shriek.

Immediately, I hear heavy footfalls from inside the house. My shadow disappears as if he were never there. The door is pulled open quickly, and Cade flies out, scanning the yard.

Turning toward me, he asks, "What's wrong?"

I lean forward, finally feeling safe enough to look away from the forest.

"I'm sorry, I—" I start, but he cuts me off.

"Stop apologizing. It's my job to keep you safe. What happened?"

Knowing he won't believe what I saw, I hesitate, but then speak anyway.

"I saw something," I say, pointing to the last place I saw the figure. "In the woods." The area is now drenched in darkness.

"Are you saying you saw—a *person*?" Cade pulls out his phone, turning on the light.

"Umm. No, I don't think so. I just saw a shadow."

"It's all shadows out here, Calli. But I'll do a perimeter check, just in case. I'll go tell Jack to check the cameras—"

"No!" I interrupt. "I'll go tell him." I rush inside before he can argue. I'm cold, and I don't want to be out here any longer.

I rush to Jack's office, plopping into the armchair in the corner.

"Cade wants to do a quick perimeter check—he says to check the cameras," I say while rubbing my temples.

Jack frowns but pulls up the feed.

I want to tell them it's pointless, that they aren't going to find anything. I know it's in here with me.

CHAPTER 8

CADE

I make my way over to the garage. Pushing the door open takes more force than it should—I need to fix that hinge.

I sift through all of my drawers in an attempt to find my spotlight. Where the fuck did it go?

I swear to God one of these days I'm going to hide Jack's controller if he keeps putting his hands on my shit. I finally find it in a drawer that I *know* I didn't leave it in, and make my way back outside to the tree line. Calli may have thought that she saw a shadow, but I know damn well that's not the scariest thing that could be out in these woods. If I made any slipups on my mission, there's a chance we could be traced back to this place.

I follow the path outside the woods, keeping an eye out for any signs of movement. I move toward the spot Calli pointed to earlier, then stop. I can hear a faint rustling about ten feet into the trees and turn on the spotlight, pointing it in the direction of the noise. I dig my feet in and prepare for a fight.

A fucking deer pops its head up and immediately books it deeper into the forest.

Goddamn it, Calli . . .

I shake my head and make my way back to the garage, tossing the spotlight onto the workshop bench. I look over my latest project, the birdhouse Calli wants for her garden in the backyard. It's not much, but that garden is the only sense of freedom I've been able to grant her. So I do my best to help her spruce it up with my woodworking. Keeps my mind busy, too.

Might as well take this opportunity to pack a bag, I think, pulling out my duffel from under the bench. I begin opening all of my drawers, examining every weapon at my disposal while imagining all the things I could do to Allen when I finally get ahold of him.

I carefully and methodically pack every weapon, along with some rope and morphine.

I lift the duffel over my shoulder, pick up a canister of gasoline, and walk it over to my truck, setting the canister in the back. I open the passenger door and toss the bag inside. The only pleasure I'll be receiving from this is knowing that the man I'm doing this to deserves it.

I'm not completely fucked in the head.

Yet.

Maybe Calli has a point. But even if she does, it won't make a difference. I have to do this. I owe her that much. She deserves a chance to have a normal life. As normal as she can, anyway. She might be a little crazy, but who the fuck am I to talk?

And who could blame her? Our parents kept her completely isolated, and now I'm doing the same. She is desperately trying to hold on to whatever her imagination comes up with. Maybe she's gone stir-crazy. I've kept her here to try to keep her safe. But she is losing it, and she's old enough now that she should be afforded a bit of freedom. Just a bit.

Jack has all the materials to make fake IDs—he pretty frequently has to make them for me. That would at least give me some peace of mind. It's been long enough that people shouldn't recognize her.

I walk into the office to find Jack sitting at his computer.

"Yo, I'm just finishing up that perimeter check. We're all clear," he says, not looking up.

"I'm aware," I say, my voice flat. "Bambi scared her."

"You serious?" he asks with a smile. "Bless her heart . . . that's adorable." He chuckles to himself.

I pull my brows together and change the subject.

"I want to make her a new ID. You think you can manage that before I leave?"

He rolls his chair toward me, a surprised look on his face.

"Uh, yeah. What made you want to do that?"

"She needs to get the fuck out of the house. Not too far, but going into town should be fine," I say, shrugging.

"Hell yeah. I have the template left over from your last one. Should only take me a few hours. I got you," he says, a little too pleased.

"Take her out, do something fun. Just get her out of her fucking head."

"Can do, boss," he says, fingers working the keyboard.

"Just don't have too much fun. Keep her safe. And just to put this out there: I'm not above cutting your dick off, shoving it down your throat, and sewing your lips shut."

Jack pauses for a moment, not acknowledging my threat.

That's fine.

He knows I mean it.

It's always been a concern of mine, those two, but despite his stalker-like nature and weak spot for women in general, he's been trustworthy and is damn good at what he does.

I found him when the Covenant sent me on one of my first missions. Jack was just a kid, but he had smuggled over a million dollars out of one of the Covenant's offshore accounts. I was ordered to execute him but instead, I decided to cut him a deal—one he was happy to take. He works for me, and I give him security, a safe place, and a purpose. He has a fetish for pulling things apart to see how they work—from security systems to people's minds. Over the years we have become close.

The plan was always to get me and Calli out of there so we could have a life. But when I found out about the Covenant's plans, it didn't take me and Jack long to organize a hasty escape. Those two became fast friends, and after all this time I know I can trust he will do everything to keep her safe.

I sigh audibly.

"Listen. I need to thank you, Jack." I grit my teeth. "If I didn't have you, a lot of what I do wouldn't be possible, and no matter what, I know she won't be alone."

He turns, a smile playing on his lips.

"Hey, man, you and Calli are the closest thing I have to family. I was off the deep end when you found me. You gave me a chance to prove myself, and I don't intend on squandering that. We're a team, a fucked-up trio going up against the man." He grins. "I live for this shit."

"I'm just worried about Calli. Maybe they fucked her up too much."

"Naw, she's more resilient than you think. We all got our own shit going on. We may not get her, but we are still here for her." He turns back to his screens. "Stop overthinking. You're doing everything you can. She may not like it now, but one day she will thank you for it."

I pause at his words. He's right. One day she will get to settle down, get married, have kids. She will get to live the life she deserves, and it will be on her terms. That's what has kept me going—I just don't want to focus so much on the future I picture for her that I neglect her now. That's why this is a good idea. Let her have a little leash, have normal experiences with normal-ass people. That's what I want for her.

I'll deal with the cesspool that lingers over us. I don't care what I have to do, or what it does to me, if it keeps her hands clean. That's why I never wanted her involved in the first place. But she isn't a kid anymore . . .

I can't just distract her from the reality of this. I can't shelter her from everything, no matter how much I want to.

She will keep asking questions, and keep digging for answers.

All that matters is that she is safe right now.

I grab the door handle and look over at Jack.

"I'm gonna go take a shower and finish getting ready. Leave everything on your desk and I'll grab it in the morning."

"No problem."

Maybe I should be less concerned about micromanaging her and more concerned about whatever the fuck is going on with me. As much as I want to deny it, these dreams—this *feeling*—is really starting to fuck with me. They feel too good, too real. I keep finding that I don't want to leave the dreams . . .

I make my way to the bathroom, the door clicking shut behind me. I turn the water on and strip my clothes off, throwing them into a heap on the floor.

I shake my head, attempting to push the thought from my mind.

It's. Not. Fucking. Real.

I step into the shower, hoping the heat of the water will burn the thought from my mind. But it's not enough.

I can *feel* you watching me.

You're always here, in the back of my mind.

The steam curls around my body like fingers. I try to hone in on the water hitting the tile, my head bowed, palms planted on the slick wall in front of me. But I become too aware of my body, focusing too hard on my chest rising with each inhale, trembling with restraint I don't understand.

Or maybe I do.

I grit my teeth and my eyes fall shut. The image of *you* forms instantly. Never your face—but your presence.

I drag my hand slowly across my abdomen, feeling the way my stomach flexes under my own touch. I wrap my hand around my cock, the pressure deliberate.

I stroke myself slowly. My thumb circling over the head, smearing the precum down my length until my grip slides. I brace against the wall, my head falling forward as I imagine it's *you* touching me. I imagine your mouth tracing along my jaw. Down my neck. Over my chest.

"Yes, just like that," I grunt.

I squeeze tighter, my pace quickening, the wet rhythmic sound filling the space. Your presence circles me as I bite back a moan, my imagination turning the water into your hands, dragging down my back.

I fuck into my hand like it's your mouth begging to be claimed. My muscles tense. "Shit," I mutter under my breath. My grip tightens. I'm so close . . . My body twitches as my pace quickens. I jerk harder as your mouth takes me in my mind. My head leans back as my orgasm hits hard, and I savor it. Milking every last drop from myself, my breath ragged. It's not enough. I want more. I want *you.*

CHAPTER 9

CALLISTO

I lie down on my bed reading the smutty romance Jack picked up for me in town. The painfully slow burn finally breaks—he kisses her. The tension spills into something hungry, and my breath catches as I feel the whisper of a hand trailing down my abdomen.

"Do you need my help, darling?"

I keep reading, stomach flipping with each word as the characters start fucking in vivid detail. "I need it," I whisper.

Pressure builds between my legs, and I let myself get lost in the hand drifting under the blanket. Attempting to quelch the growing need.

"Spread them wider for me." And I do.

The lights begin to flicker, and I'm lost in the sensation. Entirely giving in to it. I need this.

"Calli, why the hell is your door locked?"

My door handle jiggles violently, followed by pounding.

Cade.

I jump, flushed and annoyed. Fuck him. Scrambling upright, I swing the door open.

"You trap me in this house like a prisoner, and now I can't even have privacy?"

"If it means you're safe—yes."

"How about fuck you. What do you want?" I snap.

He smirks, pulling a small envelope from his back pocket.

"Jack got you a new ID. There's also a credit card."

My eyes widen, something akin to hope blooming in my chest. "Wait—does this mean I can leave?"

"You can go into town. But not without Jack. No risks. I get it—you need some freedom."

I fight the sting of tears that threaten to fall. A warmth blooms in my chest. It's not everything, but it's something. I smile and wrap my arms around him. Maybe too tightly, because he stiffens, clearly hating it, but I don't care.

"Thank you."

He pulls back, locking eyes with me. "Don't make me regret this. If anyone figures out who you are, we're done."

"I'll be low-key, don't worry."

"You'll do exactly what Jack says. Got it?"

I shrug and tuck the cards into my wallet, replacing my real ID.

"I'll be back in a few days."

He turns to leave, but I catch his sleeve. He only meets my eyes for a moment, jaw set, before I speak. "Be careful."

He doesn't respond, just nods and walks away.

I watch him disappear down the stairs, and for a second I feel it again. That same gentle presence from when I gave him the pendulum. I whisper into the silence, say, "Take care of him, okay? He doesn't know it yet, but he needs you." As soon as my brother pulls out of the driveway, Jack sidles up next to me.

"Want to get out of here?"

"You have no idea."

We've been driving for about thirty minutes before I finally speak up.

"So, where exactly are we going?"

"You'll see," Jack says with a big grin. "We're almost there."

"You better not be taking me to a fucking strip club, Jack."

He laughs as he turns into a small gravel parking lot. There's a little building with a sign that reads *Carmalitas*.

"A restaurant?" I ask, my brow raised in confusion.

"They have the best enchiladas. You'll love it," he says, pulling the keys from the ignition, stepping out of the truck, and turning to me. "C'mon, let's go."

I reluctantly exit the truck. The building looks old. Red, green, and white banners hang from the outdoor seating area.

He opens the door for me. "Ladies first."

I give him the side-eye and walk past.

"Table for two?" the hostess asks with a smile.

"Yes, ma'am," Jack speaks up.

She grabs two menus, ushering us to a booth in the back.

"Any suggestions?" I ask, sliding into my seat across from him.

He leans in excitedly, pointing to the menu. "You're gonna want their chimichangas—they are to die for. Oh! And their deep-fried ice cream, *and* they have the best margaritas," he says enthusiastically.

"I'm sorry . . . did you say deep-fried *ice cream*?" I look to where he is pointing on the menu. "How does that even work?"

"I think they freeze-dry it or something, but it's amazing. Wanna try it?"

I nod slowly. "I will admit, I'm curious. Let's get it."

After we order, Jack jumps out of the booth and jogs up to our server, whispering something in her ear before coming back over.

"What was that?" I ask.

"You'll see," he says with a mischievous smile.

It doesn't take long for our food to arrive. I pick up my fork and take my first bite, and my Gods, it's delicious. I look up and see Jack is focused on his phone. My heart drops. We shouldn't be hearing from

Cade until he gets to Allen's last-known location, and that won't be for a while. If it's him, something could be wrong.

I speak through my full mouth.

"Is everything okay?"

"Yeah," he laughs, turning the phone to show a picture of me taking a very large, very unflattering bite of food.

I reach across the table to grab the phone, my mouth still full.

"Delete that!"

"No way! You look cute," he says with a genuine smile.

I sit back in the seat, crossing my arms in protest, and decide to ignore him for the remainder of my meal. I focus on the intricate wooden carvings on the booth behind him. Images of cowboys riding horses, beautifully done. It reminds me of Cade, and when he made me the most beautiful vanity with intricate roses carved on the sides. I smile despite myself. It's one of the few things I kept from our old house—how he combined his carving capabilities with my love of flowers was incredibly thoughtful.

It's hard to picture him working on something so small and detailed. But it's his thing. Isolating himself in his workshop and eventually coming out with the most beautiful things. It took me months to talk him out of building every piece of furniture in the house. I wanted an actual couch, with cushions. Not a damn bench that looks like it belongs in a museum.

My thoughts are interrupted when a loud bell rings behind me. I jump at the sound as four servers come to our table singing happy birthday. They drop a large sombrero on my head and slide two shots of clear liquid in front of me.

Not knowing how to respond, I sit there, smiling like an idiot while they sing. Jack, phone in hand, is smiling ear to ear, clearly recording the moment. I shoot him a death glare. It's not even my birthday. As if he can read my mind, he shrugs.

"Free shots."

He picks them up, handing me one. He drinks his and slams it on the table, and I follow his movements. The burn going down my throat makes me wince, and I exhale as if I'm breathing fire. The servers are cheering. I nod and thank them as they walk away, our server setting our check down on the table as I ask for our ice cream to go before she joins them.

"Was that completely necessary?" I ask.

"No, but watching your reaction was fucking worth it," he says, smirking.

"What was in that shot?" I ask, taking a sip of the sweet tea I ordered.

"That, my dear, was tequila."

"Okay, I'll admit, this was fun," I say, admiring the rim of the hat still on my head. "Do I get to keep this?"

The server walking past speaks before Jack can answer.

"No, you can leave it at the register on your way out."

I look away, embarrassed, and Jack laughs.

"You're a dick," I say with venom before laughing with him.

"So." He takes a breath. "You ready for our next stop?"

"I don't think so."

"No, I think you're gonna like this one."

I follow him to the front, reluctantly returning the beautiful sombrero to the hostess while he pays the bill.

The sky is just starting to get dark as we step out of the restaurant, the deep blue casting an eerie atmosphere over our parking spot. Chills creep down my spine. For a moment—just a moment—I had almost forgotten about everything. Even the thing I know is watching me. I pause, staring at the shadowy tree line.

"Calli," Jack says with concern. "C'mon."

I robotically move toward the truck as he leans over to open my door from the driver's seat. I let myself sink into my seat, the leather squeaking under me.

"All right!" he says, clapping his hands together. "Ready to get your ass kicked?"

His words pull me out of whatever moment I was having.

"Uh . . ."

He pulls out a huge sack, and it jingles in his hand.

"We're going to the fuckin' arcade!" he says with an exaggerated, enthusiastic voice.

My shoulders perk up a bit. That actually sounds fun. I look at him with a faux-serious face.

"Just, please promise me it won't involve any more singing."

He laughs under his breath as he turns the key, shifts the truck into gear.

"Scout's honor."

CHAPTER 10

ALABASTER

I watch as Calli and Jack approach the large building lit up in an array of neon lights. They walk arm in arm, almost skipping. I fucking hate this guy. I don't trust anyone who is that . . . happy. It's fucking weird. But despite my reservations, I've never seen her smile like that before. Problem is, it's not me who's causing it.

Why the hell does that bother me? They seem close . . . too close.

I could always possess the fucker. That could be fun, but it would ruin her night.

Maybe another time.

I follow behind them as they go to the counter, my eyes zoning in on how well her ass fills out her jeans. For a goddess that doesn't get out much, she has the most exquisite frame. A large bowling alley sits to one side of the entertainment space, people filling the lanes. Jack shamelessly flirts with the girl handing them their wristbands. Gods, what an ass. Calli appears to agree, judging by the annoyed look she flashes him as she walks away.

It's in that moment that I sidle up next to her, my fingertips brushing her hair away from her face. Her skin pebbles with my touch—*yes, she's already molding for me, and she doesn't even know it.* "We're going to *have so much fun . . .*" My voice is a whisper, her eyelashes fluttering. I take a step back, giving her space for Jack to reapproach.

As he shoves the piece of paper with the girl's number on it in his pocket, he wraps his fucking arm around Calli, escorting her to the arcade doors.

I've changed my mind. *I'm gonna make their night a living hell.*

Calli immediately cheers at the sight of all the games, flashing lights, and neon screens beckoning her.

"Dance battle, milady?" the blond one suggests. Absolutely not on my watch are they going to be that close. I reach my hand out and grab the cord, not realizing this one cord is connected to every game along the wall, which effectively shuts off nearly half of the arcade.

Oh well.

"Oh my Gods!" She turns to Jack, clearly searching for answers.

He can't give you those, Calli.

Jack's hand grips the back of his neck. He searches the arcade for another appropriate game, till his eyes land on one I don't mind them indulging in.

"Want to play air hockey?"

Calli's face beams. "Fuck yes! Let's do it," she says, pumping her fist in the air.

They move to their respective sides, and Jack places four coins in the slot. The machine roars to life and the air makes the puck float around the table. *Interesting.* Calli cracks her knuckles and readies herself.

"Hope you're ready to get your ass kicked," she quips. I creep up behind her, just a breath away. Drawn to her fire.

"You must not know—I'm the reigning air hockey champ around these parts, Cal."

My eyes roll back into my head, *please . . .*

She hits the puck, immediately sinking the first shot before Jack has time to defend. My hands reach out, gripping her ample hips and guiding her to rub up against my growing interest for her. She doesn't even resist, but pushes harder against me. A small moan slips past her lips, so low I almost don't hear it.

My, she is impressive. Being so dirty for me where anyone can see, but nobody will know.

"Cheap shot!" he says, placing the puck back on the table.

"You must have forgotten how good I am," she says, blocking his shot.

"Oh, I could never forget how good you are," he says, his voice deeper.

I see her give him a sultry look. What the fuck is that smile?

I don't even blink. My hand snaps out and cracks against her ass cheek.

Her body jerks forward, the sound muffled by the music and chatter of the arcade.

My voice is a growl, low in my chest, as I lean in. "*You are mine, pretty girl. Don't make me take you for the first time over this table.*" She has the intelligence to bite her lip, letting out a tiny whimper.

"Do you remember, Calli?" the dick has the gall to say.

"Jack . . ." Did she just sound breathy for him?

Oh, fuck no. My hand shoots out, shadows going into the machine without thought, forcing it to malfunction. The air stops, and the lights flicker before going dark. Call me petty or jealous, I don't fucking care. This guy is toying with what is mine, and needs to be put in his place.

Calli's pale skin is red from embarrassment. She may not know who I am yet or what I will do, but she can't deny that she likes it.

"What the hell?" I hear Jack complain as he kicks the leg of the table. "I'm definitely leaving this place a bad review. They've got to have some faulty wiring."

"Maybe . . ." she says, and I can feel her lean back against me. She's upright now, her whole body shivering as she feels my chest go up and down behind her.

"You good, Calli? You're really flush," Jack says, turning toward the employee standing at the door.

"Nod for him," I rumble, low in her ear. She does. *"Good girl. Now get rid of him so we can play."*

"I'm good, Jack. Can you go ask the employee eye-fucking you, though? Maybe she can fix it for us. I'm gonna go to the bathroom."

I'm honestly shocked the hunter would allow someone like this anywhere near his *precious sister.* They've clearly fucked. And I don't think big brother knows. Maybe I don't need to kill him to be rid of him—Cade will do the dirty work for me. As I guide her, a sly grin curls on my face.

"When you said play, I really thought you were referring to something else." Is she pouting? My, my. I love seeing this side of her.

"We are playing," I whisper in her ear, my right hand trailing up and down her spine, the other guiding her to aim at the zombies on the screen. I can see the goose bumps rise on her skin at the bottom of her cropped white tank. It's exquisite.

Callisto isn't a small girl by any means, but she is dwarfed next to Jack.

I'm still taller . . . But I want her to understand how to defend herself. To feel a sense of power she hasn't been afforded.

"If you wanted to kill zombies, we could just go home and play *COD*," Jack interjects, ruining our perfect moment.

"But here we get actual guns! Kind of . . ." She laughs. "Besides, the games we play at home are not the same thing." He flashes a grin at her, nudging her shoulder. My eye twitches.

"Yeah, you're also terrible at pool."

She glares at him. "I sunk the eight ball *one* time," she says, looking over at the girls who are still lingering near where this tool came back from. "So, did you get that girl's number?" She looks at him with a smile.

"I got *two*," he says with a mischievous smirk.

Dick.

"I guess you don't need a wingwoman," she retorts, going back to shooting zombies.

"Remember that time I snuck you out to the park and that drunk group of girls came up to us? The blond ended up making out with *you*."

My eyebrows raise at that. She continues to surprise me.

"Hey, she came out of nowhere."

"Either way, if you tried to be my wingwoman, you would end up with all the ladies. Which defeats the purpose."

"That was *not* my fault. But I suppose you have a point, after all. I am hotter than you." She flicks her hair over her shoulder—her scent is intoxicating.

"Low blow, Cal. But I can't disagree." These two are fucking weird. I can't get a read on them. And although the image of Callisto making out with another woman is kind of sexy, a part of me hates the fact that he knows her so well. That he can sit there, be an asshole, and she's just having a good time. This makes no goddamn sense.

I'm back in the corner, allowing her a moment of peace, when I sense something near. One of my kind.

Guess my fun is over.

I shift into smoke, moving around the building like a blur. I stop dead in my tracks when I see Alok, staring at Callisto.

No.

"What the fuck are you doing here?" I approach him quickly, sizing him up.

He laughs under his breath. "I told you I wanted to know what had you so consumed by this one." He pauses. "Now I know."

My heart skips a beat and my throat goes dry.

"You don't know shit," I say, attempting to brush him off.

"That mark on the back of her neck."

"What about it?" I glare at him.

"She is marked for death," he continues. "Now, I wonder how that happened."

"That's what I'm trying to figure out," I answer, attempting to sound convincing.

It's not technically a lie. Humans shouldn't have ancient knowledge like that. But I know how they got it. The grimoire. I just don't know how they obtained that particular artifact.

"So you are following this pretty thing to discover the source?"

"I'm fucking warning you. Stay out of this."

He smiles. "I will do as I please. And you aren't going to stop me." He moves closer, whispering in my ear, "I think I'll drop in every now and then. You see, I like pretty things, too. You have piqued my interest and I currently have nothing better to do."

"Leave her out of it. I can deal with this on my own," I say, head down, ears back.

"Oh, I don't think I will. And if you try and stop me, I could always inform the council."

"How petty of you. All of this because you're bored?"

"Sure. You could say that." He smiles. "I'm sure they will be intrigued as to why such ancient knowledge is carved into a human's flesh. A mark that symbolizes worship and sacrifice of our kind." He looks me in the eye. "Such a binding hasn't been allowed since before the war of the titans."

"Don't threaten me with a good time, Alok. I've broken no laws."

He looks up at me with an aura of authority. "You're toeing the line, Kai," he says sternly, using my chosen name. "I will sate my curiosity, and you will not deny me, or I will say something."

"She. Is. Mine," I say as the ground rumbles under our feet, my voice a low growl. "You will do well to remember that. I'll tell you what I know when I know."

Alok chuckles, patting my shoulder.

"Don't worry, brother. I'll keep to the shadows. For now. But expect to see me again. I happen to enjoy watching the way this one affects you."

I despise being toyed with, and I hate being threatened even more.

He's not wrong, though. I've been able to keep this quiet for so long simply because my kind doesn't meddle in human affairs. But this, this is different, and my hands are tied. I clench my jaw, that fucker.

I don't respond. I want to tell him to fuck off, to threaten him. But it's not worth the trouble. I doubt he would actually say anything, but the threat is enough to accept the position I'm in. The council is a bunch of old fuckers, powerful, out of touch, and set in their ways. Keeping this under wraps is more important than ever, especially with Alok involved.

"See you soon, friend," he says ominously, grinning from ear to ear before disappearing, leaving me standing there like a dumbass. I rub my face in frustration.

"Fuck . . ."

I make my way back over to Callisto and Jack as they continue having a good old time.

I need a distraction, and since I'm here, I might as well make the best of it. I notice them playing Pop-A-Shot. Lifting my hand, I begin manipulating Jack's balls, skewing them just enough to not go in the hoop.

"Wow, you suck at this," Calli says, laughing at his failure.

Yeah, this'll make me feel better.

CHAPTER II

CADE

I slam my fists into the steering wheel over and over. I've been a real fucking asshole. I know. She doesn't deserve it. Neither does Jack, but I didn't exactly get lessons on how to be a good brother and friend. No family nights at the dinner table for me.

It was "Be sure to drive the knife in deeper" and "Attachments get you killed."

Stopping my assault, I exhale.

My eyes shift to a bright neon sign and my stomach growls.

First: doughnuts and coffee.

I pull into the parking lot, grabbing my hoodie from the passenger seat and tossing it over my head. Opening the door to the Dunkin,' the smell of fresh coffee grounds fill the air. My favorite.

The employee behind the counter gives me a half smile and takes my order. A large mocha cappuccino and a half dozen chocolate-frosted doughnuts. It doesn't take long for her to set my order on the counter.

The wind picks up as I open the door to leave, and I almost drop my damn coffee. The Dunkin' employee comes up behind me and holds the door open, then follows me out and lights up a cigarette.

I huff as I open my truck door. I am throwing my doughnuts on the front seat and setting my coffee in the center console when I hear a sound coming from the truck.

Was that a fucking *cat*?

I step back out of the vehicle, my eyes looking over the bed of the truck. Nothing.

I bend down, my hand pressing into the gravel as I look under the truck. I hear another little sound come from behind me. It's in the fucking wheel well.

I crouch down, angling my eyes up, and I'm met with glowing orbs of amber staring back at me.

It really is a fucking cat.

Reaching my hand up under my truck, I wrap my hands around the black fluffy thing. Surprisingly, it doesn't fight me. I set it on the ground in front of the truck, and it just stares up at me.

"You do know that is not a safe place to sleep, right?" Did I just speak to a cat? Eh, not the weirdest thing I've done lately.

The little thing begins stretching on my pant leg, kneading my leg like it's a scratching post.

You've gotta be fucking kidding me.

I shoo the cat, but instead it jumps onto my hood, meowing loudly, like I offended it. It snuggles up against the windshield, making itself at home.

I roll my eyes, resigned, and head back inside to ask if I can have a cup of water. Coming back out to my truck, cup in hand, I set the cup on the ground and offer my fingers to the snoozing cat on my hood.

"Psspsspss."

Surprisingly, the cat hops down and begins lapping up the liquid. I attempt another escape.

I sit in the driver's seat and start to close the door when I hear the hostile employee start yelling at the cat. "Outta here, you mangy little fucker!" The cat cowers in front of the tree near the entrance, and the man kicks it.

He fucking *kicked* it.

I sigh, opening the door, and slowly walk over to the man.

"The hell is your problem?" he asks, taking another casual drag.

I don't blink as I approach the offensive asshole. I ball my fists at my sides, attempting to restrain myself from knocking this fucker on his ass.

"I have very little tolerance for people who hurt things that can't fight back," I say in a controlled voice.

I walk over and pick the cat up, cradling it in my arms, when it hisses at the man. I look down and chuckle at it.

"Sassy little thing, aren't you? Should we make the big bad man pay for hurting you?"

I look back at the guy and, pulling out my pocket knife, walk over to him, next to his vehicle, and shove the knife into one of his tires.

"Yo, what the fuck!" I hear him yell from behind me.

"Karma's a bitch," I say, cat still in hand as I walk away, flipping him off. The cat purrs in my arms.

"Aww, you liked that?"

I may not believe in magic, but I sure as fuck believe in karma. I get in the car and set the cat down on the seat next to me, watching out the window as the employee talks on his phone. Clearly calling the police to complain about a man slashing his tire. I chuckle to myself as I start the engine and back out quickly. I shake my head.

Great. Now I've got a cat.

I look over at the small cat curled up in a little ball beside me on the seat.

I blow out a breath, resigned. "I guess you're coming home with me."

I make an unanticipated stop at the corner store. There's an entire aisle dedicated to pet food, toys, and litter. I am *not* having a shit box in my house. I look over the many options and realize I have no fucking clue what I'm doing, so I grab a couple bags of assorted toys, a cardboard scratcher, and all the bags that have cat faces on them. This cat better be fucking grateful. I walk over to the cashier, my arms full, and drop everything on the counter in front of me. The cashier jumps at the thud. I watch as he scans the items one by one, attempting to make conversation.

"You must have a lot of cats," the cashier quips.

Okay, so *maybe* I got too much. How the fuck am I supposed to know how much one of these things eat? I've never had a pet.

"Your total is $186.68."

I hand him two hundred-dollar bills, take the bags as he passes me my change, then casually exit the store. Back in the truck, I address the cat curled up next to me.

"You're shitting outside, got it?"

The cat looks up at me and yawns, settling itself back in a ball. I guess it's kind of cute.

Pulling into our driveway, I notice Jack's truck is gone. That didn't take long, I suppose. Hopefully they stay out of trouble, if that's even possible for Jack.

I open the truck and the cat jumps out, staying at my heels as I pull the pet items out of the truck bed.

Stepping through the front door, the cat runs in and hops up on the kitchen counter, wrapping her tail around her legs as she begins licking her paw.

"You have a habit of making yourself at home, don't you?" I scoff, pulling two bowls from the cupboard. I fill one with water and set them both on the ground.

I tear into one of the bags of cat food, and at the sound of the kibble, the cat jumps down and attacks the food.

"You're her problem now," I say, grabbing a pen and piece of paper out of the kitchen drawer. "But I swear if you piss on my fucking couch, you're staying outside."

The cat doesn't even acknowledge me. I check the time on my phone. Fuck, I need to leave. I quickly run to the door before the cat gets any ideas about following me and make a beeline for my truck.

CHAPTER 12

ALABASTER

I force myself to dematerialize, leaving her to enjoy the rest of her afternoon. What? I can be generous. She rarely gets the opportunity to be out of these four walls—the least I can afford her is to give her the illusion of more freedom. The image of how she molded to me so beautifully, and for the whole world to see, sticks in my mind. My pretty Calli does love to put on a show, it would seem. So shameless.

Now back in her room, I realize once again I'm not alone.

Well.

Less alone than I usually am with you watching me. What are you doing here again? Aren't you supposed to be keeping watch over the brother?

Whatever. I can understand your interest, human, but know that I'm spoken for.

I walk down the stairs to sift through the library and see a tiny black cat with beautiful orange eyes staring up at me. Oh my fucking Gods.

"KITTY!"

I jump over to the fluffball and begin to squish her little face. She purrs into my hands as she willingly accepts my aggressive cuddles. I fucking love cats.

"You're a beauty," I say, scratching the underside of her chin. Her purrs ring through the room, and I smile to myself.

Interesting. Maybe I misjudged our hunter. He must have brought this kitty home.

"I wonder what the story with you is." Just picturing Cade in a position where he felt he needed to bring home a cat is hilarious to me. "He didn't see you coming, did he?"

I carefully pick up the cat and walk upstairs, lying down on Callisto's bed. The cat makes biscuits on my chest.

Yeah, I could get used to this . . .

I must have nodded off because I hear the front door shut, Jack's and Callisto's voices traveling. The little feline is still curled up on my chest, content and sleeping. I carefully set her down next to me on the pillow and creep through the door. Calli speaks up from the kitchen.

"Thanks, Jack, I really needed that." She sighs. "Wait, what's this?" I watch as she picks up a small note from the counter, reading it aloud.

"What's up with all the cat food?" Jack asks.

"So you won't be alone. P.S., her name is Karma." She stands there for a moment.

"I see cat things but no cat," Jack speaks up.

Calli begins looking around underneath chairs and tables before her gaze catches on a window—cracked open.

"What an idiot. He brought home a cat and left the window open. It's probably long gone by now. And why did he buy so much food?"

She goes over and picks up the bags, reading the labels off. "Pro kitten plan, digestive care for elderly cats, indoor joint health? What the fuck, Cade?"

I double over laughing at the top of the steps, my stomach tightening and my face hurting from the smile stuck on my face.

This fucking guy.

I see Karma walk past me, little paws hopping down the steps. The second Callisto notices, her face lights up and she crouches down.

"Oh my goodness, you're so cute!" she says in a high-pitched voice.

Karma rubs up against Callisto's legs, and when Jack bends down to beckon her, the cat totally ignores him.

"Aww, c'mon, don't be like that." He steps over and scratches under her chin and she purrs, thrilled for the interaction.

"She likes you!" Callisto says in that sweet voice of hers.

"Look at us, we're like a little family," Jacks says with a stupid-ass smile on his face.

Their eyes meet. Jack's face softens as he continues petting Karma. *My* Callisto and *my* cat are staring up at him as if he hung the fucking moon. A low growl rumbles in my throat. How dare they look at *Jack* like that.

I'm unable to hold back my rage as the air begins to vibrate around me. I quickly glide down the steps with the intention of doing . . . something. I don't know what. When I approach Jack, Karma comes over to me. Mewing into the air, still purring.

Fuck.

I can't be mad at a face like that.

Jack is unbothered, but Calli looks up. She notices Karma trying to get my attention, batting at empty air. I hear her heart begin to pick up.

Can she see me?

No. But her eyes . . . always *feel* like they're staring straight at me.

A smirk plays on my lips—Jack doesn't do that to her, but I do. I'm gonna make sure *I'm* the only thing that makes her heart race.

"You okay?" He waves a hand over her face. "You look like you're spacing out." He gives her an awkward laugh.

"Yeah," she says, her attention back on him. "My bad. Listen, I really do appreciate everything. You seem to take my mind off things so easily."

"Must be my charming personality and rugged good looks." He gives her an exaggerated bow.

She giggles. "I'm serious, Jack." She nudges his shoulder. "You've always been there for me when I need it most. I don't know what I would do without you right now."

Oh, she's gonna find out. Cuz I'm gonna fucking kill him.

He begins to lean in closer to her. "Calli, I need you to know—"

I put my hand out in front of me, forcing the temperature of her body to rise. I feel her heart skip a beat, and she pushes her hair behind her ear. Jerks away and stands up quickly.

"Sorry, I, um, I think I need to go to my room . . . Can we talk about it later?"

"Yeah, for sure." The moment is broken, and Jack rubs the back of his neck, his face red.

Fuck you, dude.

I follow Calli up the stairs. Opening the door to her bedroom, she beelines to her balcony.

She leans over the railing, scanning the horizon.

I bring my body flush with hers again, and she inhales. Like she's scenting the air.

"I know you're here . . ." she says. "I can feel your hands on me."

I smirk, but she can't see it—it's too soon to let her see me. I'm not done playing this game.

I angle my head down, my lips brushing her ear. "This view makes me miss my world."

She surprises me by asking, "What does your world look like?" My hands completely wrap around her waist now, our bodies flush.

"It's filled with vast forests and mountains that touch the clouds," I say. "Much like this one, but bigger. Better."

"Better?" she says, like she's in awe at the prospect.

I grin. "The flora and fauna shift with every biome, evolving into strange and beautiful forms depending on the region. The flow of time feels . . . different there. The planet doesn't spin like this one. Tidally locked, one side forever facing our star, about half the size of this one. Never moving across the sky. The side closest, nothing but scorched rock and lava in an endless day. A miserable place, but I do miss their mead. On the other side there is no sun, just three moons that push and pull the tides, the surface nearly uninhabitable. But below is one of my favorite places."

She stares out at the horizon, almost like she's in a trance at the prospect. "What is your favorite place?"

"The Underground." The way her body tenses at that brings a low rumble up my chest. The Underground is a cavern the size of a continent. Bioluminescent algae coats the walls and ceiling like stars in an endless night sky. I don't miss the war on resources. We are good at war. That's probably why Alok is so dead set on bothering me, to avoid the chaos and meddle in my life. "Perhaps I'll bring you there one day."

"I think I'd like that." Fuuuck, she's perfect.

I don't know what it is about her. The way she moves, the way she thinks, her stubborn, relentless personality . . . it all makes me gravitate toward her. I want to break every rule I've been taught, to forget what I am, forget why I'm here, just to be near her.

I bring my lips down to her collarbone, just brushing it, and she arches for me. Angling her hips so that she pushes further into me.

"Why can I feel you but not see you? Are you here to hurt me?"

"I would never hurt you, unless you want me to." Her thighs clench at that, and my hands trail down her body. She's quivering in my arms. I bring my second hand up, gripping her throat. She gasps, but I don't stop there. Instead my tongue flicks out, licking from her shoulder up to her collarbone.

When she lets out a whimper, I am done for . . . my eyes rolling into the back of my head. Her taste and responses are intoxicating.

"My shadow." She finally looks up, like she's seeing me again. How does she do that?

"You're breathtaking," I growl.

"And yet you're taking my breath." I loosen my hold on her neck just a little, and she breathes in deep. Almost like she's trying to catch her breath. Her pupils are blown wide, and she darts out her tongue, wetting her lips.

"Do you like it when I touch you?"

"I don't know."

I grind my teeth at that. "Did you like it when Jack touched you?"

She blinks at that. "What?"

"I plan to erase any memory of him, every touch, every caress. When I am done, the only memory will be of me, and how I claim you."

She angles her chin up, defiant. "Jack is just a friend." I drive my hand down until my fingers edge her pussy, claws slightly out. Just for her to feel a little bit of bite.

"And that is all he will ever be." She moans at that, eyes still defiant, but her body is singing for me.

Undoing the button on her jeans, I dive my hand underneath, feeling how wet she is for me. How much the fear, fight, and I do this to her. Her eyes flutter shut. I grip her chin with my free hand, angling it straight ahead once again. "Watch the view, feel all that I do to you."

"Oh Gods," she mewls as I circle my fingers over her clit. Her whole body jerks at the movement.

"Call to the heavens, but you will come for me." I up my pace, diving a finger in between her folds, and I'm met with no resistance. She reaches behind her, trying to grip me, but I stop her with a growl.

"Put your hands on the railing."

"But I just want to touch you, feel you," she whines. I smirk, adding a second finger. Calli gasps. "Not what I meant."

I chuckle. "Oh, I know what you meant, but this is my time to play. And your time to obey." She gulps at that, biting her lip to try to hide her cries. Her head falls back as her inner walls finally clamp down, and she comes all over my fingers. "That's my good girl." I finish and bring my fingers out, licking them clean of her essence. She may not be able to see me yet, but she felt everything I did to her. The groan that leaves my lips at her taste—honey and something floral. "Time for bed . . ." I whisper.

Almost in a trance, she's still riding the high from her orgasm. Or maybe just a bit of buzzing from the idea that a *shadow* got her off. That I did that to her, and will do it again. She turns from the balcony, walking back to her room, and I follow, seeing Karma already making herself at home on the bed.

Calli pulls the covers back and climbs in. She smiles over at the little kitty there and whispers to the room. "Will I see you again?"

My answer is instant, a brush of my lips on the top of her head as she drifts to sleep.

CHAPTER 13

CALLISTO

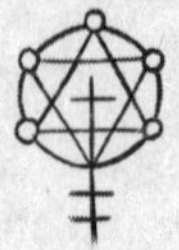

I blink the sleep from my eyes and stretch my muscles. Turning over to see the little black cat, Karma, curled up in a ball on my pillow. My cheeks heat, thinking back to earlier in the night. My body's still buzzing, even after the little cat nap. These moments that are becoming more and more tangible.

My phantom—shadow—got me off while I slept.

Rolling onto my stomach, I groan into my pillow, my mind jumping from one thing to another. He knew about Jack and me. A blush spreads across my face at the memory. Jack was acting kind of weird—and Cade! Of all people, he got me *a cat.* I mean, I'm grateful, but I've been begging him for a pet for years and he has always refused.

"Gods, what the hell is going on around here?" I mumble to no one in particular.

Maybe he's changing, I think. Maybe the pendulum is changing him for the better. I sit up and scoop Karma into my lap, caressing her soft fur. "What do you think of our shadow? He almost seems to have a soft spot for you." She just nuzzles in closer, purring. It's cute. Maybe I am overthinking everything. Maybe Cade is right—I just need to relax. I see what I want to see. But if that's true, I could just try to ignore it.

So that's what I'll do.

I stare up at the ceiling, attempting to manifest calm, cool, centered.

I think back to the restaurant and arcade. It felt so nice to just *be* earlier today, and I want to feel that again. I am twenty-one, after all, and grew up in a safe house. I've never properly gone out, cut loose, or even went to a bar.

Now that's a thought.

Jack always talks about the bars around here. I wonder if I could push my luck and ask him to go out tonight. Checking the clock, it reads 10:00 p.m. That's plenty of time to throw on something nice and go out for the night. I'm sure he wouldn't mind—it's the perfect opportunity for him to get out too . . .

Jolting out of bed, I'm careful to move Karma back onto the pillow, giving her one last pet. "Be a good girl for me . . . Yeah?" I smile to myself. "I've got to find something to wear." Giddy at the thought, I picture the outfit clearly in my mind: a shimmering purple dress that hugs my curves, backless and stopping mid-thigh, the thin straps crossing my shoulder blades, and my favorite strappy heels. I look over to the cabinet where I hid the grimoire . . . Remembering the demon I saw in the pages, golden eyes that entrance me and leave me shivering—much like my shadow does.

Out on the porch, Jack's smoking. I drop down beside him.

"I wanna go to a bar."

He quirks a brow, brushing hair from his face. "Taking more advantage of your newfound freedom already?"

I smile, and he laughs. "Fair. But don't tell Cade I let you, or I'll be next on his list."

"Can we go tonight?"

He crushes the cigarette under his boot. "Why not? Go get dressed up for me, k?"

I roll my eyes but keep smiling, jumping up to get ready.

The bar looks ancient but packed, cars crowding the lot. Pop music thumps from the open deck, and people laugh with drinks in hand.

My face must say it all.

"You're the one who wanted to come," Jack reminds me, laughing.

He comes around to the passenger side and opens the door with a theatrical bow. "Milady."

I step down awkwardly, heels sinking into the gravel. He offers his arm, and I take it—more for balance than because of his charm.

Inside is chaos—bodies everywhere. The place is packed. The bartender moves like he's casting spells. Jack leads me toward an empty pool table in the back.

"I'll get the drinks," he says, then disappears into the crowd.

I grab a cue, needing something to do with my hands. I glance back and of course he's already surrounded by women.

Typical.

I can't hear them, but I know that look. They're flirting hard and he's lapping it up. Great. I roll my eyes and turn to the table, setting up a fresh game.

Jack's a walking wet dream. Blond, broad, blue-eyed—but he flirts with anything that breathes or blinks at him. It's honestly exhausting.

Still, he brings the drinks and keeps the good vibes coming. An hour passes—maybe more, and between a few rounds of pool and a few too many drinks, I'm definitely tipsy. And surprisingly? I'm having fun.

When "Go Fuck Yourself" by Two Feet comes on, I lose it a little. Singing way too loud, hips swaying to the bass as I demand another round from Jack. I rack the table again, still dancing. The music crawls down my spine and I let it, needing this moment.

"Wanna play?" A stranger's voice asks behind me.

I keep my back turned, tone casual.

"Just waiting for my friend." I nod toward Jack, who's now laying it on thick with the bartender.

"Your friend looks busy. I can keep you company."

I look down, unsure how to respond. Then I feel hands gently grip my waist, a low voice ringing in my ears . . . *my shadow*. "You're safe with me. Enjoy this."

"Yeah, sure," I respond to the stranger, feeling a flutter in my chest knowing I'm not alone.

He grabs a cue, lining up to break. "I'll go first."

The cue cracks against the eight ball and it flies unnaturally—smashing him square in the nose.

He howls, clutching his nose as blood spurts from it.

"Oh my Gods, are you okay?" I gasp. Then, muttering low, *"You weren't supposed to hurt him."* I take a step back in shock, pushing away from his grip.

The light above the table flickers. "You really thought I would let him near you?" My stomach drops. He tricked me . . .

"Don't follow me," I say.

I push past the crowd, making a beeline for the bathroom. As I swing the door open, the heavy scent of alcohol and too-sweet perfume hits me, causing my stomach to turn.

Every stall is occupied. Of course.

I grip the edge of the sink, trying to breathe. The walls feel too close. My skin prickles, heat spreading down my arms and up my neck. I twist the faucet on and splash cold water over my forearms and behind my neck, trying to ground myself. The fluorescent lights overhead only add to my disorientation.

A stall door swings open, and I lunge for it, ignoring the slurred protests behind me. I lock the door and drop to the floor. The chill of the tile hits my skin, a harsh contrast to the burn inside my chest. I press my palms to the floor, breathing deep.

I can't escape this.

My shadow—it followed me.

After a long minute, I stand. My hands shake as I smooth out my dress, willing my expression back to neutral. I unlock the door and step out like nothing happened—until I remember I had my hands all over the floor of a bar bathroom.

I head straight to the sink and scrub my hands clean before making my exit.

"What the fuck happened?" Jack appears beside me, two drinks in hand. I grab one and knock it back in a single swallow. It burns going down my throat, and I wince, face scrunching up like I just swallowed battery acid.

"Cheers," Jack says with a hesitant laugh before tossing back his own drink.

"I need to leave. Now."

Jack doesn't question me, just gestures me toward the door.

The silence on the drive home is thick. Not uncomfortable, just . . . charged. Jack drives and I'm slouched in the passenger seat, my cheek pressed to the cool window, watching the forest blur past.

That presence didn't leave when I ran out of the bar. I can feel it with me now, and I'm done waiting. I'll show whatever the fuck this thing is I'm done being afraid. Let it come.

When we pull into the driveway, I leap out and rush inside, kicking off my heels. I run up the stairs, yank out the grimoire, and start lighting candles one by one, forming a circle in front of my bookshelf. I sit at the center with the grimoire in hand.

"Show yourself. I know you're here."

Nothing.

"Quit fucking with me! You followed me. You hurt that man. I know it was you!"

Still more silence.

I flip open the grimoire and it lands on the same page as before. The golden eyes stare back at me. I grit my teeth; a shaky exhale escapes my lips and I take in a deep breath.

"Alabaster," I whisper. "Show yourself."

The lights flicker then vanish, darkness filling the space.

I gasp, eyes straining against the void. The candles snuff out in unison, and the air is heavy, silent. My heart pounds, and I swallow hard.

"Show yourself." I say again, my voice steadier than I feel. The presence presses in—everywhere and nowhere, all at once. Silence stretches tight across the room.

Then, a deep velvet laugh wrapped in sin curls around me like smoke and I freeze, my breath catching.

"You called, pretty girl?"

CHAPTER 14

ALABASTER

The sound of my name on her lips? Like a fucking summoning. I force the lights to die, and the room goes still. My body solidifies as she holds her breath.

Smoke spills across the floor. I watch her eyes track the movement she can't quite see. Her breath catches when she sees me, lips parting like she's about to speak, instead—

A high-pitched scream. I flinch, covering my ears, convinced she's going to make my eardrums bleed.

"Would you please stop that?"

"You're real!" she yells into the air, bracing herself for only Gods know what.

"I thought I made that obvious."

She cowers, backing away until she meets the bookshelf and begins tossing books at me one by one. They pass straight through me and into the wall behind.

I hear Jack's footsteps running down the hall. He throws open the door, looking wide-eyed at Callisto.

She jerks her head toward him, then back to me.

"What the fuck is going on in here?" he says, breathing heavily.

"You can't . . . ? Umm," she says in a panicked voice, meeting my eyes.

"He can't see me, sweetheart," I say calmly.

She exhales quickly, running her fingers quickly through her dark locks, before taking a deep breath, clearly trying to calm herself.

"Callisto. What's wrong?" Jack says in a stern, manly voice. *Please*.

She looks over at him, stuttering as she attempts to come up with what will most likely be a bullshit excuse.

"I s-s-saw a spider?"

"Is that a question?" he says, confused. "All of that over a spider. Seriously?"

"It was a . . ." She looks at the ground and then slowly up to my face. "A really *big* spider."

I cross my arms and bite my lower lip.

"Okay," he says, his face red from the night's spirits and sleep in his eyes. "You good now? Is it gone?" he asks dismissively.

What a dick. I'd investigate, or help her clean up this mess, comfort her. Something! And how the hell is he buying the spider excuse?

"Uh . . . yeah. Yeah, all good. Sorry. Have a good night," she says. She's shaking, but he doesn't seem to notice.

See, she doesn't need someone who can't even recognize when she's clearly scared. Oblivious dumbass.

He waves lazily at her before closing the door and walking away.

I look down at her as she pulls her knees to her chest, avoiding eye contact with me before speaking in a quiet voice.

"You're the thing that's been following me, my shadow." She doesn't meet my gaze.

"The one and only, baby." I flash her a smile and sit on the ground in front of her. "I've been waiting for you to call me."

"Are you here to steal my soul?" She speaks so quiet, human ears almost wouldn't catch it.

"How the hell would I steal your soul?" I ask with humor in my tone.

"You're a demon, aren't you?" She finally looks at me. "Isn't that what you *do*?"

"You are adorable," I say, looking down at her.

"What the hell is happening?" she asks, throwing her hands up.

"There she is," I quip. "Let's just say, I'm invested in the story."

"Don't dance around my question—I don't speak cryptic."

Gods, this fucking woman is amazing. I'll spell it out.

"A powerful witch afraid of her own shadow hiding from a cult, a psychopathic brother hunting down each member accompanied by an interdimensional ghost—you can't deny, it's interesting."

She looks at me like I'm stupid, confusion painted all over her pretty face.

"That doesn't explain the things you have been doing." She gulps. "The way you've been touching me . . ." Her face turns red.

I lean closer to her and meet her eyes. "How else am I supposed to get your attention?"

Her brows come together in a scowl. "What you did tonight was wrong."

"Oh, darling, sometimes the most wrong things can be so right." I trail my eyes over her like a caress, then cross my arms again, straightening. "Besides, Fucker had it coming." And he did. Her brows furrow, so I continue. "He touched what is mine."

After she bolted to the bathroom at the bar, I continued watching the scene play out. The guy slinked out the back door, and I decided to follow.

He stumbles, clutching his bleeding face and reeking of sweat and regret. He lit a cigarette, probably the last comfort he got tonight.

I watched him from the shadows, eyes narrowed. Then—with one step forward, the cigarette fizzled out between my fingers. The man startled, patting his pockets for a lighter. I let him find it. He flicked the flame to life.

I chuckled to myself. One of the many perks of my powers is choosing whether I'm seen or not. Gives me the ability to mess with fools like him. I sidled up beside him and brought my pointer finger and thumb up over the flame—snuffing it out.

He blinked, startled. "What the—" I tilted my head, just slightly. Ooo, this is going to be fun.

If only he could have seen my grin. I brought my lips to his ear, whispered, "You really thought you had a shot with her?" I laughed, voice soft and mocking at his drunk stupor.

His eyes narrowed. "Fuck off," he slurred.

I stepped to the side—and then I was behind him as he spun to find me.

"You're rude," I murmured. "And you smell like rot." My voice dropped to a low hum. "You don't even belong in the same room, let alone deserve to breathe the same air, as her."

His bravado died, and he took a shaky step back. "Show yourself, pussy!"

I chuckled. This stupid fuck wants to see me? I let just enough of myself slip through.

Not my whole face. Just the shadow. A glimmer of something too inhuman to process. Black smoke curled from the corners of my eyes, teeth just a little too sharp, a smile too inhuman.

He went pale and fainted. I caught his body before it hit the ground and lowered him gently—like a lover.

"Sleep tight, creep."

Then I quickly vanished back to her.

Her voice snaps me back to the present. "I am not yours, and I don't need protection."

I just grin back at her, my eyes positively glowing.

"You broke the guy's face. All he did was offer to play a game with me."

"Oops," I say, shrugging.

"It's not a joke," she says, shooting me the most adorable attempt at a serious face while she puts up her hair with the hair tie around her wrist.

"You aren't that naive, you were visibly uncomfortable, and Jack was too busy trying to get pussy."

She huffs and rolls her eyes. "Okay, yeah, I didn't like it, but that doesn't mean what you did was right." She rubs her eyes and stands.

"Oh my Gods, I'm lecturing a demon. What the actual fuck am I doing?"

"You're right." I walk over to her. She backs away until her back is up against the bookcase. I place one arm above her, lean in, and lock eyes with hers. "I have a much better way to use your time, if you're interested."

She visibly gulps, eyes wide and heart racing.

"No." She attempts to push me but I don't move. She dips her head under my arm and throws her hands in the air while walking to her balcony. "Not today, Satan!"

I laugh.

She quickly turns to me, pointing an accusing finger. "What kind of hypocrite breaks a man's face just for hitting on me then proceeds to hit on me?"

"An *irresistible* hypocrite?" I shoot her a charming smile.

"If I asked you to leave me alone, would you?"

"Negative, ghost rider," I say, casually brushing my hair over my shoulder. "You're stuck with me. You called, so I'm bound to you. That's how it works."

"But you've been following me. You all but forced me to call you out," she says, frustrated.

Smirking, I put my hands up in defense. "You caught me, but I'm not the one looking into old grimoires. Names hold power, so I'm all yours now."

"But what if I don't want you?"

"You didn't seem to mind me in the arcade." I go to reach for her, but she turns on her heel, headed for the balcony. She sits, processing.

I reach my hands out again, gripping around her waist—and lift her to land back on my lap. She shivers at the feel of me but doesn't look at me.

Her face is in her hands, so when she speaks her voice is muffled. "Please leave me be." I smirk, proud I have such an effect on her.

"You're still drunk. You've had a long night. Why don't we try and get some rest?"

"Why don't you not pretend like you care about my well-being?" she snaps back with a glare, standing and walking to plop down in the opposite chair.

"Who said I don't?" I get up and leave the room, coming back with a glass of water and two Tylenol. "Here. So you don't wake up miserable."

She looks up at me, confused. "How does a demon know how to tend to a drunk human?"

"I've been around. Plus, where I'm from isn't too different from here. Except our drinks would burn a hole in your stomach lining."

She raises an eyebrow as she downs the pills and takes a few gulps of water.

"Finish that and go to bed," I say, turning away from her to pick up the books.

"Sure, *Cade*," she says sarcastically.

I turn back to her, taking the glass and throwing it off the balcony. I push her chair back on two legs, her feet coming off the ground. My face is inches from hers.

"Make no mistake, pretty girl, I am *nothing* like your brother. Compare me to him again and I will make you regret allowing the words to ever cross your lips."

Her eyes are wide. She speaks softly, breath smelling of whiskey.

"I'm sorry. I don't know how long you have been following me, but I don't know you." She gently places her hands on my shoulders as I place her chair back on all four legs. "I'm used to weird shit, but a demon showing up and taking care of me was not on my bingo card. So forgive me for coping with sarcasm."

I stand up. She may have a point, and I may have overreacted. I walk over to the mess of books sprawled out on the floor, noticing that Karma has made herself a bed out of one of them. I smile down at the little feline, cooing, "Let's find you a more comfortable bed." I reach down and scoop her up, noticing the cover she had occupied. A black-and-white picture of a shirtless, tattooed man. I quirk a brow. "Karma, you are dirty just like your mommy," I say, setting her on the bed before picking up the remainder of books.

Placing the stack back on the shelf, I notice Calli walk behind me and throw herself onto the bed.

"Remind me when I'm sober not to summon anything while I'm shit-faced," she says, face squished into the pillow.

Her comment pulls a smile from me as I spot a paperback still out of place. I slide it back onto the shelf, my thumb catching on yellow tabs marking the pages. I open it to a random marked page.

Oh. Literary. Fucking. Porn.

This girl is filth in angel's skin. I grin, flipping to the other pages labeled in yellow. I know what I'm doing tonight, and this could give me some ideas.

I bring the book to her bed and pull the covers over her. She's so pretty when she sleeps. Probably because it's the only time she shuts up.

Curious. Smart. Dangerous. And she has no idea.

I just know she would taste like honey. I'll have her. I will. Mind, body, soul. She'll beg me not to stop until I ruin her.

That mark on the back of her neck pulls me in, and I lean, drawn like gravity, like a moth to a flame. Her skin looks soft, the delicate little baby hairs rising at my breath.

She tenses, mumbling. "You smell good."

Good. She feels me, even while asleep.

Her chest rises as she rolls onto her side. I slide next to her on top of the blanket and open the book to chapter one.

I finish the book and look over at the clock, the sky slowly brightening.

Five a.m.

Where the hell did the time go? I close the book and get up to place it back on the shelf when she begins tossing and turning. She must be having another one of her nightmares. I sit next to her, hand on her shoulder, and she seems to calm before jolting awake. I quickly pull away.

She reaches out and clicks on the lamp, pushing herself up.

I lie back, watching her move around her room in that worn nightgown. When she strips out of it to change into jeans and an old T-shirt, I lick my lips.

"You put on quite a show," I say with a rasp in my voice, and she jumps.

"Fuck!" She turns, hand on her forehead. "Why are you in my bed?"

"I was reading. You have quite good taste in literature, I must say."

She rolls her eyes as if annoyed, but I see the pink in her cheeks.

"Nothing to be embarrassed about, sweetheart. I quite enjoyed it."

She shakes her head, snatching the book off the nightstand, and walks away.

I trail after her into the kitchen as she makes coffee. She opens the book, pulling out a stack of little tabs. She has been carrying it around but hasn't seemed to finish it in over a month.

"Are you savoring it, or are you just a very slow reader?" I ask, leaning over the counter.

"I like to annotate, so I like to reread the same book. I'm actually quite a fast reader, thank you. Now leave me be."

Then . . . in struts Jack. He's got that skip in his step that makes my skin crawl. He pours himself coffee and seats himself next to her. Her eyes quickly bounce from me to him.

"Last night was fun," he says, overly upbeat.

I lean back in the chair and cross my arms, flashing her a smirk.

Her tired eyes scan my face then quickly jerk away.

"Mm-hmm," she agrees, taking another sip of her coffee.

CHAPTER 15

CADE

After driving for almost fourteen hours, the road ahead has started to blur. I check my phone one last time to verify the last ping from Allen White: a shitty motel outside Goodsprings, Nevada. Knowing I won't be relying on Jack this time is almost exhilarating.

This is gonna be fun.

I should get there just in time to check in for the night. If he's smart, he's long gone, but I've learned not to put anything past desperate men.

The gravel lot of the run-down motel somehow looks even worse than the pictures online. Peeling paint, a busted neon *Motel* sign blinking against the dark sky.

The place looks abandoned despite the lot being full and folks lounging outside in fold-up chairs, smoking shit that's definitely not legal.

Inside, the front office smells like week-old sweat. The clerk is a balding, greasy little man glued to a soccer game on a box TV. He barely glances at me.

"Excuse me," I say, rapping my knuckles on the counter to get his attention. "Can I get a room, please?"

"Yep," he grunts, eyes never leaving the screen. He tosses the keys to room 13 onto the counter. "Fifty bucks a night."

I set the cash down and swiftly make my exit. I head down the sidewalk, passing cracked doors, when two women catch my eye—both looking disheveled, wearing too-tight clothing, makeup smudged from long hours of wear and their heels kicked off beside them.

"Evenin,' sugar," the redhead says, her voice husky with cigarette smoke. "You look like a man who's had a long day."

The brunette eyes me, lips curling into something lazy and sharp. "Damn," she murmurs, looking me over. "You're tall as hell. Love the ink. I would love to see where all those lines go." If I had a dime for every time a girl hit on me for my tattoos, I'd be an even richer man. Too bad I have enough money to last me a lifetime, and no need for it. The lines reach across my chest, up to my neck, and down my arms. I've always been fascinated with smoke—being an assassin, you learn to be one with the shadows; it comes with the territory. So, yeah, tattoos.

I pull out my phone and hold up the screen, showing them a picture of Allen. "Have you seen this guy?"

They share a look.

"Maybe. Depends on who's askin' . . . and what he's offerin'," the brunette says, tilting her head.

"I'm not here to waste your time," I say, pulling out a hundred-dollar bill and passing it to the redhead. "I just need a direction."

They exchange another glance, brief and silent. An unspoken language.

"Yeah, we seen him," the redhead says finally, sliding the bill into her bra. "Little weasel left earlier. Kept his head down. Real twitchy-like."

"Which way?"

"South. Toward Primm."

"Appreciate it." The brunette steps closer, fingers brushing my forearm. "You sure that's all you want, gorgeous?"

I swat her hand away without flinching, keeping my face uninterested. "What was he driving?"

The redhead speaks up again, voice a little tighter now. "Old red Chevy. Rusted to shit."

I walk away while they disappear into their room, door slamming behind them. I pull out my phone.

Room 13 reeks of mildew and regret but my body begs for sleep, so I give in and sink into the bed.

I drift off . . . You're here again, *I think.* I don't know how much longer I can keep pretending this isn't breaking me. I don't even know what to call you. You don't speak. You just appear. And when you do, it consumes me.

All I see is smoke curling around me until you're all I see. A beautiful shadow hovering over me. Dancing over my skin—so gentle it drives me insane. I feel a mouth wrap around me. Slow and deliberate. My abs tighten instantly, muscles flexing hard as I grip the sheets.

I feel you sink lower onto me. Swallowing me whole as my hips jerk into the feeling. A sharp breath tears from my throat. The way you move—fuck.

I twist the sheets until my knuckles ache, fighting the urge to take control, knowing I have none here.

Your mouth is a prayer and I'm your altar.

I want to hold you here, I want to *own* this. I want to keep you forever, right here.

"Don't fucking stop," I growl.

I lose myself in the feeling right as it disappears. Cold air rushes toward me and my eyes snap open.

I look over to see 3:33 a.m. glowing red on the cracked digital clock.

I sigh.

But I can still *feel* you.

You might just be in my head. But I want to stop the world and stay with you. Crazy or not. You shouldn't feel this real. You shouldn't feel like mine. But you do.

I hate it. I hate how badly my body wants you—how I react on instinct. I hate that I want to fall back asleep. But these moments . . . They are the only thing that feels good anymore.

I roll out of bed and sluggishly tug on my jeans. My eyes are heavy, my arms not wanting to cooperate as I drag a shirt over my head.

I've got to make up ground if I'm going to catch him, so I head out, ignoring the glare I receive from an old man with his gut out, beer in hand.

The front office reeks of stale air and burnt coffee, though it looks like someone just made a fresh pot. Thank fuck.

I drop my keys at the front desk and make a beeline for where a dusty coffee maker hums next to a sad selection of cereal and granola bars. I pour myself a to-go cup, scalding and bitter, then head out to the truck.

Hours later, Primm greets me like a forgotten dream. Dusty casinos slump on the horizon, their neon signs flickering like they're too tired to lie anymore.

If I were a desperate man, running from someone like me . . . where would I hide?

I notice a small bar and grill still open with a sign reading *The Tavern*. Perfect. I quickly pull in. The place is pretty packed, but I could go for a drink.

I park and grab my leather jacket from the back seat, pulling it on. The building is small and run-down. An outdoor patio hosts a group of women loudly cheering on a young woman with a little twenty-one sash over her chest.

Inside it is.

Loud hip-hop music blares through the speakers and people on the dance floor grind up against each other.

Music-themed decor is scattered over wooden, cabin-like walls. On my right, people fill pool tables and play darts. The roar of chatter almost overwhelms my senses.

I avoid eye contact as I look for an empty seat. The bar wraps around in a massive U-shape, and people group together, chatting with one another while they wait for their drinks.

My eyes drift to the side in annoyance as I approach a seat. My luck improves when three douchey-looking guys get their drinks and toast then walk away together, heading up the stairs. I quickly take the seat one of them was occupying.

The bartender stands in front of me in a low-cut black tank top. She appears to be chewing gum when she speaks.

"I'll be with you in one sec, hun," she says without looking at me.

An old man with a half-empty pitcher of beer sits to my right and an awkward-looking man with a water sits to my left. The woman standing next to him—clearly his girlfriend or wife—is flirting with a small group of women. This guy obviously doesn't want to be here—hell, I'm second-guessing the decision myself.

"What are ya drinkin'?" the bartender asks as she leans over.

"Double shot of whiskey," I yell over the music.

She nods and quickly pours my drink, and I toss a ten-dollar bill on the counter.

I don't even get a sip in before a girl comes over, grabbing my arm. I immediately jerk away, looking her over. Her long brown hair is messy and she looks up at me with large blue eyes.

"Can I sit here?" she pleads with something almost like fear in her eyes. "*Please*."

"Fine," I respond flatly.

She sits close to me as she orders herself a whiskey and Coke. She leans in closer.

"Can I help you?"

My question is quickly answered when a tall, husky-looking guy with a cheap leather vest and a buzzcut approaches us.

"Hey! We're leaving. Now!" the man says, clearly shit-faced.

I stand, pushing into his shoulder with enough force to keep him from getting closer.

"I don't know what's going on here, but it's pretty clear she doesn't want to leave with you."

The guy spits a cackling laugh. "How about you mind your fucking business? She's leaving with me." He puffs out his chest and flashes the handgun in his waistband. "Let's go, Andrea."

"You're going to back the fuck off, or I'll happily cut off your trigger-happy dick and shove it down your throat."

The guy doesn't hesitate before swinging at me. I catch his fist almost too easily as he throws another punch.

One of the bouncers quickly comes to investigate and the small girl—still clinging to my shirt—explains the situation. The man is pulled away, despite his protests, and I finally get to take a sip of my drink.

After a few minutes the confusion dies down and the girl speaks up.

"Thank you. My name is Andrea. What's yours?" she asks shyly.

"Jack. Nice to meet you." Sorry, Jack, I'm not giving her my real name.

"Would you like me to—"

"No," I say coldly. My tone says everything she needs to know.

She shrinks into herself. "I was just going to offer to buy you a drink." She turns her head and gestures to the bartender, requesting another round. "Relax, you're not my type."

Two drinks later, I'm feeling much better. Andrea's been nursing the same drink the entire time, looking straight ahead and not making conversation. She's nice enough company, quiet.

"You look like you might know the area," I begin.

"You'd be right. You look like you don't belong here."

"I'm in town looking for someone." I search for an excuse. "My uncle Allen. Short, balding gray hair, always in a pressed suit."

"Oh yeah, drives a red truck. Saw him about forty-five minutes ago when the bouncers threw him out," she says, taking a sip of her drink. "The guy was wasted. Kept hitting on the bartender, screaming about taking his business elsewhere."

Perfect. He's still in town.

Drunk and vulnerable.

A smile plays on my lips, and I feel like I've won. I look over at Andrea.

Her closed-off demeanor is a stark contrast to the woman on the other side of me who's crying to some random guy about how her dog died three years ago and that she hasn't been the same since. I turn my head quickly to avoid eye contact.

"Thanks, I owe you one," I say, getting up to leave.

She looks at me, confused. "You helped me first. Call it even."

"Right. You gonna be good?" I say, gesturing to the door in reference to the creep they just threw out.

She takes another drink and scoffs. "Yeah, that's my brother. Theo." Her face stiffens. "And don't ask, I'm not in a talking mood."

"Wasn't planning on it. You gonna make it home safe?"

"I'll figure it out," she says, waving me off.

"Thanks again." I drop a fifty on the bar and turn to leave.

"Church" by Chase Atlantic comes through the speakers, and I hear yelling—and a group of women all but stampede to the dance floor. They bump into me, all three grabbing my hands and arms, pulling me with them.

"Come dance, handsome!" one yells over the music.

What the fuck is happening . . .

They begin dancing, grinding on me in all directions, spilling their drinks in the process, as I try to sneak my way out of their human barricade.

"Aww, you're no fun!" I hear one of them yell from behind me.

I need to get the fuck out of here. This place is madness.

I quickly make my way through the crowd, abandoning Andrea at the bar, avoiding ramming into anyone else. I burst through the doors. Hands on my knees, I lean over, gulping in deep breaths.

Freedom.

The respite doesn't last long. I hear the loud roar of multiple motorcycles pulling up. One by one, they pile into the parking lot in front of me, shouting obscenities. The man who got kicked out of the bar earlier, Theo, approaches them, yelling and pointing at me.

You've gotta be fucking kidding me.

I stand up and stretch my neck to the side, preparing for what looks like a fight. Slowly, I walk down the steps, approaching the men as they hop off their bikes. Each one wears a vest similar to the one the drunk man was wearing in the bar.

A large bald man steps up to me. He starts to speak but I cut him off.

"Are we doing this one by one or all at once?" I ask confidently, cracking my knuckles.

"The young lady you were with inside—do you know where she is?" he asks, his voice deep and raspy.

"Leave her alone. She made it very clear she has no interest in leaving with her brother."

"I think there has been a misunderstanding here." He puts his hands out. "I'm Mack. Theo came to pick her up after she ran off from our clubhouse. She isn't all there mentally and hasn't been taking her meds. He's a bit drunk from the party, so maybe he wasn't able to get his point across. We're just worried about her."

Bullshit.

"So why would she beg a stranger to protect her?"

"Look, son, she moved here because her mother couldn't handle her episodes. Her brother took her in. I imagine she would say just about anything to avoid coming home. Would you go inside and get her for us? We would prefer not to cause an issue."

Well, fuck.

I make my way back into the chaos and search for the tiny brunette. It doesn't take me long to see her standing in the corner of the room, a cup of water in hand, shrinking into herself like she doesn't want to be here. She looks me up and down as I approach her.

"We need to get you out of here," I start. "Is there a back entrance to this place?"

She sighs, setting her drink on the stage.

"In the back, behind the bar." She points to the back of the wall, past a large group of people.

"All right, let's go."

"I'm sorry, who the hell are you to tell me what to do? This isn't your problem. I'm a grown-ass woman, and I'll figure this the fuck out on my own."

I can't help but laugh.

"Is that funny?"

"No, you just remind me of my sister. Now let's go. You can be stubborn when there isn't a group of men outside trying to take you."

She looks behind me at the door.

"Wait, *what*? They're here?"

"Yes." I grip her arm, not hard, but enough to urge her on. Her eyes widen at the contact.

"Okay, yeah, let's go! You have no idea what those men are capable of. If Theo called them, it's not gonna be good for you," she says, yanking her arm from my grip.

I trail behind her as she makes her way to an employee exit. She pushes the door open with force, and we are met with two men in similar vests as her brother. She stops dead in her tracks. One of them calls out, "Yo, Theo! We found her!"

No sooner does the call go out than her brother comes around the corner with rage in his eyes.

"I come to apologize, and you get some asshole to try and start a fight? The fuck is wrong with you?" he says quickly, the words almost blending together with his slurred speech.

"Get on the bike, now," one of the men commands.

"I'm not going anywhere with you."

"I don't give a fuck what the issue is here," I say loud enough for them to hear, fixing my eyes on the girl. "Do you want to leave with them?"

"No," she answers quietly.

"Good. Now that we've cleared that up, let her fucking leave."

"This is none of your business, dick," he says, grabbing the girl's arm and jerking her away.

"You just made it my business."

The bald one charges first. I sidestep clean, twist, and crack a fist across his jaw—hard enough to spin him. No hesitation. I'm already moving.

Theo barely gets his hands up before I drive a punch straight into his nose. Cartilage crunches. He hits the ground like dead weight.

The girl flinches, staggering back.

Two more come in fast. One throws a low kick that slams into my knee. A solid hit, but I drop back, pivot low, and sweep his legs. He hits the concrete hard.

The second's already mid-swing. I don't bother blocking. I slam my fist up between his legs. He folds forward, choking on his breath. I rise slowly, brushing the dirt from my jeans. They're still groaning on the ground when I turn and walk away.

I glance at the girl. She's frozen, wide-eyed. I jerk my chin toward the truck out back, pulling the keys from my pocket.

She hesitates.

"Get in the truck, Andrea." She does, and I sweep in beside her.

"What direction are we going?" I ask flatly.

"If you're willing . . . you can take me to my coworker's house. She lives about fifteen minutes from here, you're already going the right way."

"All right. Just put the address in," I say, handing her my phone.

"Why did you do that for me?" she asks, returning the phone.

"Someone had to. Your brother is an asshole."

Then I see it.

Rusted red Chevy. Bingo.

I need to make this quick.

CHAPTER 16

CALLISTO

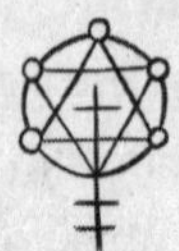

"Can you *please* get out of my toaster?" I ask, voice low and tight with frustration. "It's three in the morning, and I just want some toast."

The appliance shudders. A curl of smoke seeps from the slot just before he materializes in front of me, smile sharpened and eyes glowing faintly gold.

I flinch, unable to hide it.

He grins wider, teeth flashing.

Ding.

My toast pops up—blackened.

"Is that a normal thing for you?" I try to steady my hands as I reach for the plate. "Possessing kitchen appliances?"

He glides behind me, his breath ghosting against my ear.

"Only if it inconveniences you," he whispers, voice soaked in amusement.

I tense as the air around me shifts . . . He's playing with me.

"Dick," I grumble, trying not to pout.

"Guilty. Keep being mouthy and I'll show you just how big of a dick I can be." Alabaster trails his fingers up my silk nightie. I slap his hand away, realizing I have nothing on under it.

His eyes flash, and my cheeks heat as I avoid his gaze. In the next moment I'm lifted, splayed out on the counter—silk bunched up to my waist. My legs are spread wide. I'm completely exposed as his face dives between my legs.

He laughs softly. "You summoned *me*, pretty girl. You didn't think that would come with boundaries, did you?"

"Can't you just leave me alone?"

"You're the one who called *me*," he says, tilting his head, the move animalistic. "I'm afraid we're tethered now . . ."

"I just wanted to eat my breakfast," I whine, his hand covering my face.

"Me too," he says. I can feel his tongue darting out, trailing up my center—and I squeak, not expecting the feeling. "You make such delicious sounds when you're startled."

I gasp, my body reacting before I can stop it, goose bumps rising like a warning.

Then—

"Calli?" Jack's voice cuts through the room, casual but close. "Who are you talking to?"

I go cold with terror, my legs still spread wide, Alabaster between them. I can feel his deep growl over my clit, his claws possessively digging into my thighs. I try to close them, worried that Jack will see, but he won't allow my legs to close.

"Myself," I say too quickly. "Obviously."

There's a pause as he enters the kitchen. "You're telling yourself to leave you alone?"

"Jack, don't—" I try to tell him not to come in, but I'm too late.

His eyebrows raise. "Whatcha doin' there?" He must be referring to me, splayed out, like I'm pleasuring myself next to the toaster. I reach down, attempting to shove Alabaster away, but he's now sucking my clit into his mouth. My hand slaps to my mouth as I try not to let the moan past my lips, and my eyes are glued to Jack—who is looking both aroused and like I have five heads.

Searing pain hits my core as I feel him bite down on my clit. My eyes snap back to Alabaster. "Let him watch," he growls. "I want him to see what I do to you."

In that moment he starts fucking me with his tongue. It glides inside of me, curling up and teasing just the right spot. My hand reaches down, gripping at his hair, pulling him into me. I grind against his face like a woman possessed, as I come in waves.

Jack's voice snaps me out of my high. "Fuck, Calli. That was the hottest thing I have ever seen."

Alabaster stands in that moment—releasing me—and rises to his full height. A smirk is stuck on his face as he licks my cum off his lips.

I slowly turn toward Jack. He walks up to me, gripping my chin more firmly than I expected, and angles my face up to meet his eyes.

"If you wanted to get off, you could have just asked."

I look at him, confused. "That—no. I—"

Instantly, Jack's body begins to tremble, and his eyes roll back and then darken into an inky, solid black. His skin drains of color, muscles twitching as if he's fighting something inside.

His hands reach toward his face before stilling in midair and his movements go calm—controlled. He drops his hands and looks straight at me.

A grotesque smile spreads across his face, looking completely unnatural. It doesn't reach his eyes.

"Wake up! Jack, wake up!" My voice is shrill with panic. "What are you doing to him? Get out!"

"Burning the memory from his mind. I wasn't going to let him interrupt my meal."

I jump up and grab Jack by the shoulders, shaking him hard.

He looks down at me. It's Jack's face—but it's not Jack at all.

"Do you want this human?" Alabaster asks, voice dangerous, a brow raised accusingly.

"No! He's . . . he's my friend," I stammer. Jack's always been there for me, but I don't see him like that *anymore* . . . He's gorgeous, sure, but we both decided a long time ago that it was best to stay friends.

"I think we both know it's more than that. Don't let him touch you like you're his again."

Alabaster, inside of Jack, pulls me into his chest, fingers tangling into my hair. His voice darkens into a low, terrifying promise.

"If he does, I'll kill him. You. Are. *Mine*." He waves his finger back and forth at the counter. "And what we just did there will not be the last."

And then Jack's eyes return. Blue. Confused. His skin warms again, but he looks disoriented.

We're still pressed together.

I pull away quickly, face flushed.

"Damn . . . I just got the worst headache," he mutters, rubbing his temples. His voice is groggy and disconnected.

He stumbles slightly as he moves toward the counter, catching himself on the edge. His breaths are shallow, as if he's been running. His skin, though warmer now, still holds a sickly undertone—too pale, too slick with sweat.

"Are you okay? What do you remember?" I ask, my voice unsteady.

"What? Nothing. My head feels like I got hit by a truck." He winces, squinting like the lights are too bright. "My stomach feels off, too. Weirdest nausea."

"Do you believe in the supernatural, Jack?"

He looks at me with a perturbed expression.

"I'd say I'm a man of science, but why not?" He rubs his temples. "A hundred years ago, the tech we have now would've been considered alien or witchcraft. I believe magic is just a science we don't yet understand."

"Wow. That's surprisingly wise. I wouldn't expect that from you," I say, genuinely impressed.

"I have my moments. Why do you ask?"

"Just making conversation . . . You should get some rest," I suggest softly.

He shrugs, brushing it off, but it's forced. He truly doesn't remember, and that terrifies me more than if he did.

"Yeah . . ." His phone buzzes with a notification. He pulls it from his pocket, unlocking it.

"Is it Cade?"

"Yeah." He nods and blows out a breath, looking over at me. "He found his target."

He's so pale. "You okay, Jack?" He gulps.

"Yeah . . . Yeah, I think I'm getting sick. I'll go lie down."

"Okay. Thank you, Jack . . . I'm glad my brother has you."

He chuckles weakly as he walks away. "Who the hell else could put up with him—besides you?"

I shake my head and make my way to my bedroom, heading out to my balcony. I need air.

I sink into the chair, letting the breeze bite at my skin. Since I called his name, Alabaster has been hovering over me like a shadow I can't shake. At first, I was in shock. But now . . . I don't know. What he did to that man in the bar, what he just did to Jack. I don't know what he's capable of . . .

He *should* go. I head back into my room and go to the grimoire, flipping pages like a woman possessed. I find spells for fairies. Gnomes. Ghosts.

There—*Protection Against Demons*.

Fuck, it's complicated and I don't have half the ingredients.

But then I find another: *Protection Ward*.

Salt. Cinnamon. Blood.

I scan the room—he's gone. For now.

I bolt to the kitchen and grab salt, cinnamon, and a knife. Back in my room, I spread the mixture of salt and cinnamon around the bed. Good enough . . . it has to be.

I take the knife, press it to my palm, hesitating for a moment—then slice. A sharp sting blooms as blood wells and drips into the circle.

I press a shirt to my hand, murmuring the incantation from the grimoire, voice low and trembling. I sit on the bed, back against the headboard.

Okay. Now what?

The room is still. Maybe it worked?

I say his name in my mind—and instantly regret it.

The air tightens. Darkness blooms in the farthest corner. I see his eyes first.

I freeze.

"Playing with knives, pretty girl?" he asks, voice curling around the room.

"Stay away from me," I snap, trying to sound braver than I feel.

He steps closer and crouches. Dips a finger into the circle—blood, salt, cinnamon. Brings it to his mouth, licking it. His tongue is long and inhuman.

And yet my stomach tightens.

Heat.

Shame.

Confusion.

"Leave me alone," I say, anger laced in my tone. "You put me in this position. I won't let you hurt the people I care about."

"I have no intention of hurting anyone . . . Not yet." He grins, my blood on his teeth. "I just don't like anyone touching my things."

"I am not a *thing*."

"Cute. Very cute. But you'll need something stronger to keep me away."

"Maybe you can enlighten me. I'm not exactly well-versed in being haunted by a demon."

He pulls his finger from his mouth, seeming to savor the flavor. "Your blood tastes almost as good as your pussy."

And he's suddenly in front of me. Hovering.

His presence is overwhelming. The air around him warms, and the warmth of his body isn't comforting . . . it's invasive. My skin reacts before I do, prickling.

I hate it. I hate that I'm not pulling away.

His hand on my chin isn't rough, but it's sure.

My breath catches. I don't want to inhale him, but my lungs betray me as I breathe him in.

He tilts my head like he's inspecting prey, something to be catalogued before it's devoured.

Then his voice, velvet and jagged, is right against my lips.

"I never said I was a demon, pretty girl."

CHAPTER 17

CADE

My eyes are fixed on the yellow lines of the road, focused on my next destination. Allen is nearly in hand; we are one step closer.

"Back there you said I reminded you of your sister. What's she like?" Andrea asks casually.

"Stubborn. Always in trouble, and with a special talent of testing my patience," I say flatly.

"Well, she's lucky to have someone like you to protect her. That's what a brother is supposed to do."

I ignore her sentiment. "Does he hurt you?"

She looks away, shrinking into her seat. I notice the bruising on her arms where she has been clutching all night.

"I don't want to talk about it," she says, her voice cracking.

"You should report that." I nod to her arms.

I can tell she's fighting off tears, her voice cracking when she speaks.

"If I'm being honest . . . I am terrified of him." She shakes her head. "I should have never moved here after our dad died." Tears begin streaming down her face. "A brother is *supposed* to protect you, to keep you safe." She cries into her hands, her breathing coming too quick. "I'm so fucking stupid . . ."

"What did he do?" I ask, my voice calm.

"I don't know for sure . . . I was with them at the clubhouse last week—I only had one drink. But I don't remember what happened after that." Her voice drops to a whisper. "I moved out last week . . . he said he wanted to apologize to me, so I met up with him. Obviously that was a mistake . . ." She exhales a large breath. "If I'm being honest, I don't want to know. I just want to get as far away from him as I can."

My hands grip the wheel as the pieces begin to fall into place.

We sit in silence for the remainder of the drive due to no fucking radio signal, but I managed to cut the drive time.

"Thanks, Jack."

I look at her, confused, until I remember I gave her Jack's name, and nod.

"They mentioned a clubhouse. Where is that, exactly?"

She looks over at me, face mixed with concern and confusion.

"What are you going to do?" she asks in a low voice.

"Nothing. I just wanna talk to them."

I wait until she's safely inside her coworker's house before speeding away. That fucker Allen better still be there.

It doesn't take me long to find him.

I pull into the lot beside an old gambling hall, throw on my hoodie, and text Jack the update.

I parked a few spots over, the angle perfect.

Now we wait.

After ten minutes, the silence begins to press in too heavily, like the air's being sucked out of the truck's cab.

My chest tightens. It's too still. Too quiet. The kind of quiet I remember . . . Before the masks, before the rituals, before the screaming. I used to have to sit like this, expected to be silent, to be still, obedient, with no control. When they brought in the boy, I knew what was coming, but I didn't run.

I watched. I shook. And I never stopped.

I focus on my hands, trying to ground myself, but they blur in front of me.

I grip the wheel, knuckles white. But they don't feel like mine any longer.

They're too still. Too steady. Detached.

I blink. Once. Twice.

My mind races as the adrenaline bubbles to the forefront.

Panic rises. A sudden, choking wave that I attempt to ignore.

My ears ring, the world's colors growing too bright and hazy.

My breaths come in—shallow and sharp. A panic attack . . .

I throw the truck door open, stumble out, and slam it shut.

The world spins.

Vertigo from hell.

I fight to stay upright, my gaze stuck on the side mirror—eyes unblinking at my distorted reflection. I squeeze my eyes shut and slam my fist into the hood.

"Stop . . . Fucking stop . . ."

Flashes of blood and the dagger.

I brace myself against the hood, rubbing my eyes, as I try to focus and breathe.

It doesn't help.

The corners of my vision blur, a cold sweat running down my back.

I rip open the truck door, grab the cooler, and dump water over my head. The shock helps, but just barely.

I drop to my knees, head bowed, and try to reset my mind.

And then . . . I feel it.

A warm vibration blooms in my chest.

You're here.

I don't know how I can feel you—but I do.

Maybe I'm crazy. Maybe you're just my mind's way of coping.

But you . . .

You made it stop.

I can't see you. I can't touch you. And I don't care.

I might be fucked in the head, but I need this.

I need you.

You slip through my fingers, but I feel you everywhere. You haunt my dreams and crawl under my skin until I can't think of anything else.

Every time I'm reminded of you, it's like you're right here—your touch, your warmth. It drives me mad. In the moment, I feel like I'm drowning. You become the air I breathe, and I'm starving for every breath of you.

I shouldn't want this. It's pathetic. Desperate.

But when I feel you—fuck. I can breathe.

I don't believe in ghosts. I don't believe in anything I can't touch, can't see, can't kill.

And yet here I am, talking to you like a lunatic in the middle of the desert.

Worse than that.

I'm grateful.

My hand finds the pendulum Calli gave me. I rub the chain between my thumb and forefinger, letting the texture anchor me. This isn't right . . .

I feel guilty for allowing my own delusions to comfort me. Convincing myself that maybe . . . it's okay, as long as it helps.

Climbing back into the truck I sit, wet and still. Minutes stretch as my fingers twitch against the wheel, my gaze fixed on the entrance of the building.

It's 5:00 a.m. when the doors swing open and a man stumbles out—thrown onto the gravel by two bouncers, who slam the door behind them.

Gray, balding, pinstriped suit. My eyes lock in on him.

That's my guy. My mind snaps back to the mission at hand.

He staggers to his rusted truck, yelling slurred curses, the engine barely turning over. He drives off—slow and swerving.

He would've seen me tailing him if he weren't so drunk. But watching him try to stay in the lines is almost relaxing.

My focus is broken when red and blues light our vehicles. A highway patrol officer.

Fuuck.

The vehicle pulls in front of me and sounds its siren.

I pull into a gas station and turn my headlights off, letting the night swallow me.

Eventually, the officer drives away with Allen in the back seat, still cursing.

I look up the local station's location on my phone. The nearest one is in Vegas.

I give them a head start, then follow them into the Mojave.

When I hear the roar of motorcycle engines behind me, I sigh.

Guess we're doing this.

I pull the truck over to the side of the road and grab my duffel from the back seat, unzipping it. I pull out my serrated blade then shrug on my hoodie, tossing the hood up over my head.

I step out.

Six bikes surround me fast.

I roll my shoulders.

Theo, sobered up just enough to be cocky, pulls a gun and grins when he sees my knife.

"Hasn't anyone told you not to bring a knife to a gunfight?"

I shrug. "I've never needed one."

I throw the knife.

It hits his eye socket, dead-on. Theo screams, crumples, hits the ground hard. The others rush me. I dodge two, slipping past their swings, weaving through them like water until I reach Theo. I yank the knife from his skull—blood sprays, warm on my face—and drive it up into the chin of the closest one. I rip it out as he drops.

Another lunges. I roundhouse kick him square in the jaw. He's out cold before he hits the dirt.

I slit his throat anyway.

"Three down. Three to go," I mutter, cracking my neck.

The large bald guy throws his hands up. "Stop! I think—we're done here . . ."

I wipe my mouth with the back of my bloody hand and step into the glow of their headlights, slowly walking toward them.

"I'd say that's fair. Considering your dead friends." I twirl the blade in my hand. "Answer one question and I'll let you live."

They hesitate. I raise my brow.

"Who drugged the girl? Just out of curiosity."

One of them points straight at the bald man. "Mack. It was Mack!"

I glance over at the snitch. He's backing up toward his bike, eyes wide.

I purse my lips and nod. "Good to know."

The knife lands between his eyes. He drops without a sound.

Mack bolts for Theo's body—goes for the gun. Another guy sprints toward his bike.

I move fast. I'm on him before he can even get the engine started. I grab the back of his neck and slam him down. My boot comes down hard—once, twice, again—until he stops moving.

I turn.

Mack stands ten feet away, holding the gun sideways, one hand shaking.

"Stay the fuck back!" he shouts, voice cracking.

I take a step forward, catching the gleam of the chrome in the headlights. Desert Eagle. I drop my head, slowly shaking it.

The shot rings out into the dead night air, the gun kicking back and whacking the dumbass in the face. My head tilts back and I laugh.

"You missed," I say flatly, throwing the knife.

It slices clean through his hand. He quickly drops the weapon, screaming as he holds his hand, falling to his knees. I'm on him fast, kicking the gun away, and shove him to the ground with a hand to his throat.

"Desert Eagles have a good kick," I say, low and calm. "I'd recommend two hands next time."

I flash a grim smile.

"But you won't be getting the opportunity. Will you?"

I shouldn't be enjoying this.

But I am.

I place the blade to his cheek and drag it slowly down to his jaw. Blood beads up along the cut.

"I'd love to take my time with you . . . but I have too much going on for a side quest."

I press the knife into his gaping mouth and shove it upward. He gurgles, spasms, then goes still. I check his pockets. No ID. Just a wad of hundreds and a bag of white powder.

Figures.

I nudge the gun back toward his body and walk to the truck, wiping the blade clean and tossing it back into the duffel.

One last glance over my shoulder. Looks like a drug deal gone wrong. I walk over to my truck and strip off my hoodie, toss it in the back seat.

I couldn't have planned it better myself.

It's not the chase. Not really. It's the retribution. Someone getting exactly what they deserve. I climb into the driver's seat and leave the gruesome scene in the rearview.

This kind of silence doesn't bother me. It belongs to me. Not like the silence I grew up in—the waiting, the obedience, the quiet before the pain. That kind broke me.

No, this builds me.

The anticipation of the inevitable. Knowing I'm taking my power back one member at a time.

That thought hits low and sharp, a tightening in my chest. A half smile spreads across my face.

And then I feel it.

Soft. Warm. Uninvited.

You.

That same sensation starts creeping back in.

Those phantom hands from the other night.

That gentle touch.

My chest constricts as my body stirs.

I feel myself respond and palm my jeans. "Not now . . ."

"You know I have a mission to finish . . ." A smile curves my lips. "But after . . . after, it'll be me and *you*."

I can feel you pouting, but make no mistake. I will make it up to you.

I blast the radio, static-laced country cutting through the quiet, the only damn station out here. It doesn't help.

I busy my mind with the scenery, the desert that stretches on either side of me in the dark.

Silent. Empty.

A perfect place to hide a body.

CHAPTER 18

CALLISTO

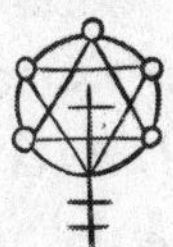

I wake up in a daze, last night's events still at the forefront of my mind. What did he mean by that? He's *not* a demon? No, he must be lying. Nothing else makes sense.

I sit up groggily, pulling my messy hair back into a bun, and head to my closet. As I turn on the light, I jump at the sight of my demon standing before me, looking down with an inquisitive gleam in his eyes.

"Get out. I need to change," I say with as much authority as I can muster this early in the morning.

"Nothing I haven't already seen, pretty girl."

"Stop calling me that." I sigh.

"You're just going to have to accept that I'm not going anywhere, *human*," he says while checking his cuticles.

I respond with a scowl. Fine. I'm not going to let him get to me. If his plan is to terrorize me and my family, I should probably try not to piss him off.

I grab a T-shirt and jeans from my closet and toss them on my bed. Pulling my nightshirt over my head, I avoid eye contact with the monster in the corner. I slip my jeans on and do the skinny jean shimmy. My curiosity gets the best of me, and I glance up at him. He's . . . staring. Hard. He isn't smiling anymore, his eyes locked on me.

I feel my face turn red—no one has ever looked at me this way. He looks . . . hungry. I hate to admit that the way he looks at me makes my body react.

I quickly pull my shirt on and slip into my house slippers, then head to the kitchen to make myself a cup of coffee. I find Jack sitting at the table eating cereal.

"Morning," I say in a husky morning voice.

"Good morning." He doesn't sound like his usual chipper self. What if he is experiencing side effects from yesterday? I need to find out how being possessed affects the human body.

"You look like shit. How are you feeling?" I say, trying to sound like myself—but it's forced.

"I'm just tired. Like I said, I think I'm just getting sick."

"Do you have any updates from Cade?" I ask, sitting down next to him.

"Yeah, Allen was arrested on a DUI. I looked into his police report. He's set to be released later today. This is his first infraction, so they'll be fining him and most likely suspending his license."

"A DUI? At least he'll be easier to track, then," I say with forced cheer.

"Calli, Allen won't be leaving Vegas alive. But I think you knew that."

"Yeah . . . This is kind of fucked-up."

"You wanted to be part of this. You know he's doing what he has to in order to keep you safe." Jack's tone is sincere, but a warning, and I shrink into myself a bit. He's right. I wanted this, I begged Cade for this. I wanted him to understand—to trust me.

"Do you think I could take the truck into town?"

"You know I can't let you go alone. Cade wou—"

I quickly cut him off. "Cade isn't here, and you're sick. I can get medicine and some soup. I just need to clear my head . . . Please, Jack." I give him my best puppy-dog eyes, and he gives in.

"Just don't get into any trouble," he says with an eye roll and a sigh.

I smile and pull the keys off the hook on the wall behind him.

"I'll be back in an hour," I say, running to my room to grab my bag and hurrying out the door.

I hop in the driver's seat and start the truck, slowly pulling out of the driveway—it's been a while since I've driven.

I get about fifty feet away from the house when I hear: "So where are we going?"

I jump in my seat, the truck skidding and jerking to a stop.

"What the fuck! Don't do that!" I gasp, trying to calm the initial shock, my hand pressed to my chest.

"Thought you weren't allowed to leave by yourself—big brother's orders. I'm helping keep you out of trouble," he says, sarcasm dripping from his words.

"I don't need a babysitter. I want to be alone."

The demon quirks a brow, unconvinced.

"Did you forget what I said? We are bound. I couldn't leave you if I wanted to. The sooner you accept that, the easier this will be."

"I highly doubt that. But I do have a question." I continue down the road, accepting my unwanted ride-along.

"Shoot."

"You possessed Jack yesterday. Are there any lingering effects? Is he in any danger?"

"Depends. I don't possess human flesh often, so I'm not as skilled as some of my brethren. He'll most likely feel fatigued and sick to his stomach, or his internal organs could start to shut down. It differs based on the length of the possession, or how often it occurs and if the vessel is willing."

"How long will it take for him to get better? What can I get for him that will help?"

"I typically don't concern myself with the host once I'm done.

I'm also not completely familiar with the inner workings of humans. Our anatomy is different."

"So, you don't know?" I say dryly.

"He's most likely just dehydrated. His body's feeling the aftereffects of trying to reject a foreign entity. He should recover in a day or so."

We sit in silence for a beat. That's actually helpful. He just needs electrolytes and rest—and I need to make sure this thing doesn't hijack his body again. I'm going to roll with this. I'll play this monster's little game. I need to understand his intentions, and I don't think he's just going to outright tell me if I ask. I can only assume he wants my soul, but if what he said is true, and he isn't a demon—maybe he has other plans. I need to find out.

I'll act as casual as possible, continue my studies—and figure out how to rid myself of this parasite. I can't let this scare me. I may not have been prepared for him to show up when I called—but now I have to clean up my mess.

I arrive in town and stop at the corner store, Alabaster trailing close behind. He is huge and seeing him walk into a store so casually is almost funny. He looks around, appearing confused. I chuckle to myself as I grab the essentials and make my way to the register. The young man rings up the items quickly, bags them, and I pay.

"Have a nice day, ma'am," the clerk says in a monotone voice.

"Thank you, you as well." As I leave, I notice my favorite chocolate bar staring back at me. I want to buy it, but there are now people in line behind me and I'm far too socially awkward to keep anyone waiting, so I walk away with a sigh.

Settling myself back into the truck, I look over the items: electrolyte drinks, Tylenol, vitamin C packets, and some chicken soup. This should be good. Alabaster appears in the passenger seat beside me, suspiciously quiet.

Back home, I grab a bottle of water, pour the vitamin C packet into it, and shake it as I make my way to Jack, who is lying on the couch watching a horror movie.

"Here, this will help."

"Aww, you take such good care of me. Thank you, Nurse Callisto."

I roll my eyes and smile at him while tossing the drink onto his stomach. He reacts with a grunt and a laugh.

"Hey, about yesterday . . ." Jack says, his tone turning serious, his eyes darting away from mine.

"Don't mention it. It was nothing."

"I don't remember pulling you toward me and maybe it was the fever . . . but I'm sorry."

"Like I said, Jack, you're sick. Don't mention it," I all but plead with him.

Seriously. Drop it.

"All right. I just wanted to make sure you knew I wasn't trying to seduce you," he says with a crooked smile, finally relaxing again.

"No, of course not. You would never dare try anything with Cade's little sister," I say in a joking tone, my eyes narrowed. His smile drops when he notices the boundary I'm placing. Jack and I have always made jokes, but Cade isn't something to joke about. I'm trying to threaten him with the only thing he'll believe. The jokes need to stop—he isn't safe. Neither am I.

"No. I wouldn't." He sounds . . . disappointed? It doesn't matter. Nope. I can't begin to overthink whatever the hell *that* reaction was.

I need to study.

"I'll be in the library if you need me," I say as I walk away with a wave, not looking back.

I open the door to my favorite room in the house. Floor-to-ceiling bookshelves and stacked cases with my parents' artifacts line the large room. I grab a book titled *Ancient Beings and Folklore* and make my way to the chair in the corner while skimming its pages. I sit down and notice something on the table beside me.

A single chocolate bar. The one I wanted to buy at the store. Did . . . did he get this for me?

"That's the one you wanted, correct?" I hear his voice coming from the ether as he materializes in front of me.

"Did you steal this?"

"Of course not. I took money from your wallet and left it on the counter." His voice is serious, and I snort.

"A demon with morals? You're joking, right?"

"I only take what's mine. I'm not a thief."

"Oh, but you can steal money out of my wallet?"

"What's yours is mine, and what's mine is yours, pretty girl," he teases, and I roll my eyes.

"Your perception is sorely mistaken."

"I was only trying to—" He trails off, not finishing his sentence, his expression unreadable.

"If this is an apology for last night, I'll accept it on one condition."

He looks at me curiously, sauntering over and dropping to kneel in front of me. Even on his knees, he towers over me. I lift my chin to make eye contact, mustering all the courage I can to keep my cool.

"You trying to make a deal with me, pretty girl?" he purrs.

"You won't possess anyone I care about again."

He takes a moment, scanning my face.

"As I said, I have no intention of hurting you, or the people you care about."

"Then what *are* your intentions?" I ask.

He continues staring at me, as if searching for something. The look in his eyes makes my chest heat up, and suddenly I feel nervous. This feels . . . intimate.

Looking at him like this—he's beautiful and terrifying. His sharp glowing eyes bore into me, his long white hair falling in his face, wrapping around his massive horns. Without thinking, I reach up and touch them, running my fingers along them gently. He doesn't move, allowing me to feel them. They're cold and smooth to the touch. I look at him. Without realizing it, he's leaning toward me, and I close my eyes. I can feel his breath on my cheek. Chills spark all over my body, and I'm lost in the moment. His lips gently graze my cheek, softly moving closer to my mouth.

I meet his with my own.

The kiss is soft, delicate. He wraps his fingers in my hair, pulling me closer—firmly but gently. I feel his tongue begin to explore my mouth as my lips part. It feels softer than it looks, moving with precision. I should stop this . . . but . . .

I wrap my hands around his waist as his lips make their way down my neck. I moan into the air, head tilting back as he yanks the neckline of my shirt down my shoulder—with his teeth—tearing a hole in it.

He pulls away for a moment and gazes down at me as my eyes flutter open. They scan his beautiful body and wander lower . . .

He's hard, and . . . Oh Gods . . .

That doesn't look normal.

"Fuck."

CHAPTER 19

CADE

I lean my elbow against the window of the truck, rubbing my temple, when I notice movement. I watch as Allen is released, his clothes in disarray. He looks confused, lost, his eyes bloodshot. Good. It's five p.m.—they definitely took their time letting him out. According to Jack, he got the bare minimum, but that doesn't matter now.

He won't be of this world much longer.

While I waited, I scouted the few chosen locations suitable for the night's endeavors. About ten miles into the middle of nowhere sits an old abandoned mining facility. No one will hear him there, not even with what I have planned.

I keep my eye on him as he hops into a taxi—most likely headed to the impound lot to retrieve his car. I tail him, staying a few cars back, knowing I need to be patient. Despite my body being still, the adrenaline has already hit me. I try to steady myself with long breaths, but they do little to calm me.

Until you.

That subtle feeling is there again. I haven't felt it all day, and the fact that I'd go so far as to say I missed it . . . is ridiculous. I can feel my resolve starting to give. Maybe Calli was onto something. Maybe it doesn't matter if it's real or not. Maybe it's about the comfort that comes from believing.

Frustration creeps in. It's not real. No, it's not.

The warmth fades, almost as if you are shrinking away.

I want it to be real.

Even thinking it breaks me, frustration turning to sadness. Knowing that whatever this is . . . is just a figment of my imagination. Me feeding into my own delusion. Desperate to hold on to the only thing that has ever brought me any kind of *true* solace. But it also makes me question my sanity . . .

I want it. I want to keep it. *Keep you.*

The comfort eases the buzzing in my chest, but it does nothing to calm the desperation I always seem to feel, wanting to keep you close to me.

Sooner than I expected, the taxi turns into a beat-up tow yard. I turn and stop at a liquor store across the street to bide my time. I pull out my phone and text Jack—this will be the last update until it's done.

Me: Package found, it will be delivered by end of day.

Jack: Be sure to handle with care. 🔪 😈

Me: You really are a fucking creep.

I don't bother waiting for his reply, because knowing my friend, it'll be unhinged as fuck. Underneath all those charming looks and charismatic persona, he is one crazy motherfucker. Hell, just the other week he was talking about his latest obsession. The guy is certifiable, obsessive, and capable of doing things so heinous it would make a psychopath run for the hills. One of the many reasons I like to keep the guy around. And would never want him to be with Calli, not that he would ever try. The guy is as loyal as a goddamn golden retriever.

I find myself spacing out, eyes on the broken liquor store sign. I hop out, entering the run-down store. I grab the nearest bottle of whiskey and two cigars. As I exit, I notice the sun beginning to dip down in the sky—the October air cool and crisp.

I take a moment to appreciate the view before climbing back into the truck, placing the bag on the passenger seat. If I'm right, once he gets his car, he'll head out of town. There's only one way out from where we are, and I doubt he'll go back the way he came.

Twenty minutes later, I see him exit the impound office with his vehicle, despite his suspended license. He must've paid them off, the greasy bastard. He pulls out in the direction I hoped he would.

Perfect. The sun is down, and he's heading into the desert.

The trap is set.

But to my surprise, he turns around and begins driving toward me. He pulls into the liquor store parking lot, parking far too close to my own truck. I keep my head low, chuckling to myself. The guy gets a DUI and his first stop is to buy more alcohol. That's actually funny as fuck.

His stop is brief, thankfully, then he's continuing on in the direction I need him to.

I turn up the radio as I follow behind, closer now. This needs to be perfect. We're several miles outside of Vegas now, no other headlights to be seen. I speed up, hitting the gas hard as I pull up right behind him then swerve into the opposite lane and speed ahead. I slow down once I'm in front and brace myself.

I brake.

I feel the impact of his car almost immediately. He was only going about forty miles per hour, so he should be relatively okay—as long as he was wearing a seat belt.

I exit the truck and walk calmly to him. The front end of his old truck is crushed in and smoking. Allen is moaning, clutching his clearly broken nose. I pull hard on the door, but it sticks and I grunt as I drag it open. He is, in fact, wearing a seat belt.

"Good. It would have spoiled my plans if you died."

Allen looks up at me, dazed, before I see the realization spread across his face, his eyes widening in alarm.

"Motherf—"

I knock him out immediately, pulling his body from the car. I drag him over to the now-very-dented bed of my truck and haul his body onto my shoulders before tossing him in the back. I climb into the driver's seat and make my way to his final destination, my blood singing with adrenaline.

About an hour later, I walk into the dilapidated building where I have the piece of shit tied up. My face is calm, my movements fluid. I can hear his muffled screams before I enter the room.

I say nothing, setting my bag down gently on the table in front of him, and begin pulling out my assortment of weapons, carefully inspecting each one until I decide how I want to start this.

The silence is loud.

I saunter over to him and pull the gag from his mouth.

"Please . . . Please, Cade . . . You want money? I—I can give you money . . . Just please . . . Let me go," he says in a tone only a desperate man at the end of his rope could muster.

I don't respond, turning my back to him once again and going back to the table, my fingers delicately tracing over my options until I land on a hunting knife. Nice and simple.

I grab the chair in the corner and drag it over, placing it backward in front of him, sitting down as casually as the situation allows. I twirl the knife like a toy as I begin to speak, my voice disarmingly soft.

"I'm going to ask you some questions, and if I don't like your answers, you lose a finger. Simple."

His breath picks up, chest heaving at a rapid pace, eyes on the knife.

"When did you last have contact with the Covenant." I don't pose it as a question, but a demand.

He doesn't respond.

"Tsk, tsk, Allen. You're going to need to work with me here. The amount of pain you endure before your death is entirely up to you." I flip the knife in my hand and stand, turning toward the table again, and stab it deep into the wood grain. It stays put while I reach into the duffel and pull out a cigar.

"You and my father partook in these often when I was a child—I remember it well. You both lit one in celebration after you brutally murdered that little boy."

He stays silent and it's beginning to irritate me, the fucking coward.

"You have to understand, Allen, that I've been hunting you all down for quite some time—an accidental death here, a suicide there. That is, until your daughter." I say it in a cavalier tone while pulling out the cigar cutter and matches. His face turns red as I sit back down.

"I know you two weren't close, but you must know I did it all for you."

I place the cigar in my mouth and cut the tip, twirling the cutter on my finger.

"You are going to tell me what you know—we both know it's just a matter of time."

He finally speaks in a quiet voice, blood dripping down his face from his shattered nose. "Your father and I were friends . . . How could you turn on your own?"

I chuckle darkly in response, my eyes on the cigar. "I was never one of you. You people disgust me."

"You were meant to take over after your parents!" He says it like I've personally betrayed him. "Why? All for a sister you barely spoke to?"

I surge to my feet, looming over him, one hand braced on the back of his chair. "Do. *Not*. Pretend you know me. Or my sister. I never gave a fuck about you people. You always took your obsession too far. My parents planned to sacrifice their fucking *daughter*. They got what they deserved."

His face whitens as the realization hits him, his voice dropping to a hoarse whisper. "It was you . . . their deaths. It was you . . ."

I lean closer to him, teeth bared as I cover his mouth and press the cigar to his cheek, burning the flesh as he groans into my hand.

"I didn't come here to fucking monologue."

I grab one of his hands that is bound to his side and slide the cigar cutter onto his middle finger. He jolts at the sudden contact of the cool metal against his skin.

"Your sister—she is doomed, Cade. She's already marked. Her soul will be his regardless. What's done is done. You don't have to do this," he says in a shaky voice, pleading with me already.

Chop.

Allen lets out a blood-curdling scream, shaking the chair as he thrashes in his bonds.

I grab his neck with a firm grip and lift his head, forcing him to meet my eyes. Tears and spittle drip from his eyes, nose, and mouth.

Disgusting.

"You pathetic son of a bitch." I hiss the words. "Don't you dare speak a fucking word about my sister. Who the fuck is leading you assholes!"

"You can't stop it," he says with a twisted smile, blood covering his teeth as he attempts a broken laugh while choking on his own blood. "Our God will come for his offering . . ." He gasps a rattling breath. "Not even you can kill a God, Cade."

Deluded motherfucker. I can't fucking stand him. Rage boils to the surface, making my hand shake as I grip his neck.

Stop. Stop. Stop. Fucking stop. Stay calm. Stay. Calm.

I don't give a fuck what he says, none of it matters. I need to keep my composure.

I shove him away and turn to grab the knife from the table, cutting the ropes binding him. Then I drag him over to the old metal sink. I plug the drain and start the water, watching as it begins to rise slowly.

"Who is leading you?" I ask calmly.

"You killed my daughter, you fucking prick. Even if I knew anything, I'd rather die in my own piss and shit before telling you. I hope she finds you and your pretty little sister so you can watch helplessly as she slits her thro—"

I dunk him under the water, pressing his head down hard, scraping his mangled cheek against the bottom of the sink. I wait until his body stops thrashing so violently before I pull him up.

"Who is 'she,' Allen?"

He's gasping for air, too weak to resist my hold, legs buckling under him.

"Fuck you, little boy. Our God will come, and when *he* does, I will meet you in hell."

I dunk him again. Water spills over onto the floor as I wait a bit longer before pulling him up, then I drag him back to his chair, tossing his limp body into it.

I give him a moment to catch his breath and ask again.

"Who is *she*, Allen?"

He just looks at me with a dead-eyed expression, clutching the hand with the missing finger to his chest. The heat in my veins boils over and my impatience gets the better of me. I grab the knife and stab it into his hand that's resting on his leg, the blade driving through to the bone.

The scream he lets out is agonizing. My frustration turns into rage . . .

"Tell me who she is!" I yell, my voice reverberating off the walls as I slam my hands into the table.

"Rosa!" he wails, chin pressed to his chest.

I halt, sucking in a deep breath. Rosa White. Calli was right all along.

I walk back over to him and pull the knife from his hand and leg, using it to cut open his shirt.

"Thank you for your assistance, Allen," I say, my voice steady once again.

"Will you let me go? I told you . . . so please, let me go . . ." He's sobbing now, already knowing his fate, but I answer him anyway.

"Can't do that, Allen. This is payback for what you did to that little boy—and who knows how many others."

Without waiting for more begging, I take the knife and shove it into his gut sideways, slicing through his internal organs slowly. No precision, not caring to spare him any pain.

He barely makes a noise as his intestines begin to spill out in a gory display that makes my stomach turn. He collapses out of the chair and onto the floor, blood pooling around him. I begin to collect my things while he twitches and groans, bleeding out slowly.

"This is the least you deserve, fucking coward," I call over my shoulder as I make my exit.

Getting to my truck, I remove my boots and gloves, placing them in a metal bin on the side of the building and dousing it with kerosene. I light the match and watch as the flames rise, waiting long enough that the soles of my boots start to melt before jumping in the truck and making my way north. The road begins to blur—

Allen's words echo in my head as I drive:

Your sister, she is doomed, Cade. She's already marked. Her soul will be his regardless. What's done is done.

Bullshit. They're a deluded group of power-hungry freaks. There is no God, and if there was, I highly doubt he'd be asking these dumbasses to do his dirty work. Sounds like a shitty God to me.

I drive for about five hours before arriving at a motel. After a shower and some fresh clothes, I sit on the bed. My wet hair drips water down the back of my neck as I absently rub the metal chain holding the pendulum.

I think of you . . .

You have crawled into my head and spread yourself out like you belong there.

I tug at the chain around my neck, breaking it away.

I can feel you, more than I've ever felt you before.

Maybe I'm fucked in the head, but I'm on a suicide mission regardless . . . So, what does it really matter?

I hold the pendulum in front of me, eyeing it. I remember learning about these things. They're supposed to let you communicate beyond the veil. I always thought it was bullshit, even so . . .

"Are you here?"

I sit in the silence and almost feel disappointed. I go to lower it—until the obsidian stone begins to aggressively move in circles.

It isn't me.

I'm not moving.

I can feel the weight of it being pulled by invisible hands. Chills shoot through my arms, and in this moment, I can't deny it, can't deny *you*.

"You're real," I say into the silence. The words feel foreign coming from my numb lips.

This whole time.

You're *really* here.

I feel the gravity of my own earth-shattering realization hit me like a two-ton truck. For the first time in my life, I feel hope, warm and heavy. Like a part of the world I never knew just opened up to me and I'm fucking terrified that it will slip through my fingers.

This *is* real.

And . . . so are you.

My little ghost.

CHAPTER 20

CALLISTO

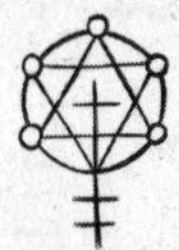

The library is still, quiet in that sacred kind of way. It's beautiful this time of night. Moonlight pours in through the tall bay windows on the far side of the room, casting silver patterns across the floor. The desk lamp hums softly, its warm glow wrapping around the space, just bright enough to read without straining. My eyes skim over the book I found on grounding techniques when the pages begin to flutter. I press my hand down immediately, holding them still.

"Could you not?" I say with a huff. "I need to figure this shit out."

"You're not going to learn what you need to from those books, little witch."

I turn around in the chair to find Alabaster leaning over, our noses almost touching. I still, trying not to let him see how he's affecting me.

"Pray tell, how do I learn, then?" I ask, cocking my head ever so slightly as I raise a brow.

He responds with a mischievous smile. "Hands-on learning is the best way I've found that works."

He brushes my jaw with his fingertips. It's light. Barely there. But my body reacts instantly, heat rushing to my cheeks before I can stop it.

Fuck him for making me feel this way.

I turn my head, roll my eyes, pretend I'm unfazed by the obvious flirtation. Like it didn't land. Like it didn't set off a fuse somewhere deep under my skin. I'm too busy to get distracted. I *refuse* to be distracted.

Even if part of me wishes I could afford to be.

"Look. You can help me or not," I say flatly, then return to my book. "If not, then leave."

"Ask me, and I will." His snide tone makes me want to say no. But I'm not in a position to refuse. He may be right about just doing. But it scares me . . .

I sigh, tilting my head back to see him above me. Staring down into my eyes.

"Will you help me?" I say, shooting him my best doe-eyed look.

His face flattens as his glowing eyes pierce through me. "Say please, pretty girl."

The look on my face drops and immediately I spit back at him through my teeth. "Will you help me . . . *please*."

"Good girl," he says, smiling that fucking smile that gets to me every time. "Follow me."

He stands and walks to the double doors at the back of the library—opening them wide before stepping onto the patio. And into the half-finished secret garden Cade and I have been building, for the coming summer.

He turns back, hand extended, beckoning me to him.

A small smile tugs at my lips as I follow, slipping into the quiet array of leafless, dormant fauna. I find him at the center of the space, standing on the concrete slab where I'd planned to put a table.

His hands come together in a loud smack, and he rubs them together before speaking.

"First thing you need to learn is to follow your instincts."

He lifts his hands in front of him, palms open.

The vines move before I can register what's happening—slithering out from the bushes on either side of me, thick and alive.

"What are you doing?"

A chill runs up my spine as I step back, my voice quieter than I mean it to be. He doesn't answer me, just watches me with a Cheshire cat grin as the vines move closer to me.

One wraps around my wrist. Then another. Cool tendrils slide around my ankles, trailing up my calves. More crawl out from the shrub wall, slipping into my hair, brushing against the back of my neck. They curl slowly and deliberately. Almost like they are teasing me.

"Stop."

My breath catches.

"Stop right the fuck now."

The vines still.

His smile fades, replaced with something unreadable. He tilts his head slightly, like I've surprised him—like *I'm* the one overreacting.

"You need to be in a situation where you have to use your magic to get out."

He walks up to me, the vines moving again, slower this time. They creep up my arms, holding me in place as he leans down, meeting me at eye level.

His breath brushes against my lips, close enough to make my heart stutter. The vines continue to move like they're thinking, like they know exactly where to touch. One traces up my thigh, curling beneath the hem of my shirt, dragging lightly across my stomach.

I shiver beneath the cool vines as they roam my body like they are alive and curious . . .

He watches me. Watches the way my breath shifts. The way I tense but don't pull away.

"You can feel it, can't you?" he murmurs, his voice smooth and dangerous. "Right under your skin . . . That power. Just waiting."

Another vine glides over the curve of my hip, and it's soft. One loops around my waist, pressing against my stomach. He leans in, mouth close enough to brush mine.

"I told you I wouldn't hurt you," he says. "But if you want out, you're going to have to get yourself out."

A pause. His smile curves up.

"That is . . . if you even *want* to."

His eyes drop to my lips, and my heart kicks up again.

"Come on, pretty girl," he whispers. "Show me what you can do."

I try to move, but the vines keep me in place. I feel them gently squeezing my thighs and arms as they wrap around my neck—just tight enough to feel it. I can't think. Between his hands slowly wrapping around my ribs, pulling me toward his body, and the vines holding me in place, I'm overstimulated in the best way. Getting lost in the sensations all at once.

I open my mouth in an attempt to speak. "I—I can't—" I say, breathless.

He bites at my collarbone, his sharp teeth piercing my skin. My head tilts back as I bite my lip, enjoying the pain. I feel the warm blood drip down my chest as the heat of him disappears. I look up. He is staring at me, his eyes hungry.

"You can."

He turns, walking over to the bucket of gardening tools next to the spigot with the garden hose.

"You just need . . . incentive."

He turns on the spigot and walks over with a glint in his eyes, dragging the hose behind him.

My eyes follow him as he gets on his knees. He looks up at me before he reaches under my skirt with both hands. My body jerks at the sudden contact and I feel him tear into my panties. The vines begin tightening and coiling around me further, as my feet lift off the ground, my weight supported.

I look down at him, waiting for him to say something—when he turns the hose on. Setting it to high pressure before immediately aiming right on my clit. The freezing cold water hits my body like it burns. I cry out. The pressure feels so good. My arms and legs attempt to thrash, but I'm unable to move.

"Fuck! Alabaster. Please!"

He stops the hose.

"Please *what*? You have a mouth. Use it. Unless you get out, I'm going to use every tool at my disposal until your body can't handle it. Maybe I'll get the hand rake next."

He looks at me and smiles.

"You want it to stop, make it stop."

He turns it back on, the pressure already drawing an orgasm from me.

The vines continue to tighten around me and I feel a prickle of heat under my skin. The same heat I felt when I knew he was near. He is warming me.

My orgasm comes fast and hard. My moans come in reckless and loud as my breathing falters. He stops the hose and stands, keeping it in hand. I lose feeling in my toes.

As I come down from the high, my body relaxes. I want down now. The vines begin to release. Uncoiling quickly. My weight dropping. He catches me with ease.

He says nothing as he carries me inside into the downstairs bathroom. Sets me down on my feet as he turns the water on, checking the temperature and adding a scoop of my bath salts before coming back over to me. Gestures for me to put my arms up. I comply, my body tired and bruised. He pulls my clothes off slowly, keeping his gaze on my face the whole time.

He lifts me and guides me into the tub, the warm water easing the ache. I relax into it.

"I thought you said you were going to keep me there," I say in a hoarse voice.

"I was. You wanted out, so you got out," he says, toying with the surface of the water with his finger.

"That's it? I just have to *want* it? That's too easy," I say, adjusting myself and sitting up.

"It takes focus, instinct, and intention. Without that, your magic is reckless. Dangerous." He stands. "I'll meet you in your room. I want to get back to that book you've been reading." He starts to dissipate.

"Don't fuck with my yellow tabs!" I call after him, loud enough to make my point.

I shake my head, smiling. Sinking back into the tub. I lay there for a moment, thinking. Though his methods are kind of fucked-up, he's right. It always boils down to me letting go—and trusting my intuition.

Makes me wonder what I'm actually capable of.

I finish the bath and wrap myself in a towel. Looking at myself in the mirror, I can't help but wonder if I would have come this far without Alabaster's help.

I can feel him changing me.

I feel . . . good.

I feel confident, despite the fact that not twenty minutes ago, I was in the most compromising position I could have *never* imagined possible.

It's late when I decide to go make myself coffee, leaving Alabaster on my bed, nose-deep in my book. I slide my house slippers on and wrap my fluffy robe around my waist as I head out of the room, Karma in tow.

I'm not even halfway down the hall when Jack steps out of his room, rubbing his eyes as he looks me over.

"You look cozy."

"And you look exhausted," I say with a smile. "How do you feel?"

He reaches down, giving Karma a pet. "Hey, girl . . ." he coos. "A bit better, actually. Thank you."

"Want some coffee?" I offer, still smiling.

"Now who's way too chipper," he says as he follows me down the stairs.

After making us both a cup, I sit down at the kitchen table with him, checking my phone for the notifications I know aren't there. I'm just lucky to have a phone at all. Took Jack and me years to convince Cade it would be safe to let me have one. Jack speaks up, breaking the silence.

"I know I made it into a joke, but you really do seem happy." He sips his coffee, watching me. "You doing okay?"

I rub my sore arms, already knowing I'll have bruises. "Yeah. I feel pretty good right now," I say honestly.

He leans back, shooting me a sweet half smile. "So . . . who's the guy?"

My eyes snap to his. "Huh?"

"C'mon, Cal. The last time I remember you smiling like that was when it was with me." He laughs under his breath.

My face turns red. He might be right, but this just got weird. And I am absolutely *not* telling him that a demon made me come with a garden hose, in our backyard, while I was tied up by sentient vines.

Nope. Taking that one to the grave.

"Umm . . . it's this guy I met in town?"

"Yeah?" He sits back deeper in his seat. "When did *that* happen?" His voice dips just enough to be noticeable. Flat and guarded.

I stutter for a second, then land on something halfway believable. "Yeah, I met him when I went into town to get everything for you yesterday."

I shrink into my seat, my cheeks hot. This is weird, talking to Jack about this. I glance over and he seems—off. There's a look in his eyes I can't place.

Anger?

"What's wrong?" I ask, concern slipping into my voice.

He leans forward, shifting like he's going to say something . . . but then stops. His jaw tightens before he responds.

"Nothing."

Grabbing his mug, he walks to the sink, rinsing it out in silence. Before leaving, he turns back to me.

"I'm happy for you."

He throws me another half smile, then disappears upstairs.

CHAPTER 21

CADE

For the first time in weeks, I slept through the night. I felt you the entire time—keeping my demons at bay. I feel different. Though nothing has physically changed, my mind has. I feel drained, empty, except for the little light in the back of my mind. *You*. My peace, my calm in the chaos. If I have never lived for anything in my life before, I would live to chase this feeling. To chase you.

With you comes the knowledge I've been missing—magic is real, that much I can no longer deny. There is much to consider. If Rosa White is pulling the strings, I need to find her. I've murdered her daughter, and now her husband. She has vast resources and no doubt revenge on her mind, with no family to speak of, and that makes her dangerous. Then there's the Covenant's God, if it's real. I need to know more about it and I need to know it *now*. I can't walk in unprepared.

I need to be ready for *anything*.

Jack will not be an easy man to convince that I haven't completely lost my mind. Because as crazy as he is, our thoughts have always aligned. But the conversation will need to be had. I'm just not looking forward to it.

I quietly creep into the house. Calli and Jack are nowhere in sight—but I'm not alone. Not anymore. I cross the kitchen and head into the garage. Placing my duffel bag on the table, I begin to methodically clean my weapons and put them away, one by one.

I pull the hunting knife from the plastic bag and start to clean off the blood. The dry dark red stains on the blade begin to fade, mixing with the running water.

The sensation of ripping his stomach open, muscles and tendons resisting and popping while I tore through them, flashes in my mind and I shiver. I drop the knife and shake off my hands as though it will remove the memory from them. I step away from the sink and seat myself in the metal chair near me.

Hands on my back calm me and delicate fingers roam my shoulders and neck. I tilt my head back, hoping to see you, but I'm met with disappointment and an empty room. I close my eyes, a picture of you forming in my mind.

"There you are." You're trying to comfort me.

Don't stop.

I grip the pendulum around my neck as if it's my lifeline.

The memory of Allen quickly dissipates, leaving only the image of your touch pulling me into the moment. I reach for where I feel you but meet my own skin. Tracing my hand down my chest, I feel myself growing hard in my jeans. Shamelessly moving my hips.

I'm *done* fighting this.

I want this.

I pull my shirt up over my head and toss it to the floor, impatiently unzipping my pants. I shove down the waistband of my boxers, my dick springing free, hard and desperate for friction. I tease the head with my fingers, squeezing out the smallest amount of precum that has already beaded to the surface.

I feel your eyes on me, and I must look pathetic, but I don't give a fuck. I spit on my hand and slowly fuck into it, teasingly moving up my shaft as I let out a quiet moan.

"Watch me, little ghost, I want you to see what you do to me." My voice is low and raspy, my muscles twitching as I continue putting on a show for you. I like this, I like you watching me.

I close my eyes again; my imagination running wild with thoughts of you.

You slide onto my lap and pull me into a kiss, rough yet gentle. Your hands wrap around my shoulders and your kisses make their way down to my neck. You reach down and place me at your entrance and I slowly ease my way inside of you. I feel myself stretching you as you begin to move your hips—while I kiss every inch of you I can reach. Wrapping my arms under your legs, I stand, lifting you, holding you close as I drag you up and down along me.

"Do you like that? Do you like the feel of my cock stretching you?" I thrust slowly and deeply. Feeling myself reach my limit, I slow down, wrapping your legs around me, gripping your ass while I push deeper. Filling you as I hold you against me in my mind. I'm lost in you—

"Every fucking part of you," I moan, holding on, desperate to not let you slip through my fingers again.

"This is our time, baby, and I can't deny your intoxicating presence."

Your phantom lips on mine pull me back to the present, as if to tell me you aren't going anywhere. When I open my eyes, I'm still sitting in the chair holding my dick. I want to roll my eyes at myself. I want to tell myself how ridiculous this is.

I want to do it again.

I. Want. More.

Fucking more.

"Cade? Are you here?" I hear Calli call from the other side of the door.

Fuck, fuck, fuck. I jump up and button my pants, stumbling and tripping over myself to get to the workbench where I was cleaning my weapons.

Calli walks in and pauses, looking around the room.

"Hey! I wanted to talk to—um, Cade? Where is your shirt?"

"I didn't want to get any blood on it," I grumble. That sounds believable enough, my voice rough with pent-up desire.

"Okay . . ." she says slowly, her voice tinged with suspicion. "Well, I need to talk to you when you get the chance, cool?"

"Yep. I'll meet you in the library after I'm done here," I answer quickly, trying to rush her off.

She walks away and shuts the door as I lazily grab my shirt off floor and pull it over my head, narrowing my eyes at the empty room.

"I can feel you smiling. Don't laugh at me, you fucking started it."

After I finish, I grab a bottle of water from the fridge and head into the living room to find Jack on the couch. I sit down next to him.

"I need you to do some research for me," I start, looking straight ahead.

He looks at me curiously. He is already aware of Rosa White, I updated him on everything except . . . I attempt to summon the words to say to him but stop myself. He won't believe me, so I settle with—

"I need to find out if there is any information on how to kill a God." I keep my voice bland, but my fingers curl around the water bottle, making it creak.

He bursts out laughing until he sees my very serious face, his jaw dropping.

"You're fucking joking, right?"

"No." I'm serious. "Our next targets are going to be more dangerous, and we need more information. We need to play their game, make them think I believe, and then we can use that knowledge against them. If there is a way to kill their 'God,' maybe I can convince them to give up chasing Calli."

"That's fucking stupid, Cade . . . but I guess I get what you're going for. Fine." He groans. "I'll do some research, but you're better off asking Calli—this is more her territory and we both know it."

"That's what I'm going to talk to her about now. How is she?"

"I don't know. I've been sick, and she has been a total hermit, either holing up in the library or her room. Honestly it seems like she's avoiding me after—" He cuts himself off abruptly, looking away.

"After what, Jack?" I say his name as a warning.

"I—um, it's hard to explain," he stutters, avoiding my eyes. I stand, staring down at him, my eyes narrowed.

"Try anyway," I hiss.

"She's been off, and weird shit has been happening, which you would know if you were fucking here," Jack says with a snap in his tone, finally looking up at me.

I raise an eyebrow and nod slowly, still looming over him.

"You're right, I'm not here. I'm trying to fucking save her."

"Tell yourself whatever you want to sleep at night. This is about what you saw, this is about revenge. You could have taken her anywhere and hid from them." His voice is rough with displaced anger.

I lift him from the couch and shove him against the wall, getting in his face.

"I don't know where the fuck this is coming from," I growl, shaking him. "They are searching for her, and if you think for a fucking second that if I thought there was another way I wouldn't have taken it . . . You know as well as I do how lucky we've been to have not been found this far, mostly because of you, and we're grateful for that, but I'm doing a fucking service getting rid of these evil bastards. So check your fucking tone when you speak to me."

He shoves my hands away and looks to the side, resentment all over his face, arms crossed over his chest defensively.

"I'm sorry," he finally grumbles, shoulders drooping. "I didn't mean that. I'm just worried about her. And you. You're my best friend, Cade, and I love you both like family, but shit is getting weird. Maybe we should pick up and leave. It's not too late."

"Jack." I sigh, running a hand over my face. "We know who is leading them, we have a target, and now we just need a plan. No one knows where we are. We are all safe here. For now."

"It's only a matter of time, Cade," Jack argues, stubborn as always. "There's a detective that's been snooping around the disappearances. Requesting files from years ago, even going as far as pulling your parents' file."

"I covered my tracks. They won't find anything," I reassure him, putting a hand on his shoulder. "How do you even know that?"

"I keep tabs on your past cases—victims, their families, any police digging around. I won't bore you with the logistics. Just know I'd see it if your name got brought up. And lately . . . I've noticed a pattern." His voice is tight with anxiety and I give his shoulder a squeeze before finally stepping back.

"Can you keep them off our trail?"

"I'll do what I can, just . . . just . . . start wearing a mask. The last thing we need is for someone to notice you, and dude, your scar is a dead giveaway. For now I'll do what I can to get info on Rosa." He sighs, slumping back against the wall, looking tired.

I nod my thanks and leave the room, heading for Calli, but as I approach the door to the library, I stop dead in my tracks. I feel frozen, like I can't move an inch. The air feels so heavy, and my skin is buzzing on its surface, hairs raising . . .

What is this?

The pendulum around my neck begins to vibrate, a warm sensation spreading out over my body allowing me to suck in a breath. I shake off the initial feeling and open the door to see Calli sitting in the chair near the window.

She speaks up first, words rushing out.

"Cade, I know you don't believe, but I need to tell you something—" she starts, worrying her hands in her lap.

I cut her off. "Me first."

She pauses and nods.

"You were right." I sigh. "About Rosa White, and about the pendulum. I won't tell you how I know, but I need your help."

"I'm sorry. *What?*" A mix of confusion and what looks like anger plays across her face.

"I'm saying I believe you and I need your help," I tell her, trying to calm that anger before it bubbles over.

"Heh. Wow. Just like that, huh?" she scoffs.

Clearly, I failed.

"After years of you chastising me, judging me, and shitting on everything I know, you walk in here to tell me you believe, like it's nothing? Like it's just another job!?" Her voice is rising and I feel my own temper rearing to face it.

"The fuck is your problem? Isn't this what you *wanted?*" I snap at her.

"Yes! I want to help, and I want you to listen, but you're acting like it's nothing!" she says, surging to her feet.

"So you're upset because I'm not reacting the way you *think* I should? You fucking serious, Calli?" I groan, letting my head thunk against the wall.

"This is huge and you're acting like it's another fucking Tuesday!" She throws her hands up. "What the fuck, Cade? Be angry—cry, scream, do anything but dissociate and internalize everything! Fucking *do* something!" She grabs one of the throw pillows and chucks it at my chest. I catch it, drop it on the ground, and stand, crossing my arms.

"Yes, this is huge. But I can't afford to let myself slip. I accept what I know is true, and yes, Calli, I'm freaking out. It's crazy, *this* is crazy, but I'm in uncharted waters here and I need to stay focused," I try to reason, and her face falls as she drops back into the chair.

"I wish I could do that," she whispers. "Just be strong all the time."

I bend a knee and gently take one of her hands in mine, dipping my head to meet her eyes.

"I'm not, Calli," I tell her honestly, my voice soft. "I'm scared, too.

Scared of losing my baby sister. I don't care how much I lose myself in the process—I'll do all of it to keep *you* safe."

"Why does it have to be this way . . . ? You're tearing yourself apart. I'm not worth it."

Not worth it? I look into her eyes, which are beginning to tear up. I remember how she never cried as a girl. How she was treated like a stranger in her own house by our parents, a fucking tool. A means to an end.

I admit we weren't close as kids . . . I probably could have done more, but she always smiled when she saw me. And I always saw her as a helpless little girl who needed to be kept as far away from everything as she could be. I was glad our parents stayed away from her. I never understood why she always seemed so happy. But then again, I never knew her. Not really.

But I see her now. She's seen things, fought for what she believes in, and tries every day. She's desperate for the attention that she deserves, and desperate to be understood. It's in this moment that I realize she and I are so much more alike than I ever realized.

But she doesn't see her life as one worth fighting for. She was ready to die, and I forgot that. I choose my next words carefully, squeezing her hand to ensure I have her attention.

"You don't get to tell me what's worth it to me. That is *my* decision and mine alone. You deserve a life where you can feel it all. I want you to love endlessly, to fight and show up for yourself. You are not replaceable, and this is only the beginning of your story. I will always fight to give you the life that I know you deserve."

Tears stream down her face as I pull her into a hug, a real hug. She needs this, and honestly, so do I. She hiccups then, swallowing back more tears.

"You're right . . . but I don't *know* what I want, Cade," she whispers into my chest. "I'm terrified. I hate that I feel so fucking helpless all the time, like everything is just too much."

I hug her tighter and kiss the top of her head, resting my cheek there.

"I know, but you don't need to know everything right now. You'll know when it's time." I gently push her back to look at her face. "You said *you* wanted to talk to *me*. Is everything okay?"

She pulls away fully and sits back down, wiping away the tears staining her face. She looks up at me with her dark brown eyes as if searching for the answer in my own. She hesitates when we both hear a knock on the bookshelf.

"I—" She sighs, shaking her head. "Ignore that. Just the resident poltergeist."

I stifle a laugh; this is so fucking weird. But I know now that she is telling me the truth.

"Thanks for the heads-up." I laugh. "I noticed you and Jack were gone when I came back with Karma. Did you have fun?"

"I, um . . . I'm . . . I—" she stutters, and I tilt my head at her, but before she can say anything, the door behind us slams shut and I jump. Eyes wide, I look back at Calli. Suddenly, I feel something hit me from behind, the sting causing me to bend over, holding the back of my head.

"Fuck! What the hell?" I groan. Looking down, I see a book at my feet. I cock my head—the cover reads *Covenant Origins.* I pick the old book up and skim the pages. I glance at Calli, who looks annoyed, arms folded over her chest.

"Is this the shit Jack was telling me about?" I mumble, still rubbing the back of my head.

She looks at me, rolling her eyes, huffing, "Yeah, you could say that."

Snatching the book from my hands, she places it on the large stack on the table next to her chair.

"Are you sure there isn't anything else going on, Calli?" I ask her, my eyes drifting from the book back to meet hers.

"I could ask you the same, Cade," she says, cocking a brow with a serious face. I roll my eyes at her.

"I told you I would tell you anything you *need* to know. Let's just leave it at that. Please?" The please makes her eyebrow raise in surprise, and she nods.

"Fine." She sighs. "What do you need from me?"

I look at her for a long moment, knowing there is no soft way of putting this, but she has to know. It's the only way, if it's even possible.

"I need to find a way to kill a God."

CHAPTER 22

CALLISTO

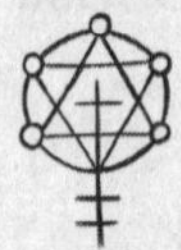

What he's asking is impossible. The most we could do is banish the thing, but I'm not even capable of banishing whatever Alabaster is. It's wrong and twisted, but I don't even want to, and that scares me. I can feel my cheeks heating at the memory of Alabaster and me in the garden.

I *can't* let him get to me.

I want to tell Cade. I want to talk about everything. Okay, not *everything*. But it would be nice to talk about it, especially now that he actually believes me . . . But I can't put him at risk. I have no clue what Alabaster is actually capable of, but what he has already shown me proves that I can't test it. Too much has changed. For both Cade and me. Everything that has happened since the pendulum appeared, gave us both shadows.

My brother's: a guardian angel.

Mine: a demon.

Both of us bound. Condemned to a fate we never asked for.

My nightmares have become my reality.

I just wasn't expecting him to be so beautiful.

I've been in the library looking through the book that was oh-so-conveniently thrown at Cade's head, but it doesn't offer much information regarding the God itself. Karma is curled up on the sofa, keeping me company.

My ancestor, Jonathan Halloway, founded the Covenant. How exactly he got the grimoire isn't specified, but family history does say that he called upon the God through a spell from its pages.

It sure does sound like the grimoire may have the answers I need.

I stand in front of my bedside table, staring at the top drawer where the grimoire has sat for days, untouched, then I stop dead, reminding myself that I'm no longer alone.

If I'm going to open that thing back up, I'll need to put up a barrier. I turn on my heel and scamper into the kitchen to grab the container of salt and race back to my room, carefully creating a circle in front of my bed: around myself and the old book. I take a deep breath and state my intentions clearly in my mind.

I need to know about the Covenant's God.

I'm carefully opening the book when Alabaster's voice booms from behind me. I jump, feet skidding, and break my salt circle—the book slamming closed as I pull my hands away.

"You have no clue how to use that thing, do you?" he says in a wry tone, Karma in his arms and a smirk plastered on his too-perfect face.

"Can you not see that I'm busy?" I say in a low, clipped tone, my annoyance obvious. "And put my cat down."

"*Our* cat," he tuts, clutching her to his chest, and the traitor nuzzles in. "And I thought we were getting along so well." He pouts.

"Karma, you're a traitor," I groan, tilting my head back. "Go away, Alabaster."

"I love that you keep pretending I'm not getting under your skin," he purrs, taking a step closer and kicking at the useless line of salt.

"That is one thing you will not do." I smirk, sitting up straighter.

"Wanna bet?" He sets Karma down on the bed, stroking her chin before turning back to me. "Sorry, sweetie, mommy and daddy need to have a chat."

He looks almost predatory now. He stands to his full height, towering over me. He must be seven feet tall. He doesn't even look real. His body shifts from a physical form into this mist-like substance, as if he is only partially here. His golden eyes darken when his voice lowers to a growl.

"Run, pretty girl . . ." The words seem to echo around the room.

He takes another step toward me, and the realization hits just as my instincts catch up. I bolt out of the room, knowing there is nowhere I can go that he won't follow.

I want him to chase me.

So, I run.

Down the stairs and outside. I make a beeline for the trees surrounding the estate, my bare feet breaking twigs and sinking into the ground with each of my quickened steps. My lungs are burning at the point when I hear him laughing in the distance.

It echoes all around me, his presence pressing in on all sides, when I trip over a raised root.

"Fuck!" I squeal as I crash to the ground, gripping my leg as I scream into the air.

I look down to see my ankle is cut deep. The sensation is so overwhelming, my vision begins to blacken. I attempt to breathe through the pain.

I try to calm myself, sending my power to heal the wound, but to no avail. It's too deep and I can't focus.

Tears burn my eyes and I sit there, silently crying to myself, when I notice black smoke creeping through the brush all around me. It nears my foot then transforms into a gigantic pale hand, before an arm slowly appears—and then the rest of Alabaster's body.

"Stay still," he mumbles, voice surprisingly gentle.

I push at him with as much strength as I have—which isn't much at this point.

"Get off of me, asshole!" I say stubbornly. As if it's his fault I'm clumsy.

He takes his other hand and leans me back against the tree behind me, not looking up from my ruined ankle. He holds me there, in a gentle stronghold, his arms long enough that I'm unable to swing at him any further.

Watching helplessly, he leans down and opens his mouth, and his tongue slowly begins licking the blood from my ankle.

My stomach rolls from the pain and I hiss, "What the fuck is wrong with you?"

He continues to hold me there, pinned, as his tongue makes its way to the deep gash. I cringe at the sight, my body jerking from the pain.

"Please sto—"

He removes his hand from my chest to cover my mouth and all I can do is sit there and watch him bent down on his knees, his tongue tracing the curve of my ankle. I close my eyes tight, unable to watch any longer, when the pain begins to subside. I slowly peek down and see him—looking up at me with my blood covering his mouth.

My wound is gone.

He releases my ankle slowly, with an almost innocent look on his face, those golden eyes blinking at me.

He *healed* me?

"You need to be more careful," he says as he leans over to kiss my ankle.

"I didn't know you could do that," I say, reaching for the spot he kissed.

"There are many things I am capable of, pretty girl."

I shift on the unstable ground and lean toward him.

"I would love another lesson," I say, smirking.

"I think I can manage that, if you're up to the task," he says, kissing me softly at first, then crawling on top, grinding himself against me. I feel heat pool in my gut just as . . . I hear Cade in the distance calling for me. *Fuck*. Alabaster glares in his general direction at the interruption and collapses back into smoke in my lap. I watch in horror as the smoke *seeps into my skin* and disappears.

"Calli! Where the fuck are you? Answer me now!" Cade calls out, his voice rough with worry.

"What did you do to me?" I ask in a desperate tone, speaking out loud.

Then I hear a voice in my head, as if it were my own thoughts.

"Relax. I can't affect you the way I did your little friend."

"Why can I hear you in my head?" My voice is high with panic.

"I told you I would get under your skin," he says, sounding pleased with himself.

"Not literally! I think I'm going to be sick . . . This is what you did to Jack . . ."

"I can't hurt you like this. I'm not very good at possession, definitely not skilled enough to possess a witch. Think of me more like a hitchhiker. Now stop talking to yourself before they think you've gone mad."

"Haven't I though . . . ?" I say in a low tone. It's rhetorical. Of course I have . . . This is madness, all of it.

"I like you crazy."

I roll my eyes and stand, anticipating pain. I wiggle my foot, surprised.

Thanks, I guess?

Cade comes storming through the forest with rage in his eyes as I brush myself off.

He grabs my shoulders. "Where the fuck have you been? Why didn't you respond? What the fuck, Calli?" he says through gritted teeth, shaking me slightly. "I had no idea what happened! We could hear you screaming from inside the house!"

"Quit yelling at me!" I snap. "I tripped. I'm fine. I'm sorry I made you worry."

"What is going on with you? I can tell you're lying to me. I can't fucking help you if you don't speak up." There's worry in his tone and something inside me breaks.

"YOU CAN'T HELP ME IF I DO!" I scream up at him, pulling free of his hands.

Cade straightens, clearly surprised at my outburst. I continue with as calm a tone as I'm able to muster, despite my voice cracking.

"I will always be broken in my own way. You can't fix me, Cade." I take a deep breath in. "Look, if I want to talk to you, I will. I have been putting everything I have into learning how to control my power. I finally feel like I'm getting somewhere. I'm sorry I scared you guys, but please . . . Don't try to parent me right now."

"Calli—" he starts, but I cut him off.

"No. I don't want your logic. I don't want you to try and solve my problems. I want you to *see* me," I say with strength. "I'm more capable than you think."

I slowly raise my hands, closing my eyes as I will the wind to pick up. I imagine it circling around us—and it does. Fallen leaves begin to pick up and form a vortex around us.

"You are magnificent." The smile that meets my lips is more genuine than I have ever felt before—*I did it.*

"Of course you did. Now open your eyes."

I open my eyes to meet my brother's, but he is looking up, taking it all in with an expression I've never seen on his face before. *Wonder.* His face is in awe as I drop my hands and the leaves float to the ground in a circle around us. He looks into my eyes as I speak again.

"I want to put my past behind me, Cade. I don't want you to see that scared little girl anymore."

He stares at me for a long moment, recognition dawning on his face.

I speak, looking away as my voice cracks. "Please, tell me you understa—"

He rushes over and wraps his arms around me, holding me to his chest, saying nothing. My confidence breaks. I can't hold back the tears, so I let them fall. My chest heaves as I let out all of the things I've been keeping from him without words—the fear, the confusion, the pain.

We stand there for a while, arms around each other tightly as he lets me let it out before finally speaking.

"I don't know how you feel or what you're going through. And I'm sorry I didn't believe you." He says it in a loving tone, but I can almost hear his mind whispering for me to *please let him try.*

My brother has never been one to show his emotions—I almost don't know how to receive it. Right now, he's accepting mine, and that is enough to break through the mask I try so hard to keep on.

I release him from the hug and step away, wiping at my face.

"I know you're trying. But so am I," I whisper, wrapping my arms around myself.

"Why didn't you show me before?" he asks genuinely.

"I couldn't . . . But I've been practicing."

"Clearly," he says, half smiling as he scoffs.

I look up at him and can't help but smile as I shake my head.

"C'mon, let's get home. Jack stayed back to wait in case you came home before me," he says, gesturing toward the tree line.

We exit the forest and head back to the house, when I hear a voice in my head.

"You handled that well."

I smile and speak under my breath. "Thank you. Now can you get out of my head?"

"No. I don't think I will. I like it in here."

CHAPTER 23

ALABASTER

Jack runs to Calli, his chest heaving, fear and concern etched on his face as he approaches. He cups her cheeks and looks her over, running his thumbs over her face. I feel the rage bubble up in me as he speaks.

"Are you hurt? You scared the shit out of me, Cal," he says, his eyes not leaving her.

"Jack . . ." She pushes his hands away, shaking her head. I see him look over at Cade and drop his arms.

Cade looks over both of their faces. "What the fuck is this?"

Calli winces at Cade's sharp tone. "It's nothing." She tries to brush it off, but Cade isn't stupid.

He sees her reaction. Big brother has put the pieces together.

He storms over to Jack and shoves him against the front door with a loud thud.

Oh, this is going to be *fun.*

"Is there something going on with you two?" he says, clearly holding back his rage.

"Nothing. I swear—" Jack speaks, but Cade interrupts him.

"I know you well enough to know when you're fucking lying, Jack. What. The. Fuck. Is going on with you two." Cade's voice is low, measured.

"I'm telling the truth. We are just friends."

"You don't look at your fucking friends like that!" Cade says with a growl, his voice louder now.

"Fuck, will you two stop? Jack and I had a thing years ago when we first met, but *nothing* is going on now, Cade. We are just friends."

"Probably not the best thing to say, my dear."

Cade turns toward Jack, swinging an uppercut to his jaw. Jack immediately falls to the floor, rubbing his face.

"Are you fucking kidding me, Cade? What the hell!" Jack screams.

"That's the least you deserve." The look in his eyes screams betrayal. "How far did it go?" Cade says, looking down at Jack.

Jack rubs his bloody nose, not responding.

"How far!"

"We were both kids—and it was a long time ago, Cade. Can we please not get into this right no—" Calli tries to speak up, but Cade cuts her off.

And by the look on his face, she all but answered his question.

"After all these years I've trusted you with her, to keep Calli safe, and you went behind my back?"

Jack stands, back against the door. "That's all I've ever tried to do. I swear to God I never—"

"You are the closest thing I have to a friend! How fucking could you? And to hide it from me, for years! I could forgive you if I thought you actually loved her, but I fucking know you!"

"I do love her!" Jack says, pausing. Cade's eyes widen.

I can feel Calli's shock from his confession. I thought it was pretty obvious by how he looks at her.

"I've loved her since the day we met. But I knew that wasn't what she needed from me, and I know I'm not good for her." He drops his head. "I'm sorry."

The look of disgust on Cade's face says more than words ever could. Anger, resentment, sadness. I almost feel sorry for the guy. But

I gotta say, watching him lay out that little shit was more satisfying than I thought it would be. Maybe I won't have to kill him after all.

"Cade . . ." Calli says, reaching out.

"Don't." He turns quickly, walking over to the steps.

She shrinks back, looking at Jack as her brows pull together with a look of concern. I can feel her mind reeling, attempting to find the right words where there are none.

Cade turns, looking both of them over with a cold expression before walking down the steps and disappearing behind the house.

Calli walks up to the door, not meeting Jack's eyes. "Please, excuse me."

He moves over as she turns the knob, walking inside. Karma runs up to her, rubbing herself on Calli's ankles. Reaching down, she cradles the cat in her arms and walks upstairs and into her room.

"Rule number one, you don't sleep with your best friend's little sister. I'm just sorry I didn't get to hit him myself."

She sighs.

"He's right. We did lie to him, and he has every reason to be upset."

"He'll get over it."

"In my defense, I was eighteen. I had no idea how close they were at the time."

"No need to explain yourself to me."

I hate to admit it, but I fucked up. I can't get out of her.

This is a bit awkward. It's never comfortable being in someone else's skin—a ghost in flesh without any control is maddening, despite how much I like the idea of being inside hers.

In all my years on this Gods-forsaken planet, I've possessed and hijacked plenty of bodies—witches included. I'm utterly perturbed and would almost be impressed with her if I wasn't so frustrated.

It's about ten in the morning and she's still sleeping. I can't say

I'm surprised, since she spent half the night arguing with me. This one is so stubborn—it's infuriating, and I can't help but like it. I can feel the soft satin sheets beneath her, her heart beating in a gentle rhythm, her scent filling the air around me. This is the only time I've felt her so peaceful.

Her dreams, on the other hand, are dark, filled with symbolism I'm sure she doesn't understand yet. A dark figure standing before a table with an old journal—next to it, a white rose. I've kept the dreams at bay all night. I had no idea she was cursed with the sight.

Her premonitions should not be ignored.

I find myself in quite the conundrum—this woman frustrates and inspires me in all the best and worst ways.

This was *not* the plan.

I was drawn to all of this by the grimoire and the question of why, oh why, do these humans have a celestial artifact?

I've been trying to figure out how they got it. I've played my part well, and I believe this beautiful creature will provide the answers I seek. There is just that one lingering issue . . .

"Are you still in there?" she says softly as I feel her slowly come back to a conscious state of mind, stretching her arms and rubbing her eyes.

"Good morning, beautiful," I purr into her mind.

She sighs—I can feel her annoyance with me and it only causes me to want to push her buttons further.

"Look—I'm tired," she groans. "Cade is leaving and I am in no mood. If you could please get out of my body, I would appreciate that," she says, voice calm yet stern.

"No can do. It pains me to say I appear to be trapped in you," I admit, mentally shrugging.

"What do you mean *trapped*? You can get out, *right*? I saw you do it before," she demands, sitting up and leaning against the headboard.

"You saw me possess a human. You, my dear, are no human."

"Wait . . ." She trails off and I can feel the spike of anxiety in her chest. "So you genuinely can't get out? Are you fucking kidding me?"

I laugh softly. *"Sorry, little human. You gotta put up with me in here—for now at least."*

I can hear her thoughts racing. She's flustered—but not angry.

How very curious.

She gets up and follows her typical morning routine like a ritual and all I can do is watch the world through her eyes, feeling what she feels. It's almost sensual how delicately she takes care of herself. I notice the way she is careful to brush her hair, observe her obsess over what to wear and defaulting on a comfortable sweater anyway.

The way she takes extra care scratching Karma's belly when she lounges on the windowsill.

I feel the sway in her hips as she makes her way to the kitchen to pour herself a hot cup of coffee—feline friend in tow. Every move this woman makes is divine, elegant. Her brother is already at the table next to that chipper little shit. She sits down across from them.

"Good morning," Jack says in his usual positive tone. Clearly pretending yesterday didn't happen.

"Let's wipe that annoying smirk off his face," I prod at her.

"You stay quiet," she says aloud, and I laugh as I watch both their reactions. Her brother's brows furrow, and he gives Jack a death glare while Jack shrinks in his seat. Cade speaks up, not making eye contact, our traitorous kitten leaping into his lap.

"Go save our baby from the bad man!" I screech, and I can feel her eyes roll.

"He's the one who brought home the cat," she breathes. "Besides, she likes him."

"Darling, when I get out of here, you are so getting a spanking."

"Okay . . ." Cade mumbles, Karma now purring in his lap. "Jack found one of the Covenant's safe houses and was able to hack the security system—I'll be heading out in about an hour to make my way there to slip in and bug the place," he says in a low, flat tone.

This is hilarious. You could cut the tension in the room with a fucking knife.

"I've had a premonition, Cade. This could be a trap. You need to be careful." She says it with resolve, but her voice comes out unsure.

Jack speaks up, his voice quiet and reassuring. He goes to reach out to touch her hand but stops himself, pulling back. Smart move . . .

"This may be one of the safest missions he's taken on, Calli."

I can feel the gears turning in her head. She's doubtful. I hear her whispered thoughts repeating: *It's a trap*. Her instincts tell her to doubt the situation, but in the end, her trust in her brother and Jack wins out. But this isn't some scared little girl—this is a woman demanding to step into the power she knows she has. She was treated like nothing, even now she has no control over her life, yet she doesn't feel small. Looking in her head, it appears she never has. That's something I've never seen in a mortal. It's . . . perplexing.

She sighs. "Okay—who's the target?" she asks as she sips her coffee.

"No one specifically. This mission is solely to gather intel. Rosa hasn't been to the property, but one of her right-hand men has—seen on traffic cams going there multiple times. Could be living there or prepping for Rosa. His name is Benjamin Teller," Jack says, shoving cereal in his mouth as he talks.

I feel the chill that crawls up her spine at that name. She may not know it yet, but that's her intuition. This man is dangerous.

Her mind flashes with worst-case scenarios—images of her brother tied up, covered in blood. This could have been one of her dreams, but it's too clear . . . too vivid.

"There are only three guards stationed—" Cade begins, but she cuts him off, putting her mug down with a thump.

"As far as you know," she counters. "Do you really think they would be so brazen after one of their own went missing?"

"If it's any consolation, Calli," Jack says, trying to soothe her, "I'll have eyes on him the entire time through the security cameras. I'll be guiding him the whole way through the house. This is a stealth op, simple and clean."

She relaxes slightly, but her mind is still torn.

"This is a bad idea," she murmurs, mostly to herself, but Cade sits up straighter, Karma leaping from his lap, his tone sharp.

"You don't make the decisions, Calli—I do. Rosa's good at covering her tracks, so this is our best chance, and we have to act *now*."

"You're going to get yourself killed, Cade," she snaps, crossing her arms, thoughts singing with worry and frustration.

"Feel lucky I'm even telling you this." He gives her a long, pointed stare. "I'm trusting you with this," he continues, voice weary and a glazed look in his eyes. Even I can see he looks off. He sighs, shaking his head to clear it before asking, "Have you found anything useful on their God or the Covenant's origins?"

"Not yet . . . I'm working on it," she tells him, not meeting his eyes.

"All right, I—"

"Fuck you, Cade." She glares as she stands with her coffee. As she storms away from her brother, again. I can feel the bitterness in her. He blatantly disregarded her. Which, if I'm being honest, is fair. I almost respect his reckless idiocy masked as confidence, knowing Cade really will do anything for her even when she betrays him.

He gets up and follows her. Grips her arm enough to stop her. His face softens. She jerks her arm out of his grip, shoulders dropping as she exhales a breath.

"I'm sorry. I never meant to lie to you. But I *need* you to know that something is wrong with this mission."

"You *always* say that, Calli. You are always paranoid or have some issue. This time is no different."

"Your *little ghost* can't protect you from physical danger, Cade. Do well to remember that." She speaks quietly, but it's laced with venom.

I see something in his eyes, a shift in his expression. *You've really gotten to that man, ghost.*

Calli stomps her way to the library, leaving her brother standing there in shock. She grabs a book off the huge stack and sits hard in the desk chair, slamming the book down.

"Gods, he's so fucking frustrating!" she seethes.

"He would do well to listen to your counsel," I tell her seriously.

"Wow. You say that like you're on my side." She says it sarcastically, but I feel her genuine surprise.

"I'm on my side," I remind her. *"You are wrong for what you did, but with this, it just so happens you're right."*

"That's ironic coming from something like you," she snorts, opening the book.

"I'm a walking contradiction, baby. Get used to it."

She brushes me off, skimming the book I now see is the one I threw at her brother.

"I thought there'd be something in here to help—but it's all generalized bullshit glorifying their intentions." She sighs in disappointment. "Talking about how their 'God' will bring them knowledge and power in exchange for a powerful sacrifice. It's all vague. This is written as though they were chosen, like they are special. It's disgusting."

"Humans are such ignorant creatures—predictable and easily influenced. So easy to see when you're inside their mind," I hum, scanning the page through her eyes.

"Sarcasm is exactly what I needed right now. Thank you." She stills, back going straight as something hits her. "Wait. No. No, that might actually be it."

"Sarcasm? Oh, darling, I have plenty of that."

She ignores me, jumping up and rushing to a corner bookshelf stacked with old journals, desperately tracing each spine.

"No, we need to see inside their minds. These journals are dated before the Covenant was established . . . I put these in here when I was unpacking years ago. We have a bunch more packed away, but this is a good start."

"And you are just now realizing this?" I say with more sarcasm dripping from my tone.

"I never had a reason to learn about their history," she defends. "I had the grimoire, so I focused on learning about my magic rather than the people who want me dead. I honestly just didn't connect the dots and forgot about them."

She pulls one down, opening it and settling back into her chair as we read its contents together.

Oct. 12th, 1847

I write this in haste and against my better judgment, for even now I feel its influence pressing upon me like the weight of sin before confession.

The thing we unearthed beneath the chapel ruins was not written by the hand of man. Its cover is flesh-bound and cold as stone even as it rested near the hearth. I watched the ink bleed anew across its pages, as if the words themselves refuse to remain still. It knows I read it. It wants to be read.

At first, I believed it to be a relic. A piece of forgotten history. But there is no history in this, only hunger. The knowledge it offers is profound. Impossible. And yet . . . it works. It answers questions not asked. It knows the names of men long buried. And when I dream, I dream not of Heaven, but of blackened altars and blood-soaked promises. Jonathan caught me reading it yesterday.

He is twelve and far too clever and curious. He asked no questions—only watched with that solemn stare he inherited from his mother. I closed the book, told him it was not for his eyes, and still—when I returned from town—I found him hunched over its pages, turning them with a reverence that chilled me. I took it from his hands. He did not protest.

He smiled.

I have locked it away, but locks are a fool's comfort. I fear I have already failed in shielding him. He is drawn to it like kindling to flame. And the book, in turn, responds to him. The symbols shift more readily when he is near. I dare not say it aloud, but I believe it knows he is the one who will open it again.

I have not told Margaret. There is no comfort to be had in the confession.

I fear we are not its masters. We are its vessels.

This book whispers of power. Thrones beyond flesh and influence, beyond coin. But its voice is sweet, and all sweet voices in darkness are lies. I feel myself slipping closer to temptation each day, and still, I cannot burn it. Something in me stays my hand.

Should I fall to this evil, may this journal serve as warning to my bloodline.

We are not chosen. We are bait.

—R. H.

I feel her heart racing. This is the first I'm learning of this as well. So, it was Rholand who found it, buried under a church no less. This just keeps getting more and more interesting. Callisto holds the old journal in her hands as she sits, trembling.

"My Gods . . . This is Jonathan's father . . . He found the grimoire. There's nothing on him in any of the Covenant books I've read," she murmurs quietly.

"And why would there be? Clearly the man seemed against it."

"Good point," she agrees absently. "They wouldn't put anything on paper that's contradictory to their twisted rhetoric. And what he says about the grimoire . . . he's not wrong. I've noticed it, too. Is that why you stop me every time I try to use it?" she asks, and I feel a small burst of pride in my clever little witch.

"Who says that's what I've been doing?" I tease.

"Don't fuck with me," she scoffs, gently setting the journal down. "Every time I use that thing, shit would happen, and now I know it was you. You've been protecting me, haven't you?"

I don't respond. She's right in a way—I don't want her to use it. However, I've haunted, threatened, and scared her . . . how could she think I've been protecting her? She speaks up, interrupting my thoughts, her voice surprisingly soft.

"Look, I hate to admit this . . . but I doubt I would have put two and two together if it weren't for you. So . . . thank you."

I pause, a strange warmth filling me.

"I didn't help you . . . I haven't helped you. I've been a nuisance at best," I say honestly, disliking the way she passes over her own strengths. She pieced that together herself. She underestimates herself far too much.

I weigh my next words carefully.

"You have me trapped in your body, little witch. That's not easily done. You care about others despite them being the cause of your suffering. You have a good heart and should stop questioning yourself. Everyone makes mistakes, but we learn from them."

I can feel her thinking and the way her emotions swirl around her. She is confused but grateful. She can feel that I'm being honest, despite still questioning my intentions. She speaks slowly.

"Do you know how I can separate us? Has this ever happened before?"

"No. Not by a human, or a witch. My best guess? It's our connection . . . or you're simply something else entirely. Or maybe you just want me inside of you," I say, my tone flirtatious as I preen at the idea . . .

She shakes her head, unable to hide her smile. "I won't begin to try and understand what you mean by that, and you wish. Do you have any useful ideas?"

"Fear is a good motivator," I say nonchalantly, mentally licking my lips at the idea.

"Yeah . . . No thank you, but nice try. Anything else?"

"You could allow me to take control. Then I may be able to pull myself out," I muse idly.

"And how do you suggest I do that . . . ?" Her voice sounds hesitant but intrigued.

I rumble softly, almost purring the words into her mind. *"It's easier if I show you. Just relax for me."*

I push my influence into her as best I can, causing warm sensations to flood her body, centralizing at her core and sliding lower.

"What are you doing?" she breathes, her face flushing as she shifts in her chair at the feeling.

"You need to let go for me." I whisper the words softly to her, dragging my consciousness along her own.

Her mind spirals and I feel her giving in. She wants to, she wants this, but there's hesitation. She sucks in a deep breath and leans into the feeling, letting go.

Her head tilts back as she quietly whispers, "Okay."

She lets go and I can feel myself begin to seep out of her skin and slowly materialize. Her eyes are still closed, chest rising and falling with her deep breaths. Once fully formed, I grab her hand and pull her into me.

"I did it . . ." she gasps, free hand braced on my chest, looking up at me with those wide eyes of hers. Those big, beautiful almond-brown eyes, and it feels like I'm looking into them for the first time. The way that the golden rays hit her irises just right, making them look like a pool of honey. I can't help but be mesmerized.

"You let me out. You followed your instincts like I showed you." I smile and continue, brushing a thumb along her jaw. "But this time, you trusted me . . ."

"And you didn't take advantage of it," she counters, raising a brow at me.

"You're going to make me think you actually like me," I tease, tugging her closer. "I'd be careful."

"You're obnoxiously cocky and a bit terrifying . . . but I thought it was obvious I liked you," she says, giggling, her head tilting back with the sound.

Shit. I've never heard her laugh like that, and I've watched her long enough to know—it's rare.

"Your smile," I blurt it out, staring at her lips, transfixed.

"Yeah, what about it?" she says casually, pulling out of my arms and closing the journal on the desk next to the large pile.

I step closer, following, craving her proximity.

"I believe there isn't anything I wouldn't do to see that again," I admit, and she smiles again, stealing my breath. I want to live in that smile. In those dark brown eyes. I have to admit, I've wanted her, in every way, but I didn't know why. But helping her come into herself, seeing what she can do—I have been alive for a long time, and I can say I have never known this feeling.

She was afraid, but she didn't fight me. She wanted it. Her vulnerability, her sensitivity, her stubbornness, and her fire . . . There may be a million women like her—but they're not her.

And she is mine.

And I . . . want to be hers.

"Careful there, demon," she teases, turning to face me, blissfully unaware of the obsessive thought process I am having. "Wouldn't want to fall for me."

But there is no doubt left in my mind . . .

I pull her back into my chest and take her lips in a deep kiss, gently brushing her hair behind her ear. She looks up at me in surprise and pulls away. I give her a gentle smile and gaze into her dark eyes, saying my damning truth.

"It's far too late for that, Callisto."

CHAPTER 24

CALLISTO

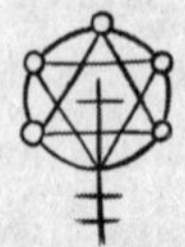

I can't get his words out of my head.

Alabaster . . . He got to me. He *really* got to me.

His words stick in my brain like caramel—sticky and sweet. So wrong, but I feel myself leaning into them. I'm already afraid that whatever game he's playing is working.

"Hey, girl," I say when Karma walks over, weaving between my legs. "I can't cuddle right now." I scoop her up, being sure to give her an extra scratch before carefully placing her back down.

I hold the bag of runes carefully in my hands as I sit cross-legged on the floor of my room. I reach in, mixing them before I cast them on the ground before me, my question clear in my mind.

Is Cade in danger?

Three runes stare back.

Hagalaz. Thurisaz. Isa.

Something unexpected will happen. Maybe an ambush. He's going to be trapped—isolated.

My breath catches. Fuck.

I feel Alabaster's presence behind me before I hear him.

"And what do we have here, little witch?" he purrs in that silky way of his, leaning over my shoulder.

"Cade is walking into a trap," I say softly, worry clear in my voice.

"These are far too vague," he hums, eyeing the runes. "This could also mean an internal struggle."

I huff, my eyes still locked on the runes. "I don't like this. I'm going to talk to Jack."

I get to my feet and turn, only to see Alabaster fade into my shadow on the ground. He's been hiding out in my shadow since this morning when he kissed me, giving me the illusion of privacy. At this point, I honestly don't care. His energy—though overwhelming—is a welcome buffer for my anxiety.

I hurry to Jack's office. I can hear him talking to Cade through the door and pause before knocking.

"Can I come in?" I call, wringing my hands nervously.

I hear his muffled voice on the other side of the door, tone low and ominous.

"Enter . . . if you dare."

I walk in with a raised eyebrow.

He swivels his chair toward me slowly, a shit-eating grin on his face. I roll my eyes at him.

"How is he?" I ask calmly, but the worry is clear in my voice.

"He just left, Calli." He sighs, rubbing his eyes. "We can't do this all night, you know."

"Okay . . . How are you?" I ask him, almost afraid of his answer.

"It's Halloween. Why don't you get out of the house? There's a festival downtown. Go." He shoos his fingers at me, grinning again.

"Wow." I shake my head, walking further into the room. "Deflection *and* trying to get rid of me? Nice, Jack, but I'm not going anywhere."

I stand my ground, hands on hips—when I notice my shadow vibrating. Something shifts from it, moving too fast for my eyes to process.

"It's not that, Calli . . ." He sighs. "I just think there's nothing either of us can do at this rate. I see no proof that this is a setup. I get that you're worried, I really do, but it does nothing for you right now. Go—meet people. Have some fun for once." His voice has softened, eyes pleading with me.

"You want me to ignore my instincts?" I cross my arms over my chest and he groans.

"No. I'm just suggesting that nothing you say is going to make him turn around. I'll do everything I can to make sure he's safe on my end. Just . . . trust him, like he trusted you."

Jack still has no idea Cade believes now, but he's right. Cade gave me the benefit of the doubt in the only way he knew how. And while I don't like this . . . trying to convince him out of it is useless. I gave him the pendulum. He still wears it every day. All I can do is pray it's enough.

Before I'm able to respond, the landline rings. Jack's eyes bolt to me—concern flashing in them as he picks up the phone, a muffled voice speaking on the other end.

"Uh, who is this?" he asks, voice tinged with suspicion and confusion.

More muffled speech. Jack makes a few unreadable expressions then hands me the phone.

"It's the guy from the corner store. He wants to know if you'll go with him to the festival," he says, wiggling his brows up and down in mock flirtation.

I take the phone and press it to my ear hesitantly.

"I'm taking you out, pretty girl. Get your ass ready," Alabaster's smooth voice purrs through the receiver.

I try to hide my face, my eyes widening.

"Sorry, I'm kind of busy ton—"

Jack swipes the phone from my hand and answers for me, standing to hold it above my head . . .

"She'd love to. Pick her up at six."

I smack the back of his head when he hangs up, grinning at me.

"Oops," he giggles, rubbing at his head. "Guess you have a date."

I motion like I'm going to punch him in the arm, and he flinches. I barely stop myself.

This is a terrible idea . . . but maybe Jack *is* right.

"You'll call me if anything gets fucky. Got that?" I warn, pointing a finger at him, my eyes narrowed.

"Yes, ma'am!" he crows with a smile and a salute, victory written all over his face.

I groan and stomp out like a child, and his laugh echoes behind me as I slam the door. But deep down, I feel . . . relieved I wasn't given a choice. My stomach flutters at the thought of being out for the night with my demon. Almost like something normal—if that's even possible for us.

I open my closet, staring at my clothes in thought, Alabaster nowhere in sight. I pull out a black dress that stops mid-thigh and some tights, closing my eyes and trying to picture a costume idea. Maybe I can tape some black paper to a headband and dress up as Karma.

I move to toss the dress on my bed and freeze. There's a small black box that definitely wasn't there before.

I sit down on the edge of the bed, unwrapping the intricate ribbon with care.

It looks expensive.

Inside is a black lace mask with catlike eye holes and pointed tips. It's exactly what I would've chosen. I grin to myself and jump up to finish getting ready.

I throw on some eyeliner—a sharp cat eye and some red lipstick. I slip into the dress and tights, placing the mask over my eyes, and when I look in the mirror, I barely recognize myself. I actually look . . . stunning. I smirk at my reflection.

Not bad.

I grab my purse just as I hear Jack shout from downstairs: "Your date is here, Calli!"

I open the door and immediately trip over the hallway runner, nearly rolling my ankle. I catch myself on the wall and carefully descend the stairs in my six-inch heels. At the bottom, Jack stares up at me, wide-eyed and slack-jawed.

And there, in the doorway, is Alabaster.

His eyes aren't glowing—but they look hungry. He fills the doorframe with his massive body, horns in full view, wearing black jeans and a fitted V-neck.

My breath catches. Damn.

I reach the bottom step and Jack clears his throat.

"You guys look fucking amazing! You two kids have fun, you hear? Be careful," he whispers to me as he gently nudges me toward the door.

"Cool-ass costume, dude," he calls to Alabaster, laughing as he closes the door behind us.

Alabaster says nothing, just smiles slowly and places his hand on the small of my back, guiding me to the driveway.

That's when I see it: a bright red Ferrari. The same color as my lipstick.

"Where the fuck did you get this?" I gasp, my eyes going wide.

"Don't ask questions you really don't want the answers to. Just get in, my little feline." He opens the door for me, with a wink that definitely flashes some fang.

I pause, one foot in the car as I peer up at him. "Thanks for the mask. I really like it," I murmur, almost shyly.

He tilts his head, curious eyes flicking to the mask. "I didn't give that to you." Leaning in, his breath hits my ear. "But I like it."

A shiver crawls down my spine at the rumble in his voice.

I quickly slide into the passenger seat and he shuts the door, getting in beside me.

"I didn't know you drive," I say casually as I turn to face him, legs crossed.

He grins wickedly, teeth flashing. "I don't."

My eyes widen as he starts the engine and peels out of the driveway, his laughter echoing through the night.

Downtown is packed. Costumes, music, vendors, and a whole-ass carnival. This town must take Halloween seriously, I muse to myself.

Alabaster rolls down the windows, blasting R&B so loudly that people turn and stare as we pass. He's loving it. I roll my eyes at him.

We park in a grassy field and he comes around to open my door, holding out his arm.

"Playing the gentleman tonight?" I ask with a smirk.

"Only for you, pretty girl," he replies smoothly.

I step out—and my heels sink into the grass, making me wobble immediately. My hand flies out, clutching his arm.

"I may have chosen the wrong shoes for this," I say with a laugh, and then squeal when he lifts me with one arm, carrying me like a purse.

"What are you doing?" I squeak, feet kicking as I try not to flash everyone around us.

"Helping." He says it seriously, looking down with his brow furrowed in confusion.

I burst out laughing. "This isn't how you're supposed to carry a lady!" I scold him, but the words are light and playful.

He hums, adjusting me. Pulling my legs around his waist and wrapping his arms under my thighs, holding me flush to his warm body.

"This better?" he asks, completely serious as he watches my face.

Our faces are close. Too close. I'm still in his arms, my breath fanning his lips.

"Uh . . . yeah," I whisper, knowing my face must be bright red.

He carries me to the edge of the field and gently sets me down, holding his arm out for me like the gentleman he isn't. I take it with a soft laugh.

We make our way to a churro stand, grab two, and sit on a nearby bench. I take a bite—crispy on the outside, soft on the inside. Perfect.

I moan as the flavors burst along my tongue. "Mmm. Good choice."

He's staring, that glowing gaze fixed on me like *I'm* the dessert, and I feel my cheeks flush.

"Let's go. I'm bored," he says suddenly, standing and grabbing my hand. I drop the rest of my churro with a laugh as he tugs me to my feet.

He leads me through the crowd toward a huge gothic building with a big painted sign that reads *Nightmare Manor*.

"A haunted house? Seriously?" I deadpan, but I'm unable to hide my excitement.

He grins down at me. "It'll be fun."

He tugs me along and we pay the ghoul at the entrance then make our way inside. It's darker than I expected—I reach for Alabaster's arm but he isn't there. I look around for a moment trying to find him in the dark hallway.

"Where are you? . . ."

A chill creeps up my spine when I feel breath against my ear.

"Come and find me."

I whip my head around, but he's not there.

"Stop playing around." I hear a whisper coming from farther down the hallway. Walking around the corner, I am met with a gory-looking skeleton with flesh hanging off the bones. A shriek is pulled from my throat as I bolt farther down the hall.

"I'm over here . . ." An ethereal whisper comes from a room at the end of the hall, a dim red light spilling into the hallway.

That's not creepy at all.

Inching my way forward, I hear noises coming from behind me and turn around. "Found you!" But nothing is there. I turn back around and come face-to-face with a black mass with bright glowing eyes. My heart stops for a moment.

"I was supposed to find you!" I call out, and have to spin around again, his voice appearing behind me now.

"And you did. C'mon, I want to show you something."

We step into a room with a massive pentagram drawn messily on the floor. The room glows under red lighting. Cobwebs hang around the ceiling and walls and a round table sits in the center.

"Looks like a seance room," I comment over the creepy music playing.

"Wanna commune with the dead?" He smirks, wiggling his brows, and I shake my head and laugh.

"I think I have my hands full with you," I say with a roll of my eyes.

"Are you suggesting I'm too much to handle?" he teases, and I scoff.

"Please. I can handle you."

He turns suddenly and presses me against the wall, arms on either side, caging me in. Eyes glowing bright gold.

"You think so?" he hums, head tilting in that unnatural way of his.

My voice stays casual, but only barely. "What are you doing?"

"I want you," he says bluntly, catching me completely off guard.

"In what way?" I breathe out softly, my heart pounding so loudly I'm sure he can hear it.

"*Every* way."

Then he kisses me. His lips crash into mine, tongue sliding against my mouth before tracing along my cheek and curling under my jaw. One large hand finds my waist, sliding up to cup my breast as he sucks at my neck. I moan, gasping into the air, my back arching.

I grab his face and drag his mouth back to mine to kiss him back—messy and rough—until he spins me, lifting me onto the table behind us. He steps between my legs, my dress hiked up high on my thighs as he grinds against me. He's hard. I can feel those ridges.

Another moan escapes me as I reach down, fumbling to unbuckle his belt and popping the button on his jeans. I reach for him—

And freeze.

It doesn't feel like it's supposed to.

My eyes fly up to see he's smiling down at me, teeth flashing.

He grabs the belt, ripping it free.

"Put your hands together, pretty girl," he demands, his voice a low purring thing.

I raise an eyebrow, but I do it, holding my hands out to him in offering.

He wraps the belt around my wrists and lays me back on the table, lifting my arms above my head. Then he walks around, kneels down, and ties the belt to the leg of the table.

"Does that feel okay?" he asks, voice low and serious, and I blink slowly in surprise.

I nod slowly, breath catching as I watch him, waiting.

He returns to me, placing his hands on my knees and slowly pushing them apart. My body reacts before I can think, my thighs falling open for him . . .

"Kiss me," I whisper, my voice a plea.

He leans over me, his mouth devouring mine. My hips arch up, desperate for friction, and he tangles a hand in my hair, pulling tight as I feel him reach into his jeans and free himself.

He bites my lip gently as his other hand trails under my dress, shoving it up further. He slides my panties aside and presses his fingers against me, and I jolt at the contact, whining.

"Fuck, you're soaked," he growls against my lips, fingers circling my clit, and I cry out, pushing into them, my hands curling against the belt.

He pulls his fingers away and I make a sound of denial at the loss. He lines himself up, rubbing the thick head against me. My breath shutters. Fuck . . . He's huge. The ridges catch and I whimper.

"Tell me you want me." His voice is rough with desire.

I gasp, lost in the moment, trying to arch my hips for more . . .

He teases me—just the tip pressing in—

"I want to hear you say it, Callisto." He says my name like a purr and my body trembles.

"I want you," I breathe, meeting his eyes so he can see the truth in my own.

His face darkens as he thrusts, filling me slowly, inch by inch. The ridges stretch me further than anything I've ever taken, one at a time. I moan loudly, the sound echoing throughout the room. He pulls at my hair, using it to arch my neck before sinking his teeth into the soft flesh. He thrusts deep and slow, until I can take all of him to the hilt.

He moans, the sound not low like I would expect . . . It comes out high—almost a whimper into my ear as he pushes fully inside of me.

It sets my body on fire.

"Rub my clit—please," I beg, squirming under him.

He lifts himself up, hand sliding down my body until two fingers find the perfect spot, his rhythm never faltering. His cock fills me so completely, every ridge dragging against my walls.

"Fuck—I'm coming. Don't stop. Please," I plead, my voice a trembling mess as my thighs shake.

He doesn't.

He grabs my hips, lifting them higher and slamming into me hard enough to make the table groan beneath us. His breath pants against my ear, ragged and desperate, and then I feel him pulse inside me—filling me in a way that feels possessive, like a claim. I cry out as the heat spills over, coating my thighs with his cum.

He slowly pulls out, then reaches up and breaks the belt binding my wrists. He drags me into him as he kisses my forehead, his breaths still as unsteady as my own.

My bag buzzes and I blink, reality crashing back into me.

It's my phone.

Jack.

My stomach sinks with a feeling of dread as I fumble for it, answering, my words shaky.

"Hello?"

His voice is low and clipped with worry.

"You need to get home. Now."

CHAPTER 25

CADE

I park the truck half a mile out, killing the lights and slipping out into the darkness. The walk through the forest is slow—dense, with low visibility. Good. That works in my favor.

Pushing branches and brush aside, I hit a clearing with a narrow path that cuts through, leading toward the house. I glance up—the trees splitting just enough to reveal a clear night. No clouds. Stars spilling across the sky in sharp, silver constellations.

I creep closer to the house . . . but something feels *wrong.*

The forest is dead quiet. No crickets. No wind. No rustling.

Just . . . silence.

It's fucking creepy.

Then it hits me—this . . . *pull.* A sudden, overwhelming urge to turn back, to leave. Every nerve in my body lights up, screaming that *this is wrong. This is a mistake.*

I turn—instinct driving my movements—only for the sensation to snap like a thread. Gone as quickly as it came.

The pendulum against my chest vibrates, buzzing faintly against my sternum, the weight settling. The panic fades.

Huh. I still have no clue what this thing does, besides tethering me to you. But that? That was new. I shake my head and continue forward.

The tree line breaks ahead and I crouch down, watching the property.

Jack's intel checks out—three main guards with cameras on every corner. No blind spots yet. Someone's definitely monitoring the feed.

The black Cadillac in the driveway confirms it—Benjamin's here.

Jack dug deep—Benjamin's family launders money through antiques auctions, art deals, dig sites, and restoration projects. Artifact smuggling. A front. How deep the Covenant ties go is . . . admittedly still unclear. But I know this much—

He's Rosa's right hand. He's brutal, rich, and untouchable as the head of Teller Enterprises.

I shift, angling my head, but freeze, my eyes narrowing as I focus.

A faint shimmer wraps the house. Thin and glistening in the night air, like heat waves off asphalt.

What the hell is that?

A knot tightens in my gut. This isn't paranoia. This is *magic.*

I remind myself to breathe. Wait for Jack's all clear. The plan is for him to loop the camera feed and catch the next guard rotation.

Get in and get out.

"Cameras are set." Jack's voice filters through my earpiece, right on time. "Two guards at the front. One east by the alley. You have an entry point on the west side—first-floor window."

Two in front. One east. Nothing on the back or west, despite the cover.

They're not expecting *me.* But they are expecting *someone.* That's clear as day.

I move up slowly, slipping behind a tree. Dry leaves crunch underfoot as I drag the mask up—a matte black half mask stretched into a sharp-toothed, demonic grin, covering just enough to hide my scar.

"A ski mask would've sufficed," I mutter into the coms, feeling ridiculous.

"C'mon—it's Halloween," Jack shoots back, voice grinning in my ear. "I even convinced Calli to dress up. She's at that downtown festival. The girl needed to get her mind off . . . well, you know . . ."

My chest tightens and I still. "*She went alone?*" I growl, almost ready to turn back just to throttle him.

"Nah." He sounds far too casual about my sister's safety. "Some guy she met from the gas station picked her up. Killer costume, too. Chill—her phone's being tracked. Be grateful she's not in our ears right now giving both of us hell."

I release a sharp breath. "Yeah, because you know what's good for her, isn't that right," I concede grudgingly.

"No, I don't. But I care about both of you."

"Drop it, Jack."

"You started it."

I roll my eyes—this is no time to be petty. At least she's distracted.

I shove the worry and bitterness down and set my sights back on the house.

The cool wind stirs the trees, muffling my steps as I creep around to the back.

"You got eyes inside?" I ask, my voice barely a whisper.

"Only four cams. Front and back. No movement . . . but keep an eye out."

I crouch under the west window and test the latch.

It's unlocked.

My stomach twists.

No one leaves a window unlocked out here. Not unless they're sloppy . . . or it's a trap.

Carefully, I shove the window open. The wood sticks, groaning, but gives enough for me to slip through. My feet land on thick, plush carpet.

I stay crouched, looking around to find an empty room with a bookshelf and two lounge chairs.

I turn to shut the window—and a shadow cuts across the glass. My breath stalls for a moment, but no one comes.

I lock the window, backing further into the room. A light is on. A dull golden glow spills from the hallway ahead as I creep forward.

"Hallway's clear," Jack says softly. "Make a right, there is a door at the end of the hall. You'll need to pick it."

I move quietly, wincing as the floorboards creak beneath my boots. I kneel at the door, lockpick sliding into place before I fiddle with it.

Click.

I open the door to an office, the smell of fresh paint stinging my nose. There is a desk sitting in the center of the dark room and a suitcase on the floor. A laptop sits open, waiting, casting a soft blue glow into the room.

I slip into the chair—the cushion sinking beneath me as I pull out the USB Jack provided and plug it in. Lines of code that mean nothing to me scroll across the screen.

"Give me a few minutes . . . oh—wait. Fuck, Cade. Someone's coming. Find cover. *Now.*"

I quietly close the laptop, being sure to leave the USB where it is, and scan the room, seeing a closet with bifold doors.

I hurry from the desk on light feet and squeeze inside the small space, sliding the doors shut just as the lock clicks.

I hold my breath as the door creaks open, the sound of heavy footfalls entering the room.

"I'm almost in . . . stay hidden," Jack mutters, voice strained. Tense. "We need this guy alive," he reminds me. Again.

Through the slats, I spot him.

Not a guard.

A large man in a fitted black suit.

Clean.

Sharp.

Benjamin Teller.

He strides in, grabs the suitcase, and walks out—locking the door behind him.

"I'm in." Jack exhales with relief.

"Wait . . . this doesn't make sense . . ." Static chews the feed and my stomach sinks. "Cade—no—ri—Get ou—"

"We've be—intercept—"

Crackle. Then nothing. Silence hangs in the air until—

"Hello, Cade." A smooth voice hums in my ear. Confident and almost bored. "I was hoping we'd run into each other."

My stomach caves and I fling open the closet door and bolt for the window only to find it's been sealed.

Shit.

"Not gonna talk?" He chuckles in my ear and I grind my teeth. "Credit where it's due. It took my witch over fifteen minutes to jam your comms. You're good. Damn good. Wouldn't have caught it if Genevieve hadn't spelled the grounds."

"Benjamin Teller," I growl, turning to face the room once again.

"Cade Halloway." His tone softens into something like amusement. "Call me Ben. No need for formalities. I hear your name so often . . . it feels like we're old friends by now."

"What the fuck do you want, *Ben*," I snarl, running a hand through my hair.

"See . . . my boss wants your head."

I snort. They can join the club. "Planning to deliver it?"

"Mmm . . . not exactly. You're my leverage. Now that your friend's inside my files—he'll figure it all out soon enough. But you . . . you're going to help me."

I begin pacing like a caged animal, trying to calculate my escape.

"Why the hell would I help you? You're just another Covenant lapdog." I grunt, going over to try the door. Locked.

"Yeah . . . about that. I'm not as loyal as you think." He clicks his tongue, voice still amused. "Rosa? She's unraveling. Not shocking considering her daughter is dead and her husband is rotting in the desert."

"It was necessary."

"Oh, I'm not judging." He laughs, sounding almost gleeful. "Honestly? I'm impressed. You've got balls."

"Get to the point," I snap, going back to the desk and leaning against it.

"Simple. I give you what you need to finish the job . . . and you help me disappear. My family's ties to the Covenant have long since soured and I've grown tired of them."

I laugh, but the sound is anything but happy. "I don't know you. And I don't trust you."

"Trust isn't part of the deal. Information for freedom is." He pauses, his voice going mockingly soft. "You do want to save your sister, right? Isn't that what this is all about? Big brother . . . doing the right thing."

I drift back toward the window, testing it again.

"And you just . . . want out?" I confirm, keeping him talking.

"That's it. I don't give a damn what happens to them. But Rosa? She suspects my hesitance. Hence . . . this fucking dump. Middle of nowhere, heavy security. The magic barrier." His voice lowers and then echoes in my ear and behind me at the same time. I tense. "You've got someone to protect . . . and so do I."

Metal clicks, cold steel pressing against the back of my skull.

"I'll help you . . ." My voice turns razor-sharp as I remain stock-still, my hands curling at my sides. "But you need to let me leave."

"Yeah . . . Not gonna happen."

I twist, lunging for his wrist when pain explodes against my temple. I see stars as everything tilts and I fall to the ground. My ears ring as warm blood runs down my face.

Benjamin stands over me, revolver in hand.

And behind him . . . a woman holding a tire iron.

Straight red hair. Freckles. Pale as porcelain. The scowl on her face looking like a permanent feature.

Fuck. I can feel myself losing consciousness, the room going blurry around the edges.

Calli . . . she was right . . .

Benjamin crouches slightly, tilting his head as he watches me. I hold his gaze as I feel myself slowly blacking out.

"As I said . . . I need you as leverage," he hums softly. "You'll understand . . . soon enough."

Something sharp pierces my neck—a cold fire racing down my spine before everything fades to black.

CHAPTER 26

CADE

I'm falling.

Another dream? It must be.

I'm alone and it's quiet.

So quiet that my heartbeat fills my ears, pounding against my head.

I lay there surrounded by a void and it's consuming me, eating everything that I am.

I slowly sink down, the surface below no longer supporting my weight.

Panic rises in my chest as I try to shift, attempting to grasp for something—anything.

My body slowly sinks into the unstable ground, like quicksand.

I reach out into the void in vain.

I feel my body submerged into a thick weight, pressing into me, pulling me under.

The sensation reaches my face, pulling my head down despite my desperate protest.

Suddenly a light appears, far above me, and it rushes down, fast as a bullet, into my chest.

The pressure fades, and I slowly rise.

Not flying—just floating. Like something is holding me, guiding me up. The light pulls from my chest and hangs in the air, pulsing like a heartbeat that's not my own.

Relief washes over me as I feel it. That warmth, that calm . . .

My little ghost.

"Where am I?" my voice echoes dully.

The void doesn't answer. Just the sound of my own breath, too loud in my ears. I try to trace my last memory—but my mind is blank.

The light bursts—spilling into a shifting smoke, soft and glowing. The smoke reaches out—caressing my skin.

I feel you. How the fuck can I feel you?

I reach out, clutching at the smoke, but it slips through my fingers like it's teasing me.

A hum stirs under the surface of my skin and the smoke curls around my arms, across my chest. My skin prickles at the sensation, like electricity radiating through my body.

I shiver involuntarily at the feeling.

I look down at the glow clinging to me—iridescent, fading, and unreal . . .

You're beautiful.

The smoke curls around my body and seeps into my skin slowly and I see . . .

I see my house, I see Calli . . . She looks scared as she paces Jack's office, her hands in her hair.

Why is she scared? How am I seeing this?

I turn my head to see Jack typing away at his computer, fingers flying over the keys . . . But in my peripheral vision, I see something else . . . I narrow my eyes, trying to focus. A massive black figure in the corner is looming behind Calli, surrounded by smoke.

What the fuck is that—

The vision rips away as suddenly as it came and I'm swallowed by darkness again—the smoke bleeding out of my skin.

"Was that real?" I ask, my voice echoing once again.

No response.

"Speak to me!" I plead. "Please . . . What is going on . . . ?"

The glow pulses then flares—searing white-hot behind my eyes. Then it's gone. I feel myself slam back into my body.

My head is spinning as the memories rush back to me, flooding my mind.

I was taken . . . By Benjamin . . .

That vision . . . I saw Calli and Jack—but I saw something else. *Something* was with her.

My eyes drag open in a slow, uneven blink. I try to move but find myself bound to a chair, duct tape over my mouth.

The room is dark—lit only by a dim lamp in the corner. Brick walls, no windows. The air is stale, metallic, smelling of blood and mildew—most likely a basement.

The door cracks and light creeps in, the heavy hinges groaning as it creaks open all the way. The silhouette of a man steps into the room.

"You're finally awake," a familiar voice says cheerfully.

My brow furrows as his features sharpen. He reaches out and rips the duct tape from my mouth.

"I thought you wanted help," I spit out, face stinging as I glare up at Benjamin.

The blow to my jaw is immediate—sharp and ringing. My head whips sideways, vision spotting as the room spins.

"This *is* you helping me. As I said—you are my leverage. Now keep your fucking mouth shut if you want to live long enough to make it through this," he snarls, all false cheer gone from his voice and face.

I don't respond. Clearly, he has his own agenda—otherwise, he wouldn't have given me the information he has.

"So, I'm just supposed to trust you?" I say, ignoring his warning—blood spilling from my mouth.

"Something like that."

Another hit. The chair topples and my skull cracks against the floor, my shoulder taking the brunt, bone grinding against concrete. Pain bursts hot down my spine. He bends down on one knee and speaks to me softly.

"This is necessary, sadly. Boss's orders. She wants me to rough you up a bit—but I imagine you can take it." He smiles at me like we're buddies. "You see, she needs information that you have. And I need to know you aren't going to talk."

I choke out a laugh. "F . . . fuck you." It barely comes out as words—mostly just air and blood. I taste copper as my head rings.

"Perfect." He claps me on the shoulder and I groan. "Let's hope you can keep that attitude."

He lifts the chair, sitting me back up. I watch as he pulls out a pair of brass knuckles. My thoughts lag. My body is slow to respond to the ringing pain. I feel like I'm underwater—maybe I'm already dying.

"You need to be ready—this is nothing compared to what she has planned." He says it like he's doing me a favor, but then he swings again, brass knuckles connecting with my temple. The world doesn't spin. It just . . . cuts out completely.

I'm falling again, but it's not cold this time. It's warm. Soft. Like sinking into silk and static—like my body no longer matters.

I'm in my bed. I think?

Moonlight spills through the curtains, but it feels too bright, too quiet. Like everything has been muffled.

My skin twitches, anticipating another blow. But it's warm. Gentle. No, not pain.

There's heat on me—wet and slow. Lips wrapping around my cock. A breath shudders from me.

My brain can't catch up. It's too much, too sudden.

Hands roam my stomach. I flinch under their touch—my nerves raw, confused, like it shouldn't feel this good.

But it does.

Fuck, *it does.*

I move before I can think, flipping, pressing their body beneath mine on instinct.

How can I feel you . . .

It's not you, not really. Just a dream, one I will take advantage of.

My hand finds your back, firm between your shoulder blades as I pin you down—gently at first, then harder. Like I'll lose this if I'm not careful. Like I *know* it's slipping.

I slide in deep.

I can't see you . . . But I don't need to. The sensation of you alone is enough to break me.

My cock throbs with each slow thrust—heat gripping me tight, the slick pressure unreal, like velvet strangling me. Too good to be real. Too good to stop.

You're fucking made for me. That thought cuts through the haze—feeling obsessive and wrong.

Fuck. Yes. Just like that.

My breath catches as the pressure builds, nerves buzzing under my skin like live wires.

I stay there, cock twitching, before I draw back just enough to feel every ounce of pressure dragging along my length.

Then I drive forward again, slow and forceful, a groan ripping from my throat. Pain hums somewhere in the background—distant, a bad signal that I attempt to ignore.

"Fuck," I growl, my voice cracking.

I come hard—grinding in deep, clinging to the feeling like it'll anchor me. When I finally still, I'm shaking, then exhale hard as I collapse. My hand drifts over skin. Searching. My fingers gently brush along a shoulder, moving up the neck and to the jaw.

"You're so soft . . ." I whisper, my voice raw.

I pretend, just for a second, that this is real. That I could actually have this with you.

I feel myself falling back into consciousness, the pull slowly dragging me from you again.

No.

I don't want to go back. I fight against the pull—desperate to stay buried in the lie that feels better than the truth.

"*Please* . . . just a little longer."

But it's gone. The warmth. The stillness. The dream.

My chest aches, my limbs cold. I blink, and I'm back in the dark—alone.

No. Not alone . . .

A faded glow hovers in front of me. I squint—uncertain if I'm awake or still trapped in some fever dream.

"Are you really here?" My voice is a rasping, raw thing in the quiet.

I feel like I'm unraveling.

The smoke shifts closer, slow and deliberate. A hand forms, misty, barely there, and rests on my arm. Coming from it I feel a strange mix of confusion . . . and concern.

"It's okay," I sigh, wanting to comfort you instinctively. "I promise."

My head spins, the edges of the room blurring as disorientation digs its claws into me.

A gentle caress traces my skin, brings my awareness back slightly.

"I had a dream about you . . ." I whisper hoarsely, the words dragged out with a dry, humorless chuckle.

Pressure again, soft and grounding.

My face stiffens as the haze lifts just enough for the pain to return. My shoulder throbs as I adjust, my jaw clenching against it.

"Why do you stay . . . ? I don't deserve your comfort." My words are as bitter as I feel.

Warmth settles around my shoulders—a phantom embrace. Goose

bumps ripple across my skin and I flinch. It hurts . . . but the pain dulls, like you're trying to soothe it away.

Frustration tightens in my chest and my words are rough with it.

"You've seen what I've done, little ghost. Yet you stay."

I search the air for judgment, for disgust, for something that reflects the monster I know I am.

But I find none. Only empathy.

"Why don't you care!" I shout into the silence, my voice echoing around the empty room. "You know what I am. Why do you still make me feel . . ." My voice cracks and I lower my head, filled with shame.

"Loved."

I don't trust this. I don't trust anything. Fuck . . . but I want to.

The pressure deepens. Not possessive. Not demanding. Just . . . here.

I scoff, the sound breathy, bitter, defeated. "You haven't left."

You've seen the worst of me. And still, you stay. Somewhere along the way, you became the only thing holding me together in this.

"And . . . I—I need you . . ." I ramble weakly.

The truth of it sinks deep in my chest. I was raised for a mission. Shaped for a purpose. I never let myself want more—never believed I deserved it.

But now, despite everything . . . I feel it.

Hope.

And it's because of *you*.

Pain pulses through my temple and I grit my teeth, forcing my head up.

How long have I been here?

I try to take in the room again, scan for details—anything useful—but my vision tilts, everything swimming.

My eyes flutter, heavy, and just as I'm about to let them fall closed, the door in front of me bursts open.

Two men enter. Benjamin and another, and behind them, a woman dressed in an all-white suit. Her hair is pulled back in a neat bun, and she looks polished in the dirty room. She steps ahead of the men and looks me up and down with a straight face.

"Rosa White, I presume," I say, my voice coming out broken and deep.

She spits in my face. Calm. Unbothered. Then lifts the hem of her skirt, slow and methodical, revealing the holstered gun strapped to her thigh.

"You do not get to speak. Monsters do not get words, they get cages." Her voice is steady and poised as she paces around my chair. "You took my husband from me. My baby girl. You left me nothing but purpose. You. Do. Not. Speak to me."

She stops in front of me before pulling the gun free and placing the barrel under my jaw, then she lowers her lips to my ear and whispers, "You are going to suffer for what you have done, Cade Halloway." Pressing her gun harder into my jaw, she snarls, "And you are going to tell me where my sacrifice is."

I force my head up to try to meet her gaze, but my tired eyes struggle to stay open, to focus on her.

"Looks like Ben has done his job well—too well." She stands and turns to the men, anger in every line of her body.

"I need him alert enough to talk," she says accusingly, hands on her hips.

"It'll wear off just in time. He'll be sharp enough for what you need," Benjamin says with assurance, casually leaning against the far wall.

With a single, deliberate nod she pivots on her heel but pauses just before reaching the door.

"We will start tomorrow. Tonight, you will stay with him, Ben."

She turns, her gaze pinned on me.

"You've done well to bring me a gift," she says to Benjamin, her voice smooth. "But one act of obedience doesn't earn trust. Not with me."

Leaning in, she pats Benjamin's cheek, as if mocking him, treating him like a good pet.

"Come now, Frank." She flicks her fingers in a lazy wave and the other man hastens to her side. The two disappear through the door. It shuts with a hollow thud, leaving Benjamin and me in ringing silence.

"I'm not going to babysit you—so don't do anything stupid."

"Wouldn't dream of it," I say dryly, coughing, blood on my lips.

"You joke, but I mean it. I need you alive, asshole. This will only work if you do exactly as I say," he says seriously, hands shoved in his pockets.

"Please enlighten me on your plan to keep that bitch from killing me." My head rolls to the side, aching, my eyes heavy.

"It's all about timing. I need her to trust that I am on her side. I'll fill you in on the details when it's necessary," he says over his shoulder, tone bored as he exits the room, not giving me the chance to ask anything further. The door clicks shut and I'm alone again—with only the ghost that refuses to leave me.

I don't trust him and Rosa is unstable—that makes her impulsive, dangerous. The odds of me surviving this are not high and I could accept that if I knew Calli would be safe.

After everything I've done . . . Rosa has every reason to want me dead.

I made myself into a monster so I could end the Covenant, so Calli could be safe, only to end up in the hands of the very people I swore I'd destroy . . . I failed her when we were kids. I will not fail her now.

I will do what no one else is willing to do. What our parents failed to do.

Let them take my body. Let them tear out what's left of me. If she survives—if she escapes them—then I'll die knowing I finally did one thing right.

I am a monster, but I'm the monster *they* made.

And I will make them fucking choke on me.

CHAPTER 27

CALLISTO

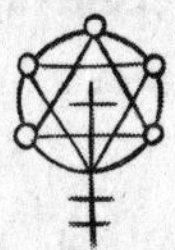

I pace Jack's office, back and forth so fast I feel the air shifting behind me. The tapping of keys digs into my skull—sharp, repetitive, mocking me.

We've been at this all fucking night. Karma is curled up in the spare chair, her little head perked up and tracking my movements.

I've ripped through every tracking spell I could find—the scent of incense still clinging to my hair, reminding me of my failure.

None of it worked.

None of it even came close.

I can feel my magic buzzing under my skin with no direction, and I can't seem to get it to settle.

"Have you found anything, Jack?" I ask again, for what feels like the hundredth time.

"If I find anything, I'll tell you," he mutters, exhaling hard—frustration bleeds into his voice, and I know it's from both the situation and from me.

"Can you at least tell me what you're doing?" I ask, my tone tight, eyes sharp with my own bubbling emotions.

Jack stops typing and the silence stretches—long and loud enough to press against my eardrums.

"Calli," he breathes, trying to keep his cool. "I'm trying to pin his last-known location. I'm in Benjamin Teller's system. I'm combing through everything: logs, messages, even fucking cached browser data. I'll find something. Just *please* let me work."

His voice is controlled, but I hear the undercurrent of words not spoken. He's scared, too, and he's trying not to show it.

"They need him alive," he repeats again. "Take that as a good sign."

That doesn't help. Alive doesn't mean okay, and it sure as hell doesn't mean safe.

"This is *Cade*, Jack. My brother. And they have him!" My voice cracks, fear a raw and hot thing in my throat. "I can't just keep sitting here with my thumb up my ass and pretend any of this is going to be okay!"

Jack's jaw twitches, but he stays locked in place, his fingers flexing on the keys as he watches me unravel before him.

"Benjamin wants out and Cade is his ticket. That means he's useful. That he's leverage. We don't know yet if the Covenant has him or if Ben's working alone. Something's blocking me from accessing his full system, but I'll get through it."

"You have no idea what's really going on here, Jack! You have no idea what he's really up against . . ." I run my fingers into my hair, gripping the roots as I try not to fall apart.

"What are you talking about, Calli?" Jack asks slowly, eyes sharp on my face in that calculating way of his. "If you know something, you need to tell me."

I need him to believe me . . . I think, and even my inner voice is hysterical. He needs to know what we're really up against. My decision made, I close my eyes and focus—allowing my emotions to take over.

My eyes open wide as the lights begin to flicker, Jack's monitors blinking in and out—his own eyes darting from me to his computer.

"Calli . . ." he says, paranoia lacing his voice as he shoves away from his desk, "What's happening?"

"It's no longer safe for you not to know," I say, my voice seeming to echo eerily around the room as the air vibrates with energy.

"Know *what*, Calli?" His voice is raised now. "What the fuck is going on?" I can tell he's scared, can almost taste his fear in the air—but I need to show him. Cade is in more danger than any of us know.

If the Covenant has him—their God isn't far behind.

I inhale sharply, feeling the buildup of power in the base of my spine expand—static crawling up my arms and into my fingertips. Every light bulb in the room shatters with a *pop*, Jack's computer screens going black as his PC begins smoking.

"Is this you . . . ? Calli! Stop!" His voice is high with panic as he stumbles farther from the desk—away from me.

I don't stop. The air vibrates more as I allow the built-up energy to flow out of me, my hair lifting in a nonexistent wind.

"Calli, stop!" Jack yells, but I ignore him, my head falling back, eyes closed. I don't want to stop. A euphoric feeling sings through me, pulling me into something dark until—

"I've got you . . ."

I feel large arms wrapping around me from behind, gripping me in a tight but tender embrace—one hand pressing against my chest, right over my pounding heart.

"Come back to me, I need you to come back to me, Calli."

His voice is gruff and deep and comforting, my eyes shooting open as I drag in a deep breath—exhaling slowly. The chaotic energy in the room syncs with my heartbeat as it slowly calms and then fades altogether, leaving me trembling in my demon's arms.

I turn around to see Alabaster placing his finger to his mouth, telling me to stay quiet.

I look back at Jack to see he is now standing pressed against the back wall, papers, pens, and other items strewn about the room. He can't see Alabaster—the look of horror on his face is because of me.

"Jack," I breathe out, my eyes watering at the look of fear in his eyes as he stares at me. "I'm sorry. I didn't know I—"

He cuts me off, his shaking voice tight with demand. "What the fuck was that, Calli?"

"It's the reason the Covenant wants me," I confess, my eyes lowering to the floor.

"But—no. That doesn't— Does Cade know?" he asks, stumbling over his words as he shakes his head, like clearing it will make this all make sense.

"He does now. He found out recently, actually . . ." My own voice is soft as I watch him struggle to come to grips with his whole world changing under him.

"So the Covenant—the *God*—it's real . . ." He trails off, staring at the wall with unseeing eyes.

"Yeah." I hesitate, worrying my lower lip. "If they have him, Jack . . . He isn't safe." There's a plea in my voice as I beg him to try and understand. "I have next to no information on the God they worship, but I know he is their only means of finding me."

"No . . ." He shakes his head again and shoves away from the wall, skirting past me. "This is fucking crazy." He leaves the room quickly and I follow, my hand reaching out for him when he spins.

"Stop," he commands, hands up, as if to hold me back, and I freeze. He's . . . shaking. "I—I need a minute." I bow my head and he turns, stumbling his way down the hall, not looking back. I stand in the doorway. Defeated.

"I didn't mean to scare him," I whisper, wrapping one arm around myself. "I don't know what happened. I thought that if I could show him, he would let me help." I rest my other hand over my forehead, my eyes falling closed.

"Five more minutes and you could have killed him," I hear Alabaster say from behind me, his voice tight.

"Please—don't say that." I sigh, keeping my back to him. "I don't even know what I did."

"You're scared for your brother and you have too much power built up inside you. You're basically a walking energy bomb right now."

"I just wanted to show him . . . I—I didn't know . . ." My voice cracks as I take a step into the hallway. "I need to talk to him . . ."

"Let him go," he says seriously, large hand clasping my arm. "He needs to process, and you need to ground yourself. For both of your sakes." Tears begin streaming down my face and I drop to my knees, a wounded sound ripping from my throat.

I'm finally able to access my power, and I almost killed my best friend with it. I've only ever done anything like that by accident, as a kid. One of the many reasons my parents kept me away from everyone—including Cade.

I choke back a scream, my head bowing, my nails curling into the rug.

Why didn't he listen to me?

Why the fuck does he have to do everything alone?

My blood feels too hot in my veins, my skin too tight, and my magic is coiling in my gut like it wants out—like it wants *violence*. Alabaster is right . . . I need to leave Jack alone until I get a handle on myself.

Stumbling to my feet, I head toward my room before I do something even more reckless, my feet dragging against the hallway floor. The house feels smaller than usual—like it's closing in around me . . .

I need to focus.

I can't lose myself. Not again.

As I stand in the middle of my room, I look around and I feel all of my jagged edges . . . The memory of the day my parents carved the mark on me flashes to the forefront of my mind.

It was a Sunday morning. I remember I was so excited because my mother had brought me a beautiful pink dress to wear. She had brushed my hair and helped me get ready. It was the most time I can remember ever having spent with my mom. She told me we were going someplace special before she placed the sack over my head. She told me we were going to play a game and I was to count to five.

One, two, three, four, five.

I felt a prick on my shoulder—it stung, leaving a dull ache in my muscle.

"Mommy, that hurt!" I had whimpered.

"Shh. It's okay, Callisto," she said while caressing my hand. "It's all part of the game." She spoke the words softly as my eyes got heavy and I fell asleep.

When I woke, I was in a chair in a strange room. The marble floor was covered in intricate markings that flowed in a big circle—with me at the center. My mouth was covered in a soft cloth that was tied around my head.

I looked up with hazy eyes and saw dark figures entering the room—chanting something I couldn't understand. One of them held a dagger in their hand as they approached me and let their hood fall down. It was my mom.

"My little girl," she cooed so sweetly. "I am so proud of you. You have shown us that you were meant for great things, that you will be the one to usher us into the next era."

I tried to tell her I was scared, but my pleas were too muffled.

They all surrounded me as my mother, wielding the dagger, went behind me. I felt them grip a large handful of my hair and force my head down. I cried out as I felt the blade begin to carve into my skin—

I rip myself from the memory, instinctively reaching for the jagged scar on the back of my neck.

I wasn't supposed to live long enough to be able to use this power . . .

I sigh as I plop down on my bed, flinging myself back and pulling the covers over my head.

Fuck me . . . I grumble in my head, *I'm so selfish . . . Cade is in danger and here I am thinking about myself . . . I'm not helping anyone right now . . . If anything, I've only made things worse . . . I just destroyed Jack's computer and his perception of reality all at once.*

"Get out of your head," I hear Alabaster say above me, and I clutch the blanket tighter.

"No . . . I need to think," I mumble, turning to bury my face in the pillow.

"No, you need to *act*. You have all of this energy, so use it—when directed it can be useful," he says, pulling the blanket off my body. I glare weakly up at him.

"I didn't even know I was capable of that kind of power until five minutes ago!" I can't help but whine, my words bitter. "How the hell do you expect me to know how to use it?"

"You may not realize it—but you are far more capable than you believe. Materializing that mask, for example? You didn't think, you wanted it, and you gave it to yourself."

"But I didn't *want* to try and kill Jack," I counter. "You fail to prove your point."

"No, you wanted to show your power, and that you did." He says it calmly, not at all rising to the bait of my attitude.

He's right, I realize. Everything I've ever done has been on instinct. I shake my head before speaking, my words softer now.

"How? What can I possibly do right now?"

"Use them," he says, pointing to seemingly nothing. I look around, confused.

"What the actual fuck are you talking about?"

"You've been around me for too long. My energy must be hiding them from you." He sighs, taking a step away from the bed and then fading into the shadows. "Focus. We aren't alone here," he says softly.

I cock a brow and sit up, curling my legs under me and closing my eyes as I attempt to search the room in my mind's eye. My spine goes rigid as I feel a faint, gentle presence. One I have felt before.

You . . .

I snap my eyes open to meet Alabaster's burning gaze as he once again steps from the shadows.

"The spirit attached to Cade? Why are they here?" I breathe, my voice hushed like I might scare them away.

"You called them for him. You are both bound to them," he tells me, his tone matter-of-fact. "But your brother has formed a soul tie with them, tethering the two to each other. If you can manage it—and if they're willing—you can create a temporary soul tie. You should be able to see him."

"Is that even possible? Why haven't you told me about this before?" I ask, my voice laced with accusation.

"I had no reason to." He shrugs. "And honestly, I didn't think you would be able to perform such a ritual. You proved you had the power in you last night when you asked about the mask and I realized that you had conjured it. Now it's worth trying, considering you're currently out of options."

"I'm willing to try anything if it will help Cade," I tell him, determination making me sit up straighter. "How do I do it?"

"I've never done something like this personally," he admits, "but do you remember how you let me take control when I was trapped in your body?"

"How could I forget?" I mumble in a low tone, goose bumps prickling along my arms at the memory.

"You need to let the ghost in like you let me out. If they're willing—it will work. You just need to focus your intentions," he says. His voice is soft and he's looking at me like he believes in me. I try to hide the self-doubt in my eyes.

"Close your eyes." He sighs, bending down on one knee and placing his hand on my thigh. "Picture the presence and focus on it."

I close my eyes and steady my breathing, searching my mind and—

"I see . . . an iridescent smoke," I say with soft surprise in my tone.

"Tell them what you want," he says quietly, his fingers gently tightening on my thigh, as if to ground me.

I pause, trying to think of the right thing to say, knowing I need to get this right . . .

"Show me Cade," I say with intent, my voice ringing with power. "*Please* . . . " I add mentally.

The smoke begins to pulse, becoming brighter and brighter as my head throws itself back. I feel pressure in my eyes, and the bright light fades into the image of a dark room . . .

"I—I can see him . . ." I gasp breathlessly. "I'm with him."

CHAPTER 28

CADE

My body feels heavy in the seat when I wake next. My eyes trace the tattoo on my forearm, trying to ground myself.

I'm here. I'm still alive.

My temples feel like they're caving in, crushing my brain. Nausea hits me like a wave—bitter at the back of my throat, my stomach lurching. The hangover from whatever Benjamin injected me with is finally wearing off, leaving only the pain—raw and loud.

I scan the room. Low light bounces off brick walls, casting everything in a hazy blur. I search again—desperate to find my little light in the shadows.

But I see nothing.

My stomach drops and my jaw clenches as a sharp spike of panic hits me in the chest, eyes moving frantically now.

I want to see you. Why can't I see you?

But then I feel you.

It washes over me—faint but consistent, no sight, no sound.

Just your *presence*.

"Stay close to me, little ghost . . ."

The words rasp out, far quieter than I mean them to.

I pause, swallowing hard, trying to wet my dry throat, my jaw ticking.

"Please don't leave."

There's no comfort to offer, just the sting in my ribs and the weight of knowing what comes next. I lean my head back, eyes falling closed once again.

Multiple sets of footsteps draw closer at a steady pace, rousing me from my fitful rest.

Benjamin and the man from yesterday—Frank—enter the room, saying nothing as they lug in several bags on their backs, tossing them onto the floor in the corner.

Ben claps his hands together with a loud smack, the sound ricocheting off the walls and around my aching head.

"All right, let's get started!" he says with a smile, his tone cheerful as he pulls his brass knuckles from his pocket and slides them on slowly, approaching me.

"So, this is how it's gonna work," he starts, eyes bright in the dim light of the room. "We've got some questions, and you're gonna answer them to the best of your ability. You got that?" He looks down at me from under his brows, like he's talking to a child. "But I think you know how this goes by now." He says it with a smile. A chuckle.

Fucker.

"Do what you need to—you know you're not getting shit." My voice is a gnarled, mangled thing.

He drops his head back in a laugh. "I love that you think that." He snickers. "C'mon in, baby girl."

He gestures to the door like he's calling a dog, and a small woman walks in. It's the redhead I saw at the property—the one who hit me with a crowbar.

Cute.

She keeps her head down slightly as she enters, her pale fingers wrapped around something she hides under her arm. She avoids my gaze. She remembers. I remember, too.

She's the witch who put up the barrier.

"Thought you fuckers killed witches. What are you doing with one?" I ask, spitting blood to the floor near my feet.

"Damn, I'm glad you asked that. And I'll answer—but if I scratch your back, you scratch mine, yeah?" He says it playfully, like we're old buddies at a card game.

I stare at him, deadpan.

"I'll take that silence as a maybe!" he says cheerfully. "See, Genevieve here, she's our backup. You know it's Callisto we want. Gen here is mincemeat compared to what your sister's capable of—but she's useful. For now." He says the words pointedly, like the woman needs the reminder.

"So, people are just disposable to the Covenant?" I scoff, the words bitter.

For a moment, I see a break in his confident facade and my eyes dart to her with realization: It's her. The witch—*she's* the one he wants to protect. That's his leverage. He gives Rosa my sister's head—she spares her life. But he has to know that's not realistic.

They won't stop at Calli—he must know that. That's why he wants my help.

"Yeah," he says, his voice soft as he eyes me, watching me put the pieces together. "Something like that, pretty boy. Now it's your turn to answer a question." He turns to look at Frank, who is behind him. "Hey, Frankie, go get me the thing."

Frank gives a single nod, then turns and walks out without a word.

I wait for the door to slam shut before I speak, my voice steady. "I take it you have a deal with Rosa to save the girl?"

He lets out a short, humorless laugh, shaking his head . . . then slams an uppercut into my jaw.

My teeth clack and my ears ring, the taste of blood filling my mouth.

"Shut the fuck up." He sneers, shaking a finger in my face like he's teaching a lesson. "But yeah—something like that. Rosa's word is bullshit, though; I don't trust that cunt."

"Why . . . the f-fuck do you care . . ." I spit, my jaw numb and slack, blood dripping down my chin.

"Oh, I'm sure you put it together—smart guy like you." He rolls his eyes at me.

"Y-you're desperate," I mutter, head still spinning from the hit. "You love her."

"Bingo." He sighs, like just hearing the words pains him. "So I'ma need you to work with me and stay alive like the stubborn bastard you are."

Frank returns, silent as ever, and stops beside Benjamin. In his hand is a thick, worn book—leather-bound. It looks older than any of us combined.

Ben takes it, his smirk returning like a mask.

"Appreciate it, Frankie," he says, clapping the other man on the back.

Frank doesn't respond. Doesn't even blink. He just steps back against the wall—his silence louder than anything Ben could say.

Ben turns back to face me, cradling the book like it's sacred.

"Now, this part—this is where things get interesting."

He crosses to Genevieve and hands it to her carefully, brushing his fingers against hers with a softness that doesn't match the energy in the room.

"Go ahead, sweetheart. Just like we practiced." He speaks to her gently, eyes on hers.

She nods. Her voice is barely audible as she opens the book and begins to chant.

"Wha . . . what is she doing . . ." I manage to rasp as the air shifts—dense and pressing, like the walls are caving in.

"Tell me where your little sister is, or my girl here's gonna put you in the worst pain you can imagine. Trust that," he says, tone hardening, his eyes locking on my face.

A pressure tightens around my ribs, my pulse skipping.

That panic swirling around me—it's not mine.

It's *yours*.

You're scared for me.

Fuck—I need you steady, little ghost. I'm not going anywhere.

"Fuck you," I say, spitting blood onto the floor at the witch—just to feel like I have control over something.

She glances at Ben, her brows twitching—concern hidden behind a mask of duty.

"Yeah," Ben sighs, shaking his head. "That's what I thought. Go ahead, baby girl. Do it."

The lights flicker.

Then—shadows stretch unnaturally, reaching across the walls like fingers. The room seems to fold in on itself, and a low hum claws through my skull. Smoke seeps from the corners of the ceiling, curling around us.

One breath and I'm gone.

Then my vision snaps to black. I try to move—to scream—but I'm nothing.

No voice. No limbs.

The silence is total. Deafening.

This is magic.

And it hates me.

I'm alive. I'm alive. I'm alive.

I am still myself. This isn't real.

I begin to feel like gravity has been sucked from my being—unable to discern up from down.

Up, down—meaningless.

My lungs inflate like foreign machines. Every swallow is deafening. I can hear the slick churn of muscle, the wet tick of tendons shifting, the flex of my jaw. Even my teeth feel wrong in my mouth.

It's so quiet, I begin to hear my organs squelching with each attempted movement. The rush of my blood moving through my veins.

I'm hyperaware of every part of my body.

I become too aware of my tongue as the roof of my mouth begins to feel too tight. Panic rises in my chest. My heart pounds like it's *trapped* in my ribs—too fast, too loud.

I can't take it.

"Stop. *Please*."

It slips out sharp. Uncontrolled and desperate.

The darkness fades immediately. But I'm not in the room.

The silence is eerie. The shift is too smooth. Air presses against my skin like breath, cold and wide. I blink—once, twice.

I'm outside.

This is the old Halloway property, the field behind the manor. Where the air always smells like iron and damp stone.

And there she is—

Genevieve.

Small. Still. Waiting.

"Where are we?" My voice is my own again, no longer raspy from thirst and screaming.

"This is where your ancestor found the grimoire," she tells me in that soft voice of hers. "It's just an illusion, but if you're asking where your physical body sits—you are in the Covenant headquarters in Topanga Canyon."

"Why are you telling me this?" I ask, suspicion clear in my voice.

"I've been under the hand of the Covenant since I was a child," she says, and there's a sadness in her voice. "They took me from my parents and raised me as their own. I stayed quiet, I read their books . . . People tend to ignore the ones they think are small."

The thought hits me hard in the chest. She reminds me of Calli. Not just the magic, not just the eyes—but the way she speaks like she already knows how this ends.

A girl called to the fire. A life they never planned on letting her live.

"What can you tell me about the God they serve?" I ask her, and this time my voice is softer, the image of my sister strong in my mind.

"Why do you want to know such things?" She tilts her head, curious.

"I want to end him," I tell her truthfully.

"He can't be killed. Not by a mortal." She lets out a quiet laugh—not mocking. Just . . . tired. "Do you know how absurd that sounds? You have no idea what's really going on here, do you?"

"Enlighten me."

"Ben wants to save me." She sighs. "He may be rough around the edges, but he truly loves me. He's convinced that you have the ability to end the Covenant. But . . . even if you do, that still won't stop the thing they worship." She pauses, watching me like she's measuring whether I can take it.

"Ben knows that. Calli has been marked." She says the words gently. "She will be claimed."

I narrow my eyes at her, bristling at her words. "Why would you tell me that and risk me not helping you?"

"Because you need his help getting out." She says it matter-of-factly. "And even though I just told you it's impossible . . . I can feel it. You're going to try anyway. You'd die for her." There's a wistfulness in her voice that softens me once again.

She's not wrong.

"She deserves a chance at life." It's my turn to gentle my voice. "Both of you do. And these fuckers need to die."

Genevieve gives me a look that's both soft and scared, her fingers trembling around the book she still holds. "I hope you survive it,

Cade Halloway. Because the path you're now walking . . . it will cross with the being they serve."

"I don't need prophecy," I tell her, barely containing the eye roll I desperately want to give her. She really does remind me of Calli. "And I don't need magic to help me."

"Bold words," she whispers, eyes on my face, "coming from a man in love with a ghost."

I freeze. Just for a second. The words dig deeper than they should.

In love with a ghost.

I hadn't . . . I never thought about it like that.

I want to deny it.

I want to laugh.

I can't.

She watches me carefully, letting my silence say enough.

"I know they're here with us, and I can feel how bound you are to them. There is a way for you to reach them." Her voice is low, like she's telling me something she shouldn't. I take a step closer. The air between us feels strange—charged.

"Tell me," I say, dark and direct, my heart pounding, barely stopping myself from reaching for her.

"Get us out of this," she says quickly, taking a step back like she can read my intentions. "Help Ben, and I promise I'll tell you what I know."

"I have absolutely no reason to trust you," I growl, matching her step.

"You're right. You don't know me. But I know Calli." I pause, head tilting. "We were kids. We played together before the Covenant pulled us in."

Her voice wavers just enough to feel human. "I don't want her to die, Cade," she promises softly. "And I don't want to die either. I gain nothing by lying to you."

She's right. She could be lying—but if she is, it's not for gain. There's nothing in this for her, nothing but survival. She must see the decision on my face because she takes a small step closer, voice urgent now.

"I brought you here to let you know that I'll heal you, but you need to be ready. Ben can't afford to go easy on you. He has to make Rosa believe you're broken."

Her eyes shift slightly, going distant.

"She's already arrived," she whispers, the fear in her voice making it tremble—I clench my jaw at the sound.

"I was told to make you afraid. Full and total sensory deprivation. I'm sorry it lasted as long as it did—but Frank had to see it."

I look at her, steady now that I have more information. And a plan.

"I'm ready. Let's get this over with." I grunt, closing my eyes.

My lungs seize as I choke on nothing—

And then I'm *back*. Gasping like I'm surfacing from a drowning.

"There he is! Good morning, sunshine." Ben grins wide—too wide.

I bite through the pain as I continue to fill my lungs with air, my chest rattling. Genevieve stiffens and her eyes drop when I try to meet them—her shoulders curling forward like she's bracing for impact.

"Don't look at her, big guy," he snaps. "Eyes on me." He points with his fingers from his eyes to mine and back again.

We all hear the sound of heels clacking outside the door and Genevieve backs herself into the corner—making herself smaller than she already is.

Ben straightens, turning his gaze to the door, and quips, "Right on time, boss. Our friend here was about to tell us where his baby sister is."

"Is he ready for interrogation?" Rosa says calmly, stepping into the room, nose wrinkling with disgust.

"As ready as he'll ever be. We had Gen warm him up for us."

Rosa stalks over to Ben, running her hand over his shoulders, and I see Genevieve flinch.

"You've done well, boys—but I can take it from here." She turns to me with a grim look and snaps to the room, "Get out. All of you."

No one responds as they exit the room, Ben wrapping his arm around Genevieve as they leave me and Rosa alone.

I don't know if this was the plan, but they'd better keep me alive.

"I'm sure you are thinking I'm going to kill you," she says coolly as she tugs leather gloves from her pocket and slips them on. "We all die in our own time—and this isn't your time, my dear boy."

I carefully measure my words, avoiding eye contact as I keep my face blank and my eyes down. No sudden movements. Let her think I'm scared, not thinking clearly. If I am careful, I may be able to get information out of her.

"I understand why you feel this is necessary," I rasp as she goes to a bag and pulls out two wood clamps and begins to press my hand flat against the arm of the chair.

"After what I did—torture is the least that I deserve. Do what you feel you need to."

She forces a dry laugh, continuing to clamp my hand down until I feel the tendons pop under the pressure, the bones in my hand giving way.

"Don't patronize me," she says, looking down on me, her voice like a whip. "After your parents' untimely demise, I planned on silencing you, anyway. They were fools to think you had the capacity to lead this Order. You were never loyal."

My bones grind together, a white-hot pain pulsing through my wrist, but I don't scream. I won't give her that.

Crack.

My breath hitches and I bite back a groan.

"Anyone with a conscience would understand. The Covenant is corrupt; you kill people in the hope of gaining more power. It's wrong—you know that," I say, breathless—forcing the words past my numb lips, the pain causing me to see stars.

"You speak of a conscience when you take lives brutally without remorse. We at least have a purpose—a reason." Her voice raises as she begins placing the other clamp on my opposite hand.

"So do I," I tell her through gritted teeth, as I look at her with an expression that shows no regrets. I know pain, I can deal with pain.

"Ah yes . . . Your little crusade to save your sister. Very noble of you." She sneers as she winds the clamp, crushing my other hand. "Your agenda is flawed. He will have his offering and I will be the one to deliver her." She stands up straight and goes back to the bag, pulling out a soldering iron.

"Who is he?" I groan, doubting I'll get an answer. "I'm dead anyway. I just want to know the name of the God that claims my only blood."

She turns the iron on and the tip begins to heat up, glowing softly. She keeps her back to me.

"He goes by many names—only showing himself when needed. I have laid eyes on him only once." Her voice is quiet and filled with reverence.

"What do *you* call him?" I ask, steeling myself for the pain as she adjusts the iron in her gloved hand, studying the heat as it glows red.

"There," she says softly, almost admiringly. "Hot enough to leave a lasting impression."

She kneels beside me, a knife in her other hand, and slices open the fabric of my shirt with clinical precision.

"You'll carry his name," she murmurs to me sweetly. "Right over your heart. As it should be."

The iron touches my skin and the sound—*flesh searing*—rips through the room.

I'm barely able to stay quiet, sucking sharp, hissing breaths through my teeth.

Each letter burns slowly, and she moves with methodical precision as she engraves the letters into my skin.

"I want you to look at it," she tells me finally, stepping back to admire her work, a twisted smile on her face. "And remember who owns your bloodline."

CHAPTER 29

CALLISTO

"Calli! You need to come back!"

Alabaster's voice slices through the dark like a blade. My vision blurs, body too heavy to hold upright, and I slump back into the mattress.

"I know where he is!" I gasp, trying to stand—only for my legs to buckle, the room spinning. Alabaster catches me before I hit the floor.

"Easy," he murmurs, cradling me to his chest. "You're bleeding."

It's the way he says it—gentle, careful.

My eyes sting, my face wet. I glance toward the mirror and freeze.

My nose. My eyes. Blood streaks down my cheeks like tears in a horror film.

"What is this?" I ask, voice trembling with a hand frozen halfway to my face.

"You pushed too hard, stayed too long. Magic always takes its toll," he tells me, his own voice steady. "Your body wasn't built for what you just did."

I groan, resting my head against his shoulder. Karma comes up, rubbing against my side. "What does that even mean?"

"It means you have limits." He says it too gently, like I'll break if he raises his voice. Then he looks down adoringly at Karma. "She really was worried."

I look up at him, narrowing my eyes.

"Don't talk to me like I'm fragile. I'm fine," I snap, lifting a shaky hand to wipe at my cheek, my free hand caressing Karma's soft fur.

He doesn't flinch at my tone, his golden eyes steady on my face.

"No, that you are not." His tone stays flat, but there's softness buried beneath it. "Just take it easy, pretty girl."

He carefully leans me back against the headboard and leaves the room for a moment. I hear the water turn on and off again, and he comes back in with a wet hand towel. Then, without asking, he starts gently cleaning my face.

"I'm not a baby," I grumble as he wipes away the blood with soft, even strokes.

"Shut up," he replies sweetly—brushing me off like I didn't just almost die.

My thoughts spiral—images I can't unsee clawing their way to the surface as he cares for me.

Genni.

She's a witch . . . and *they* have her.

She was the closest thing I ever had to a real friend . . . The realization that she's trapped—suffering in a place far worse than this—splits something open in me. Then Cade flashes behind my eyes. His pain. The sound of him.

The way his voice cracked. The look in his eyes.

The smell.

Gods—the *smell of his burning flesh.*

It punches me in the gut so hard I double over, knocking Alabaster's hand away from my face. Karma scurries out of the room.

Crack.

The memory of bones breaking echoes in my skull and my body convulses. I lurch forward, heaving onto the carpet.

"We have to get them out," I gasp as bile and drool slides from my lips, hanging off my chin like strings of guilt, tears welling in my eyes.

Panic flares in my chest like fire—wild and out of control.

I can't sit still. I can't wait.

I shove out of Alabaster's arms, shaking and unsteady but driven by something feral.

"I need Jack."

I stumble toward the doorway—my legs aren't ready, but I make them work. Weakness be damned. If Cade can be strong, so can I.

I don't stop until I'm downstairs, clinging to the railing, knees trembling. The door creaks open under my hand as I spill out onto the porch—barefoot, breathless, and still bloody—to find Jack with his back to me, cigarette between his fingers, smoke curling around him like fog.

"Not now, Calli," he mutters, voice low and worn, defeat clinging to his body.

"I know where Cade is," I tell him, my voice barely holding together. My chest is rising too fast, and I force my breaths to slow.

He spins around, shock wide in his eyes as the cigarette slips from his hand and dies on the wood.

Jack doesn't ask questions. He just ushers me into the living room, steady hands guiding me to the couch. I sink down, still trembling, and he drops beside me with his laptop in his lap, already in motion.

Tabs spring open, one after another—maps, traffic cams, databases I don't recognize.

"I tracked him on the freeway," he tells me absently, eyes scanning fast. "Caught a few glimpses near the 101—but I lost him just outside L.A. I know the general direction, but nothing concrete."

"He's in Topanga Canyon," I say, my voice firm, surprising even myself. "Rosa's main house. That's where they're holding him."

He freezes, fingers hovering over the keyboard before I can see him mentally shrugging. He begins hammering down on the keys again, faster this time. More tabs. More frantic clicks. His mouth parts slightly when he pulls up an old photo, then cross-references another—his pupils flicking back and forth.

"Holy fuck," he breathes, shock in his voice. "You're right. If I match Rosa's tagged location history with this address . . . It's the same house. It's right there, hiding in plain sight." He laughs, looking over at me. "How the hell do you know this?"

I hesitate, my fingers twisting in my lap.

"I saw him," I say softly.

Everything in him stills and I flinch.

Recognition flickers behind his eyes, the kind that carries weight. Fear, maybe. Or awe. Or both. I can see him holding back—deciding whether to ask the question forming in his throat.

"Is he . . ." Jack swallows hard. "Is he okay?"

The question settles something in me, knowing that he's at least trying to accept this. It's the answer that breaks me.

My throat closes, and tears rise before I can stop them. My head shakes slowly, and I try to breathe through the pain of it—but I can't. The moment he asked . . . It made it real.

Made it too much.

Jack shuts the laptop and turns to face me fully, his hand finding my shoulder, grounding me with slow, steady pressure.

"He's alive, though," he states. Not as a question. As a tether.

I nod, barely. "Yes."

His expression softens, and he reaches up and brushes my hair from my face, tucking it behind my ear. His fingers still when he sees the blood, swiping a thumb across my temple.

"Is that . . . is that blood?" His voice tightens, his eyes dancing over my face in that clinical way of his. "Christ, Calli, are *you* okay?"

"No," I confess in a whisper. My voice cracks, and I can't hold it back anymore. The comfort—the *kindness*—undoes me.

The sob hits before I can brace for it. My chest caves, body trembling as hot tears stream down my face.

Jack pulls me into him. Strong arms wrap around me, and I let myself fall apart against him, sobbing into his chest.

"Hey . . . hey," he whispers, holding me tight, rocking me slowly. "It's going to be okay. We're gonna get him back. I promise."

He pulls back, cupping my face and forcing me to meet his eyes. There's no room for doubt in his voice when he says, "I'm going to get him out."

"You won't need to," I say, my breath still shaky, my fingers curling around his wrists. "That man—Benjamin. He wants to save someone. A girl. I think he loves her. But he needs Cade to do it."

Jack's jaw ticks, his eyes narrowing. "We can't rely on that."

"I know her—knew her," I say, my voice low and almost pleading. "Genni. We played together when we were kids. We can trust her—at least enough to count on her wanting out. She wants to help Cade. She *has* to. She's stuck there, same as he is. Same as I would've been."

Jack doesn't hesitate, already on his feet, storming off toward his room. "Then I'm going to go get them."

"No—Jack, wait. You have no id—" I surge to my feet, panic at the thought of losing him sending me stumbling after him.

He whirls around, jaw clenched. "No, Calli. You *don't* get to keep secrets from me, then turn around and tell me what I can't do."

I flinch at the heat in his voice, the betrayal there.

"This whole time," he spits, shaking his head in disgust, "you've been pissed that we kept you in the dark. But you've been doing the *same damn thing.*"

"I didn't think you'd believe me," I say, exasperated, throwing my hands in the air. "I barely believed it myself most days. And I only *just* started learning how to control it. I *still* don't know what I'm capable of." I plead with him to understand as I trail him to his room, hovering in the doorway.

He grunts sharply, dragging a duffel from under the bed and shoving random clothes inside like he's on autopilot, his frustration and anger bleeding into every movement.

"Fine. Whatever. I hear you," he snaps back to me as he rummages through his bedside table. "But I'm still going. I'm not leaving this up to that *asshole*. I saw what he's capable of—your little possession trick fried my PC, but I saw *enough* of Benjamin's files to know he's not safe."

I move to him, placing my hands over his to stop the frantic packing, gently squeezing them.

"Then let me help you," I say, voice steady this time, my eyes catching his.

He blinks at me.

"What are you thinking?"

I exhale and sit down on the edge of his bed, pulling him down with me.

"I'll tell you everything I know, I promise." And I do. I give him everything I know: Genni's a witch. She plans to heal Cade. Ben's involvement—maybe for love, maybe survival. Frank's a brute. Rosa's the one in charge.

The only thing I leave out is the ghost.

Some part of me feels like I'm not supposed to know. Like I've been let in on a secret that was meant only for Cade.

Jack sits quietly, absorbing all of the new information with quiet resolve. When he finally speaks, his voice is low. "Cade asked me to research how to kill a God. I thought it was just part of the game he plays—one of his weird power fantasies." He looks up at me, eyes serious. "What's its name?"

"I don't know," I whisper, unable to hold his gaze, guilt heavy in my chest. "I got pulled out before I could hear it."

"Can you go back to him?" he asks, calculating.

"No." I shake my head, lower lip trembling. "It was too much. I barely made it out. I'm sorry."

He doesn't push, taking my hands in his again. "Don't apologize. I don't know anything about magic or spirits or whatever the hell this is, but that was brave, what you did. That couldn't have been easy."

I stare at the back wall, trying not to cry again. "No," I whisper. "It wasn't."

He's silent for a beat, then runs a hand through his hair, letting out a puff of air. "Okay. Do I have a plan? Not really. Other than driving straight there and winging it—actually, wait."

He grabs his laptop from his bag and settles it on his lap, tapping quickly.

"What?" I ask, watching the flurry of motion as his fingertips dance across the keys.

"I might be able to recover the files you zapped. If I can, I can find Ben's number. Maybe contact him directly," he informs me as he works.

"You think that'll work?" I ask, completely at a loss when it comes to computers.

"Maybe." He shrugs, flashing me a grin. "But it's better than nothing."

He snaps the laptop closed and stands, slinging the duffel over his shoulder.

"I'll do it on the drive and I'll keep you updated," he promises as he heads for his office, me trailing behind him. "But you get why you can't come, right?"

I nod.

I do.

He doesn't have to say it—we both know. I'd slow him down, I'd be a target. I'm not built for rescue missions or fights.

Not like Cade. Not like Jack.

So, I help him pack. I watch him load up the car. I wave as he drives away.

And then I pray.

Please come back. Both of you.

"He handled that well," Alabaster says behind me.

"Please, don't." I lift my hand in a weak stop gesture, not even looking back as I lean against the doorway, eyes on the empty driveway. "Not right now. I can't handle sarcasm."

Silence stretches between us, heavy and uneasy.

Then—heavy footsteps approach, slow and deliberate.

"You did what you could," he says, his voice closer now, his warmth almost stinging. "Stop carrying guilt that doesn't belong to you, Calli."

I feel the shift in the air just before his arm wraps around me—solid and warm, grounding me in a way I hate to admit I need. I lean back against him and sigh.

"If it weren't for your efforts," he continues softly, "you'd still be guessing. That pendulum you gave your brother saved his life."

My throat tightens.

"Cade is in love with the being connected to that pendulum," I whisper, my eyes closing.

"I know." Alabaster chuckles, soft and knowing. "Though your brother hasn't quite figured that part out yet."

He says it like he sees it all—the threads, the bonds, the things we pretend not to feel.

Like none of us has any secrets from him.

"They must be why he believes," I mutter, eyes still closed, head resting against his chest. "Why he's even open to all of this."

"You say that like it's a bad thing." His tone sharpens just slightly, not cruel—just pointed. "Didn't you want that? For him to believe?"

"I did. I do." My voice catches, the truth in the words making my heart clench. "I'm just glad he's not alone."

"Then what's the problem?" he asks, cocking a brow, already reading me if the twinkle in his eye is anything to go by.

I hesitate. "I don't know. How does that even work?" And the second it's out of my mouth, I regret it. I make a face, nose wrinkling. "You know what—never mind. I don't want to know."

Alabaster grins, slow and deliberate. That devilish, too-knowing smile he wears so well.

"How do we work?" he asks, tugging me more fully against him, his arms sliding down around my waist. He holds me still.

"I don't know if we do, yet," I say, voice low and teasing, my lip twitching like it wants to smile, but I don't let it. I can't—not until I know they're safe.

But something deep in me—*wants*.

He tilts his head, studying me with a look that's far too tender for someone like him.

"You've played your part," he says quietly. "Now you wait."

He leans in closer, voice brushing my skin like a secret. "Let me create a distraction."

I shake my head. "I can't get it out of my head," I admit, clenching my fists. "What I saw. What I felt. There's nothing you can do to distract me—"

"Watch this."

He slips away and walks down the porch steps to my flowerpots, plucking one of the cosmos buds—not yet bloomed. When he returns, he places the stem in my palm.

"Close your eyes," he says.

"Alabaster . . ." I groan wearily but he just grins down at me.

"Humor me."

I sigh and shut them.

"Good girl," he purrs.

"Now," he whispers, "imagine it, bloomed. Fully open. See it in your mind."

I do as he says. I picture the petals. Pale pink and delicate. Cade brought them home our first week here—said they were low-maintenance and pretty, just like me. A joke that stuck.

A tear slips down my cheek at the memory.

"Open your eyes," he says gently, thumb softly brushing away the tear.

I blink my eyes open and when I look down—the flower in my hand is fully bloomed.

I stare at it, stunned. The bloom is delicate. It's beautiful.

“How did you know I could do that?” I whisper, barely trusting my own voice, my eyes still on the flower as I spin it gently between my fingers.

Alabaster steps closer, looking down at me with unreadable eyes. His fingers ghost over my palm, lifting the flower with care before he tucks it behind my ear, then lets his hand drift—trailing along my jaw, his thumb brushing the edge of my temple. A touch far too soft for someone who’s supposed to be untouchable.

“I didn’t,” he says, voice low and steady. “But it’s like I told you . . .” His eyes meet mine, and the usual sharpness is gone. Just him and those golden eyes.

“You’re capable of so much more than you think.”

CHAPTER 30

CADE

My chest heaves, each breath scraping through torn lungs as my body begs for sleep—but the pain denies me the escape I crave. Copper still clings to the back of my throat, thick and metallic, dripping like rust down my sinuses and burning as I swallow.

They only ever stop the torture at night. It's quiet now—too quiet—so it must be late. A few hours, maybe, since the last round? I've lost count. I've lost everything but the rage simmering in my chest.

It seeps through me—my last ally in this hell. A slow, steady burn that holds the line, sharpening my thoughts as I claw through the haze, planning my inevitable escape.

I don't know *how* I'm getting out of here. But I will. And when I do, I'm going to make every single one of those fuckers wish they'd killed me when they had the chance.

The door creaks open with a sound too soft to match the weight it carries.

My head lolls, barely able to lift, but I catch the voice. Fucking Benjamin.

"Hurry—he's no good to us like this."

He says it hastily and then Genevieve is moving to me, her body a hazy outline as I blink slowly.

Hands press to my chest, then I feel a vibration. A low hum at first, then a searing warmth blooms beneath my skin. It spreads—up my neck, down my arms, and across my stomach like wildfire licking through nerve endings.

The pounding in my head dulls then fades altogether.

I lift my gaze and lock eyes with Ben.

"I need you to listen, got it? I don't have time to repeat myself." His voice is sharp and steady, his eyes darting back toward the door.

I nod once—still dazed, the world slowly reassembling itself around me. The pain's not gone, but something is stitching me back together. I can feel it—my skin knitting, torn muscle crawling into place. It stinks like burnt blood and charred flesh—and it *hurts*.

But it's a *relief*.

"We're doing this fast and quiet." He pulls out a handgun—a sleek, silenced 10mm pistol with an extended clip—and places it on my lap. Then he's at my wrists, cutting the ropes, my heavy arms falling limply to my sides.

"Your buddy's smart. He contacted me," Ben informs me quietly as he bends to work my ankles free.

My eyes snap open again. "Jack?" I say, barely above a whisper. Of course.

My body keeps heating, the feeling almost unbearable now. My chest feels like it's on fire, like something inside me is boiling, and I let out a hissing breath.

"I can't go further right now," Genevieve says, pulling her hands away. The heat leaves with her, sudden and jarring. "It's too much at once. We'll have to do this in sessions."

Ben leans in, eyes steady on my own, appraising. "Ready?"

I shove the ropes off, fingers already reaching for the gun. I cock it—clean, smooth, loaded. The bullet gleams in the chamber, the clip full.

It's not my style—I tend to prefer knives—but this'll work.

"I'm ready," I rasp, throat still dry as fuck.

"Your guy's waiting about half a mile up the road," Ben says, quick and clipped as he shuffles toward the door. "You'll follow me down the hall, up the stairs. The window in the parlor's unlocked. If we get caught"—he nods toward the pistol—"use that."

I stand, breath hitching at the pain that shoots through my ribs, and look down at Genevieve, brow raised.

She nods—tight but solid, her hands fluttering.

"What's security look like?" I ask, already mapping the path in my head as I roll my neck, cracking it.

"Frank's out cold. Guards at the front and back. Side patrols rotate every ten minutes. We've handled the cameras. If we time it right, we're ghosts. I'll stay close—cover you if anything goes sideways."

I nod once, mind focused on the plan. "All right. Let's go."

Pain claws through my skin like barbed wire dragged across raw muscle—but I can walk. I can kill. Let's get the fuck out of here.

I slip out the door and into the hallway, leaving the stench of rot and mold behind. The shift in the air hits me like a slap—cleaner, colder, *wrong*.

Overstimulation crashes down hard; the lights too bright, the walls too open. My body's screaming, and my brain is lagging behind. But I force myself to move.

One step. Then another.

Up the stairs. Down the hall.

The parlor looms ahead of us.

I stop just before crossing into view, pressing myself to the wall. My eyes scan the room: heavy curtains, aged wood, the faint scent of dust and wood polish.

Ben is a shadow behind me, his gun raised, jaw tight. Genevieve's between us, shoulders curled inward, making herself small. Her eyes flicker to mine—wide and terrified. She's trying not to shake. I nod at her and turn back.

I slip into the parlor, slow and deliberate, each step a silent promise.

Ben follows, stopping just beyond the doorway. He nods, gesturing toward the window with a tilt of his chin.

He throws his fist in the air and I still.

Footsteps crunch outside. They are slow, deliberate, shadows moving across the curtains. I hear armor shifting and clinking, the unmistakable sound of rifles brushing tactical vests . . . Then, the sound fades.

I creep to the window, unlatch it, and ease it open inch by inch, cold air kissing my face.

I duck and lower myself through the opening, dropping into a silent crouch on the grass below. My eyes scan the area—we're clear.

I look up—Genevieve is hesitating at the window. I reach up, catch her waist, and slowly pull her through, her body pressed against mine. Her breath is quick against my neck as I set her down, eyes already back on the window.

Ben lands beside us with a quiet thud, pistol still drawn. He points toward the front of the property, and we move silently through the night.

Backs pressed to the outer wall, we inch toward the road. Our every step is calculated, every breath shallow. The open air feels too exposed compared to the stifled air of the basement. The gravel crunches beneath my boots despite how light I try to move.

I fight the urge to sprint, my legs twitch with instinct, bracing to bolt. But as I glance at Genevieve—she's trembling. Her eyes lock on mine, her pupils blown wide with panic. Her breath catches in her throat, chest rising slow and deep like she's trying to stay calm, trying to match my rhythm. I give her another nod, a hopefully reassuring look.

I peek around the edge of the structure and see the two guards, standing right where we need to be. Their stances are loose but alert.

Trained.

We're not getting past them without blood.

I turn and grip Genevieve's arm, and pull her in tight, my hand sliding around to cover her mouth before she can protest. My other hand raises the gun, pressing the barrel to her temple. She jerks, a muffled squeal escaping against my palm.

I lean in, my lips brushing her ear.

"You're gonna have to trust me," I growl, my eyes locking with hers.

She nods fast, the motion jerky—terror written in the whites of her eyes.

Ben rounds the corner behind us, eyes immediately catching the scene, his expression tightening into something hard and dangerous.

"Stay back," I whisper, just loud enough for him to hear. "There's no way past them without being seen."

His jaw clenches, eyes darting to the guards ahead. He doesn't like it, but he nods once, tight and slow.

I take a breath and step into the light.

Genevieve is rigid in my arms, the gun still to her head, my grip iron around her waist. I walk fast—confident—like I'm delivering something.

The first guard turns. Point—clean shot. Right between the eyes.

He drops.

The second pivots with a shout, raising his weapon. I fire and miss, tearing through his shoulder instead. He screams, stumbling over his feet, clutching his arm.

I realign. The second shot is buried in his temple.

He's down.

Shouts erupt behind the house. It's too late now. We gotta move.

I drag Genevieve toward a thick tree near the edge of the path, shoving her behind the trunk as I crouch low beside her. She's shaking but silent. Shock, maybe?

I lift my head just enough to gesture sharply toward Ben to stay back.

Let them come to me.

A guard charges from behind Ben.

Ben doesn't hesitate. He intercepts him mid-sprint—grabbing him by the vest and slamming him into the siding with brutal precision. Then, with a voice cold enough to freeze the air, he shouts: "I don't have eyes—he's got the witch! Shoot to kill!"

And without flinching, Ben pulls the trigger, point-blank.

Blood sprays. The guard drops.

"Man down!" Ben roars, loud enough to shake the trees.

Another shadow moves on the opposite side of the house. I spot the glint of a weapon, raising mine in response.

Shoot.

He crumples instantly and I grin to myself. Ya know . . . I think I like this gun.

I pull Genevieve behind another tree closer to the road, shoving her behind cover. She squirms in my grip, her small hand around my wrist, trying to wrench my hand from her mouth—but I hold firm. Not yet.

Footsteps thunder behind Ben. Another guard incoming, and fast.

Ben turns just in time to meet him—two shots crack through the night.

The man falls with a thud.

"Behind you!" Ben shouts—right before he collapses to his knees, his hands clutching his side, a wet sucking sound rattling his chest.

Genevieve lets out a muffled scream against my palm and I whip around—Oh shiiit.

CRACK.

A hard blow to the side of my skull sends me crashing back against the tree, Genevieve tumbling to the ground next to me. My vision spins, stars bursting across the darkness. My weapon is gone—thrown somewhere behind the brush. I blink—dizzy. I'm bleeding. Motherfucker.

And then I see him.

Fucking Frank.

Towering and monstrous—his mouth curled into something uglier than a smile. He grabs Genevieve by the throat and yanks her off the ground like she weighs nothing. She kicks wildly, clawing at his hands as she gasps for air, face turning a blotchy red.

Frank sneers at her, voice dripping with venom.

"You're not going anywhere, little bitch."

Still on the ground, the world still spinning, I throw my leg out—my boot connecting with Frank's knee.

Crack.

He stumbles, balance broken, and his grip loosens. Genevieve crashes to the ground with a sickening thud, her hands flying to her throat as she struggles for air.

I scramble—my chest burning, ground still shifting—eyes on the gun.

Almost. Fucking. There.

Frank's hand seizes my ankle as my fingers brush the grip and he yanks me back hard across the dirt. Before I can stop it, he throws his full weight on top of me, straddling my legs, massive hands clamping down around my throat.

Pressure—white-hot and crushing. I fight, squirm, and claw at him, but his grip only tightens, that sick smile back on his ugly face.

I can feel it. The cartilage folding. The air being locked out.

Everything dims as my vision tunnels, the edges blackening.

Somewhere in the chaos, I glimpse Genevieve crawling toward Ben, screaming, begging, but her voice is distant . . . like I'm underwater.

And then it hits me. I'm dying . . .

I think of *you*.

My little ghost.

I'm sorry . . . I—I lov—

BANG.

The weight on top of me goes limp, Frank's body slumping forward as his grip slips from my neck.

I inhale a jagged, desperate breath. My lungs seize and I cough violently, tears springing to my eyes from the force of it.

As my vision slowly clears, I look up.

Ben stands over me, bleeding and shaking, the barrel of the gun still pointed at Frank's skull. His hand is pressed to his side, blood spilling between his fingers.

He saved me.

I stay on the ground a beat longer, forcing my lungs to work, my throat raw and spasming. Then I push Frank's body off me, his dead weight thudding beside my leg. Motherfucker weighs a ton.

Each breath still feels like fire as I fight to steady it—my voice torn and broken when I finally speak.

"You good?" I garble.

Ben grimaces, shifting his weight. His hand's slick with blood and he nods sharply.

"I'll live. Gen fixed it enough so it won't kill me." He exhales in a hiss, biting down the pain. "But you two need to get the fuck out of here."

"What?" Genevieve's voice cuts in, tight with panic. "No—no. You're coming, too." Her hands are already on him, clinging.

Ben pulls out his phone without meeting her eyes.

"That was never the plan, sweetheart. The plan was to get *you* out."

She shakes her head, tears falling as she clutches his arm. "No . . . no, please. You can't stay. You *can't*."

"I didn't do all this to blow the one ounce of trust I earned from that bitch," he tells her bluntly, already dialing. "If I was coming with you, I never would've brought him here."

Genevieve lunges, trying to grab the phone, but he pushes her back with a soft shove as he speaks.

"You need to get here," Ben says coldly into the receiver, his eyes on hers. "They escaped. He's got the witch. Frank's down. Bring backup."

Click.

He lowers the phone, letting it fall to the ground with a soft thud.

"Fuck you, Ben!" She pounds against his chest with both of her small fists and he lets her. Doesn't even flinch.

Then quietly, to me, his eyes still on hers, "Get her the fuck out of here."

He reaches out with trembling fingers and cups her cheek. She freezes under his touch, sobs caught in her throat, her fists curling into his bloody shirt.

"Go with him, baby," he says in the softest voice I've heard from him. "I'll find you."

His smile is thin, pain laced behind it. "Always," he promises, pressing a kiss to her temple.

He steps back and meets my eyes.

I don't say a word, just nod.

I stoop to grab the gun, flip the safety on, and slide it into my waistband. Then I lift her, arms beneath her knees and shoulders, cradling her gently. She doesn't fight it, just presses her face into my neck, crying silently.

I take off down the road, fast and steady, breaths rattling through my fucked-up windpipe. Through the trees, I catch sight of Jack's truck, the headlights off, dark and ready.

I don't look back.

I reach it fast, my legs threatening to give out as I throw the door open, placing Genevieve gently in the back seat. She curls in on herself, hands over her face, sobbing into her palms.

I climb into the passenger seat, biting down a groan as pain radiates through every single nerve, my body slumping.

Jack says nothing as he whips the vehicle around and speeds off, his hands gripping the wheel with white knuckles.

In the rearview, silent tears drip from Genevieve's chin.

I glance back and get her attention, pointing to my neck.

She wipes her face with a sniffle and crawls forward, placing trembling hands at my throat.

The warmth blooms instantly.

A sharp pulse radiates down to my chest, searing but familiar. The dull ache starts to melt, though it takes my breath with it.

Jack watches in the mirror. "What are you doing to him?" he asks sharply.

"I'm accelerating his metabolic rate—stimulating the healing response," she says, voice flat, eyes red from crying.

Jack's eyebrows lift, looking incredulous. "What, like cell regeneration?"

"Yes. But the body wasn't meant to heal this fast. Too much heat for too long will kill him."

"It's fucking hot," I mutter, my head dropping back to rest against the seat.

She pulls her hands away immediately. "That's enough for now."

I let out a breath, wiping the sweat from my brow.

Jack huffs, shooting a look at me. "Useful. Wonder if Calli could do that."

"She told you," I comment, unsurprised.

"More like nearly killed me," he grumbles under his breath. "Fried my rig, too. But . . . she found you. So that makes us even or whatever." He glances at Genevieve in the mirror. "I'm Jack, by the way." He gives her one of his soft smiles.

"Gen," she mumbles back without emotion.

We fall into silence, just the hum of the engine and the ever-present ache between my ribs.

I let her calm down for a few moments before I look back at her again. "Rosa's not going to stay there," I say to Jack. "If Calli found me—maybe she can find Rosa."

Jack's mouth tightens. "Calli said it was too much—she didn't look good." He winces, shooting me an apologetic look. "I'll find her," he adds quickly. "Eventually."

I don't respond. Instead, I turn—my voice lower now, steel buried under exhaustion.

"Genevieve."

She doesn't look up, just stares blankly out the window.

"You said you'd help me if I got you out," I remind her, my eyes locked on her face. She still won't look at me, but now the avoidance is pointed, her lips drawn tight.

"So, tell me—*who the fuck is Alabaster?*"

CHAPTER 31

CALLISTO

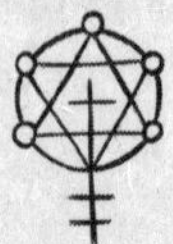

I can't stand this. I've been sitting in the library, staring at my phone, waiting for it to ring for over an hour. Alabaster is Gods know where. I've been trying to find ways to reconnect with the spirit that won't *kill* me. But I haven't found anything useful thus far. An entire library full of books, and I can't even find a damn locator spell that works. I can't deal with this: the not knowing. I spent years in the dark, only now finally getting Cade to open up to me. Finding common ground, just for him to be taken. There is no way this is how it ends. He's too capable, too stubborn to die.

I rub my face and allow myself to crumple to the ground. Everything he has done to keep me safe just for me to go behind his back. He was right. I've been selfish. He isn't just protecting me—he's preventing them from ever being able to hurt *anyone else*. I drop my head, my hands running through my hair. I've been an asshole. He deserved better and now I may never have the chance to make it up to him.

I refuse to accept it. I can't accept it. I won't.

I stand and head over to the bookcase, trying to find anything I can. A locator spell would work. Anything . . . Just one shred of hope. The thought comes to me in an instant—

My tarot cards! I hurry to my room and go to my nightstand. They're there, nestled right next to . . . the grimoire. I can't use it. I shouldn't. I haven't touched it since I read Rholand's journal entry . . . I accept that it is out of my depth right now. Dangerous.

So I sit, pull out the cards from their pouch, and begin shuffling. Questions fill my mind: *Is he alive? How can I help? Will he forgive me?*

I can't fixate on just one question. Frustrated, I shake my head and put the cards in front of me. Splay them out. I take a deep breath and think of Cade, choosing a card in my mind. *The king of swords.* If I choose that card, he is alive, but if I pull *the devil* . . . he's not.

I slowly hover my hand over the deck. I have no idea if this is going to work but it's worth a shot, even just for peace of mind. I close my eyes and pick a card.

The king of swords.

Holy shit. My heart skips and a rush of relief washes over me. Still alive. Thank the Gods . . . I almost can't believe that worked. I close my eyes once more, a single question in mind.

Where can I find more information?

I breathe and pull one more card.

The high priestess.

Of course I would pull this card. Alabaster's words echo in my head.

Trust your instincts.

I close my eyes and search my mind when I remember—

The attic . . .

When we first moved here, I remember we put everything we couldn't fit in here in the attic. There has to be something. Anything that might actually be able to help me. I quickly jump up and run out of the library, up the stairs, and to the hall opposite my room. Open the door, the dusty wood creaking under my feet. I reach for the string and tug, the dim light glowing over the cardboard boxes that litter the floor. I sit myself on the ground and begin to open them one by one. Most of them contain books. One book in particular catches my eye. It's old. Really old. Leather-bound and wrapped tight. The pages look uneven and tattered.

I slowly untie the string and unwrap the book. It looks a lot like R. H.'s journal. I open the first page and skim over the words . . .

It's indeed another journal, but the name at the bottom makes my heart drop into my stomach: Jonathan Halloway.

Holy shit.

I pull the entire box off the floor and lug it down the stairs and into the library, carefully setting it next to the desk. I feel for the seat with my free hand as I begin to read.

September 8th, 1848

Father caught me with the grimoire again today. He scolded me and took it away, claiming I've no business meddling with something so evil. When will he understand . . . it calls to me.

I watched him try to burn it once. By morning, it lay in the ashes, untouched, covered in soot but still whole. He doesn't see it. He doesn't feel what I feel. I am bound to it. My magic grows stronger with each passing fortnight.

The last time he took it from me, I made the walls tremble. The ground shifted beneath our feet. It frightened Mother terribly, but I couldn't stop myself.

I try to control it. Truly, I do. But it's beginning to overtake me.

I'm nearly a man now. Soon, Father will no longer be able to command me. And once I learn to harness this power without bleeding . . . I will take what is mine. He won't be able to stop me.

—J. H.

Goose bumps rise over my skin as I stare down at the old journal.

My Gods . . .

He was like me.

The bleeding. The loss of control. Is that why he built the Covenant? Because of the grimoire?

My hand drifts to the back of my neck, fingers brushing the raised scar—all I've ever known. What they taught me was that the Covenant sacrifices people to gain power from their God.

But . . . is that even true?

My thoughts spiral. If Jonathan Halloway had magic—if he was *born* with it—why create a system that kills people like us? None of the books on the Covenant mention his power. Unless . . . they didn't know. Unless it was erased. Hidden.

The whole foundation of the Covenant was built on gaining power through blood. Sacrifices. That's the point, isn't it?

But if he had power . . . Why would he need to *take* it from others?

Why would he kill what he already was?

My brain tries to make sense of it, but it's not clicking. The pieces don't fit. Something's missing. What if the Covenant wasn't about worship? What if it was about *control*?

But all I know right now is that everything I believed about the Covenant might be a lie—and that Jonathan Halloway was never just a founder.

I try to see the pieces how Cade would. He'd put the emotion aside. Break it down. Trace the motives. Connect the patterns.

He'd know what this means.

Cade. Fuck. I pull out my phone and check again for any notifications. Nothing.

Doubt creeps in. What if the cards were wrong? He may be *alive* . . . but that doesn't mean he isn't in a living hell.

This journal changes everything, but I don't know *how*, exactly. I begin to feel the overwhelming presence I've come to see as a sense of comfort: Alabaster.

"You've been busy," he says, placing a finger on the journal, seeming to skim the page. "Find anything interesting?"

"I—I don't know, honestly." I turn toward the window. "The man who established the cult. The one that's after me . . . He was like me."

"Is that so?" His response sounds almost like he's baiting me. The tone of his voice pulls the realization from me. I whirl around to face him. His glowing eyes are akin to a creature from the deep, dangling its luminescent lure. Drawing me in, beckoning me to ask the question.

Why is *he* here?

I walk up to him quickly, my gaze fixed on his face.

"Why do you say that like you *know*?" I focus on his eyes, searching for answers.

A small smirk plays at the corners of his lips.

"What do you know?" I ask again sternly.

His face is unreadable. I straighten myself and wait for him to break the silence.

"What do you want to know?" he says, crossing his arms.

"Why are you here?" I demand.

He drops his arms to his sides, exhaling a slow breath as he sits on the same chair where we shared our first kiss.

"Let's call it . . . curiosity." He places his elbow on the arm, hand to his chin. "I was drawn to the grimoire, you see. That's a very interesting thing for humans to have. Items like that are quite dangerous when left in this world for too long."

I sit down on the ground, crossing my legs. "Define dangerous."

He glances up like he's weighing the risk of telling me as Karma comes in, jumping on his lap. He pets her head as he speaks.

"It's artifacts like that," he says slowly, "that sparked the worship of Gods across your world. Whole religions built around them. We thought they'd all been confiscated. Removed from this realm a long time ago. Not all of those Gods were worth worshipping, Calli." He leans in.

"Wait. Why? Why would your kind take them?"

His eyes glint as though he's recalling a memory.

"There was a war. A war on worship. The more a God is worshipped, the stronger they become. That's the way of the world. That's what humans were made for."

"Made?" My voice catches. "What do you mean *made*?"

He chuckles in a low voice.

"Oh, little witch . . . you really think your kind evolved that fast? You think you crawled from the mud and learned to build temples on your own?" He smiles. "Mortals are the prey of many species. Your blood feeds vampires. Your souls feed what you call demons. Your worship feeds the divines. The list goes on."

I stare, wide-eyed. I've never known a religion, not like I imagine other people may have grown up with. I've always accepted that I know nothing—so anything could be possible. Vampires, Gods, ghosts, demons. All concepts I have accepted are possible and now know to be true.

But this . . . this is a creature who has seen things, one who knows things that I couldn't even fathom. I look up at him in a different light. One where he isn't the obnoxious demon who has been terrorizing me, or the thing that has made me question myself, or the form I may have feelings for. But something completely otherworldly and powerful. A being capable of great violence, a being *I* called. A dozen questions crash through me all at once.

How much does he know?

How old *is* he?

What even *is* he . . . ?

My voice drops to a whisper.

"What . . . what are y—"

My phone rings in my pocket and I jump, pulling it out and quickly answering.

"Cade!" My heart thumps in my chest. "Oh my Gods, you're alive!" Without realizing it, tears begin streaming down my face, my voice cracking.

"Please tell me you are on your way home."

CHAPTER 32

ALABASTER

My eyes trace Calli's body as she paces, the phone pressed to her ear, her bare feet padding across the floor. I catch the relief softening her face.

"When will you guys be home?" she asks, her voice tight, her nail between her teeth. A pause and then her shoulders finally ease.

"Okay . . . please be safe."

She lets out a long sigh as she lowers the phone, her hand pressing to her chest. She smiles up at me, eyes teary.

"They're safe," she breaths, "but they won't be here until late tomorrow."

Thank fuck that little shit survived. His death would've been *thoroughly* inconvenient for me.

"Perfect," I say, drifting closer, my voice dropping into a purr. "We can have some fun in the meantime."

I brush her hair aside and press a kiss just beneath her ear.

"I can't believe I get to see Genni again . . . it's been so long. I wonder what she's like now," she says, eyes fixed on something in the distance.

Right. *The witch.*

She'll be a thorn in my side. I know that girl and I know she knows about me—knows enough to give me away.

I could always kill her. Now, that's a thought. Not a bad idea.

But that would hurt *her* . . .

Fuck. *This* woman.

I slide my arms around her waist and bury my face in her neck, breathing her in. She smells like flowers and honey: sweet and maddening. My cock stirs instantly.

"Hey. Chill. We need a plan," she says, turning toward me.

My ears flick as I hum against her skin, not bothering to lift my head.

"For what?"

"She's going to know you're here. There's no way she won't. So we need a plan to hide you in plain sight—seeing as I'm stuck with you," she says with a half smile.

My clever little witch. Perfect in every way.

"What did you have in mind?" I lift my head, just slightly.

She turns to face me fully—and grabs both of my horns.

"Can you hide these?" she asks, eyes flicking over them. "I mean . . . *Can* you look normal?"

"Normal to *whose* standards?" I grin, clapping back with a devious smile.

She shoves me, laughing.

"Are you able to suppress your presence?" she asks with a giggle.

I stand up straighter and smile down at her, cupping her chin as I pull her into a deep kiss. I guide her hands to my neck, keeping them occupied while I begin the shift.

My horns retract slowly, clipping through my scalp with a tingling pressure. My hair and skin dull with pigment, the sigils carved into my flesh fading into nothing. My fangs begin to reshape as I kiss her deep—tongue sliding between her lips, tracing the inside of her mouth while it rounds and softens into something more . . . human.

She freezes. Pulls back. Stares.

"Whoa," she whispers, wide-eyed.

I let out a deep, rumbling chuckle.

"Other than the fact that you still look like a God . . . you almost pass for human," she murmurs, fingers combing through my now-black hair.

She quirks a brow. "Can I cut this? It's beautiful, but we should try and make you look as *normal* as possible."

"Whatever you want, pretty girl," I say, smiling.

She does a little dance and darts to the hallway closet. Pulls out a small box and carries it to the kitchen table.

She's so fucking cute.

"Please—take a seat." She bows, dramatically gesturing to the chair.

I roll my eyes, smiling as I sit. She immediately starts shifting my head around like a damn rag doll.

"We're going to have to give you a different name," she says, pulling out a pair of scissors and lopping off a massive chunk of hair.

"How exactly do you see this working?" I ask, turning my head—only for her to grab it and snap it back into place.

"Stay still," she mutters, focused. "I've been sneaking into town to see you. Jack's already met you, so that helps."

Snip.

"So what's the excuse for me living here now?" I say.

"Right . . ." She pauses. "You lost your job at the corner store and got evicted?"

I slowly turn and give her a flat, unimpressed look.

"It's good enough. Cade will already be suspicious. Oh fuck—Cade," she says, the realization hitting her. "He's gonna kill you. Or me. Or both."

She has a point. That little fucker is wildly protective of her. Watching his big brother complex kick in will be hilarious. My connection with his sister is going to *wreck* him—especially once he realizes I understand her in a way he never will.

Oh, that's perfect.

"We could say I'm a witch, too. I have been helping you hone your magic. That you told me your situation—but not Cade's part."

"So you know I'm hiding from a creepy cult, but not that my brother is out there trying to murder them all?" she says, thinking it over. "Do you really think this could work?"

"Clearly you underestimate me. Fooling a mortal witch is nothing."

"Well, I could feel you," she says, and I smirk, hand reaching up to grip her biceps.

"I wanted you to."

She smiles down at me, and I bring my lips to the top of her forehead. "If I didn't you never would have seen me coming."

She pulls out an electric razor at that and flips it on, pressing it to the side of my head without warning.

"It would also explain the magic I still give off," I add. "I'm limited in this form—but not completely useless."

She finishes trimming around my ears, then grabs me by the wrist and drags me to the bathroom—shoving my head toward the sink and turning on the water.

"You really love manhandling me, don't you?" I say, head bent into the basin.

"Maybe," she replies, and I can hear the damn smile in her voice.

She towel-dries my hair and steps back. I lift my head and catch a glimpse of myself in the mirror. Jet-black hair. Shaved sides. Longer on top.

Aside from the hair?

What a fucking downgrade.

"About that name. Any ideas?" she asks, eyeing me like she just finished an art project and nailed it.

"My friends call me Kai," I say plainly. It's true. Where I'm from, names aren't shared freely, they're sacred—but it's the name I'm known by. My given name? Too many humans know it already. It's almost embarrassing.

I look forward to her brother correcting that.

She squints at me. "You have friends?"

I chuckle and scoop her up, setting her on the edge of the sink. I nip at her collarbone, then trace a line up her neck with my mouth. She laughs softly into me, melting just a little.

"Kai is perfect," she says, her eyes heavy and full of hunger.

I hear her heartbeat stutter, then race. She pulls me into a kiss, hands already tugging at my shirt, clumsy and impatient. I break the kiss just long enough to rip it off and toss it to the floor, then lift her and carry her to her room like I already own it.

I lay her down and lean over her, kissing her neck—slow and greedy. She lets out a soft moan, the sound driving me insane. My dick is already standing at attention, ready to ruin her.

She grabs my neck and pulls me closer, rolling us so she's on top. I grin up at her as she straddles me. My hands slip under her shirt and tear the fabric clean down the middle.

She's already unbuckling my belt—quick, practiced fingers—before she pauses. Holding it up.

"May I?" she asks, sweet as sin.

I groan softly, cupping her breasts and rocking my hips against her. "Yes, please."

She loops the belt around my neck and pulls—tight but careful. Just enough to claim me.

I unfasten my jeans, sliding them down enough for my cock to spring free. She glances down and grins.

"At least that didn't change."

That wicked little smile is going to ruin me.

I reach beneath her skirt and grip her thighs, pulling her closer. My voice drops.

"Take it off."

She drops the belt, backing up with a slow, deliberate sway. Her shirt, already ruined, falls off her shoulders. Her bra joins it. Then she hooks her thumbs into the waistband of her skirt and peels it down—inch by inch—never breaking eye contact.

Fuck.

My head tips back as I bite my lip, hips shifting—desperate to feel her.

"Eyes on me," she commands, sultry and sure, looking down like she owns me—and fuck, she does.

She strips the rest of the way down, then drops to her knees.

I push up onto my elbows as she crawls to me across the floor, slow and deliberate.

"You're so pretty on your knees," I murmur, breath catching.

She slides between my legs and wraps her fingers around my cock, stroking me with an achingly soft touch. I twitch in her hand, groaning.

"Fuck, that feels good."

She circles her tongue around the head—slow, teasing. Just enough to drive me insane.

I moan into the open air as she reaches up, grabs the belt around my neck, and pulls. She rises from her knees and straddles me.

Grinding against the length of my cock, soaking my dick before lining me up—then she drops her hips.

Fuck.

My hands fist in the sheets. Every ridge along my cock catches on the soft, wet heat of her as she takes me inch by inch.

I inhale sharply. She's so fucking tight. So fucking perfect.

My jaw clenches. I try to hold still, to let her move at her pace—but it's agony. The way my ridges rub inside her, snagging gently against all the right places—it's too much.

She sinks all the way down with a choked moan, and I swear I black out for a second.

I stay still, savoring it—until she tightens the belt, pulling slow and hard. My throat constricts, just enough. My hips move on instinct, thrusting into her.

Her moan tears through the silence, raw and beautiful.

She places her other hand on my chest and works herself on me. Dropping down, bouncing up, holding herself just above me before sliding back down slow.

I grip her hips, guiding her—pulling the best fucking noises from her pretty mouth. She looks down at me, pupils blown, eyes dark, tugging the belt tighter.

A feral grin curls my lips.

"Yeah?" I say, then move.

In one motion, I lift her off me and toss her to the bed. Her giggle is cut short as I flip her over, pulling her hips up and spreading her legs. I smack her ass, hard—skin meeting skin with a sharp crack that echoes.

"Fuck—" she gasps, but I'm already sliding back inside her.

She screams into the pillow, and I groan at the sound.

I move—rough, desperate, and greedy. I can feel every curve dragging inside her. She's soaked and clenching around me like she's about to break.

I reach between her legs and rub her clit—slow, just enough to make her jump. She moans so loud it echoes.

"I'm coming—fuck—I'm—" Her voice cuts off as she groans through it, legs shaking.

Her body goes limp as she moans beneath me. I don't stop. I can't.

The pressure coils tight in my gut, and I feel my dick pulsing inside her as I come. I stay there, savoring the feeling. I drag out slowly, relishing the way her body clenches—every ridge catching, making her twitch and tense until I'm fully out. Her back arches like she's still trying to keep me in, but I'm already looking down, staring at the mess I made. My cum slipping from the hole I stretched. Dripping. Ruined. Marked.

My fingers trail down the arch of her spine as she trembles beneath me. I grip her hair, tilt her head, and kiss her forehead. I drop beside her and drag her onto my chest.

She's still gasping when she looks up at me—her dark eyes glossy.

"I think . . . I love you, too."

I close my eyes, and I feel it. The urge to keep her. To break her. To ruin her sweet little mind until she only sees *me.*

Instead, I kiss her softly.

As though that's enough.

It won't be.

She quickly falls asleep in my arms.

It's past one in the morning when I feel a shift in the air. Heavy and electric.

I scan the dark room, my eyes locking on the balcony. The glass doors are shut, but I see those glowing white eyes, clear as day through the dark. Alok.

I slip out of bed carefully, keeping quiet so I don't wake Calli. The floorboards creak beneath me as I move toward the door. I open it and step outside, the wood cool beneath my feet as I lean against the railing.

"Haven't seen you in a while," I say, my voice calm. "What happened to keeping watch?"

He steps forward, materializing beside me like a shadow finally choosing form.

"I've been here and there," he says. "Watching. From where I'm not seen."

He turns to me, eyes still glowing. "I warned you, Kai. You know the risks of falling for a mortal."

"I know," I say, rubbing my jaw. "I just don't care."

I pause, staring out into the dark beyond the trees, then continue. "She's like her ancestor. Strong blood. Powerful. They always seem to be drawn to the grimoire."

He hums low. "Humans tend to be drawn to it."

"No," I say, slower this time. "It *calls* to them. It speaks. I've watched her use it. It doesn't resist her—it serves her. As if it knows exactly what she wants, and gives it willingly."

I turn to meet his eyes. "Her ancestor found it buried beneath an old church. No telling how long it had been there. But I'm starting to believe it didn't end up there by accident."

He narrows his gaze, sensing where I'm going.

"There's only one being it could've belonged to."

The name tastes bitter in my mouth.

"Ashur."

Alok's posture shifts. Just slightly.

"He was the only titan known to have crossed into this realm after the war. The place it was buried . . . It was too intentional. A prison. A warning." I exhale slowly. "It's just a guess. But it's the only one that makes sense. He's the only one who was never recovered. No remains. No relics. Just . . . silence."

Alok looks at me, something unreadable behind his eyes. "Funny that *you* would be the one to find it. Considering you follow in his footsteps."

My expression darkens. I look down at him, my voice steady and measured.

"I know she will die. I accept that. But I can love her while I have her. I don't have delusions."

Silence stretches between us. Heavy with everything that can't be undone.

"I'm surprised you chose to don a human form." His voice is calm, but the air between us is thick. "I've never known you to willingly weaken yourself."

He doesn't look at me, just stares out at the night with that detached stillness I've come to hate.

"It's necessary," I say. "I need to understand what's happening here. Too many things don't add up."

He finally turns his head, and the shadows shift across his face.

"Her ancestor called on me," I say. "Begged for help. He couldn't control the power inside him, and in his desperation, he created the Covenant. Used *my* sigil to channel divine magic. It consumed him."

He speaks calmly. "You've been busy."

He leans forward against the railing, his eyes glinting with starlight, like he's amused by how small everything is. "They called your true name," he continues. "They used your sigil against your will. You should have razed the earth beneath them."

I shrug, unconcerned. "It's fascinating, really. The way humans scrape at power they were never meant to wield. I underestimated them."

A sharp sound cuts through the tension. A doorknob turning downstairs. Both of us go still. Our ears twitch.

"Looks like they're back," I mutter.

I turn toward him, keeping my voice low and clipped. "You need to go. They brought a witch with them—she'll sense you."

But he doesn't move. Doesn't even blink.

"Oh no," he says. "I think I'll be staying."

My stomach drops.

"I'm well-versed in possession," he continues, his voice smooth like oiled metal. "And I believe I've found a *prime subject* to host."

My face hardens. "No. You can't."

He raises a brow.

"Her brother is essential to all of this. You know that. You *know* what's at stake."

"Not the brother." His head tilts, the grin creeping up again. "I'm well aware of his little ghost. I imagine it would take issue if I possessed him."

The grin widens. "I'm talking about the new addition."

He says it like it's nothing. Like it may not cost us *everything.*

"You take no issue with that, do you?"

Fuck.

He's cornering me. Putting me in a position where any move I make is the wrong one. If I stop him, I risk losing my only link to the truth. If I let him—Calli will know. She'll feel it. She'll know I let it happen.

"You can't," I say quietly. "She'll know."

He hums, unbothered. "They've been estranged. How would she know? She won't be able to sense me in a host. The witch is perfect. Strong. Gifted. *Isolated.* Your girl doesn't need to know. And you . . ." He glances at me, a gleam in his eyes. "You won't tell her."

I hear doors opening. Footsteps. Voices drifting in from downstairs. They're all settling in.

He smiles again.

I take a step toward him. "No—"

But he's already smoke. Gone, he slips beneath the crack of the door like a silent mist on a tide.

I'm moving before I can think, my feet barely touching the ground. I race after him, every step calculated, every movement as quiet as these human feet allow. But not quiet enough.

I hear a door open—just outside her room.

The bathroom.

I catch his shadow sliding along the floor like a serpent, then rising. Phasing through Calli's door.

I don't hesitate. I reach for the handle and ease it open as silently as I can. Just in time to see his shadow settle, shift, and take shape.

A body twitches in the dark. Limbs stiffen then go still.

It's *Jack*.

I freeze.

He lifts his head slowly—mechanically. Then his neck turns, unnaturally smooth. Our eyes lock, and he smiles. That's not Jack anymore.

He turns, not saying a word, and walks calmly into the hallway. Back straight. Shoulders steady.

Like *he belongs here.*

He disappears into his room. The door closes with a soft click.

I stand there, my pulse hammering, the silence pressing in around me.

Fuck . . .

EPILOGUE

CADE

It's late when we get home and Calli is nowhere to be found—I imagine she is exhausted. I don't want to wake her. I see Karma curled up on the counter. I pet her head as Jack escorts Genevieve to our spare room upstairs and I make my way to mine—collapsing onto the bed.

After everything, I'm finally home. My body is sore, the cuts and bruises half-healed. They sting.

I try to clear my mind and push it down, but I can't get it out of my head. I grip the pendulum around my neck—like it'll summon you.

When Frank was choking the life out of me—I didn't think of Calli—or how she would survive without me. I thought of you.

Only *you*.

You have no idea how badly I want to drag my fingers down your throat just to feel you shudder. To hold you down, pin your wrists, and watch the way your body betrays you as I whisper all the things I would do to you if I had you in front of me.

The thought of losing you—I can't accept it.

I won't.

You are mine.

I don't know how this works. But I know that my every thought is consumed by your presence . . .

How am I supposed to get anything done?

I don't know how, but I know you are here.

Hear me, my little ghost—when this is over . . .

When I destroy them all . . .

When I kill the God they follow . . .

You are my final mission.

I want to consume your every thought like you've consumed mine. I want to devour everything you have to give. I will become yours, as you have become mine. The concept of existing without you is no longer an option.

I will find you, little ghost. And when I do—there will be nothing left of me, but you.

HAUNTED HEARTS

Book Two of the

BOUND DUET

Coming Soon

ACKNOWLEDGMENTS

I did it! My first novel—this is completely surreal in the best way. There is a good chance that I am only now processing that I have made it to the other side. Every chapter, scene, and word I have poured my heart into. The love, pain, and heartbreak I have put on these pages. I was fully prepared to do this on my own, but life had other plans. I met some of the most amazing people along the way, and I want to take this opportunity to thank every single person who has helped me through this journey. Supporting me every step of the way, reminding me that my story needed to be told. The first of many to come. To Chris, for taking care of our beautiful baby girls so that I could step into the light. I have to thank you, for everything you do for me, the many sleepless nights, the endless snacks, and the moments when you would just be present for me. You are my rock. I love you more than french fries. To my best friend, Lee, who has been so supportive and understanding—one day we will see each other again and go to the arcade. I miss it. To Tommy, I wouldn't have been able to do *any* of this without you. Thank you for believing in me. To Jess, you have been such a pillar of strength for me. To my wonderful editor Antoinette, who stayed up countless nights with me to make this perfect. I cannot thank you enough. Ariel, my sister. No words can describe how grateful I am to have found you. So many of you I have met, all because I decided to dedicate myself to bringing *Haunting the Hunter* to life. So it is with this message that I say *thank you*.

ABOUT THE AUTHOR

Hanna Harp is an artist and voice narrator with a deep love for dark, paranormal romance. She began writing her debut novel, *Haunting the Hunter*, while navigating the lifelong realities of dissociation, using storytelling as a way to stay connected when the world feels unreal. Hanna lives in the Midwest with her partner and two daughters, learning to accept her mind as it is and still reaching for her own version of happily ever after.